# A Dark Night Hidden

ALYS CLARE

# A Dark Night Hidden

Hodder & Stoughton

First published in Great Britain in 2003 by Hodder and Stoughton
A division of Hodder Headline

1 3 5 7 9 10 8 6 4 2

A CIP catalogue record for this title is
available from the British Library

ISBN 0340 793317

Typeset in Plantin Light by Palimpsest Book Production Limited,
Polmont, Stirlingshire

Printed and bound by
Mackays of Chatham Ltd, Chatham, Kent

Hodder and Stoughton
A division of Hodder Headline
338 Euston Road
London NW1 3BH

For Joey, my mother,
and in memory of her mother Mabel
and all the wise women

*Siqua sine socio,*
*caret omni gaudio;*
*tenet noctis infima*
*sub intimo*
*cordis in custodia.*

If a maid lacks a lover,
She lacks also all joys;
She keeps in her heart
A dark night hidden.

*Carmina Burana:*
*cantiones profanae*

Author's translation

# The Maternal Family Tree of Josse d'Acquin

Herbert of Lewes
born c. 1115
died 28 July 1148,
in Damascus
=
Ediva
born 5 Feb 1118
died 1168

Geoffroi d'Acquin
b. 10 Jan 1126
d. 22 July 1176
=
Ida
b. 5 Sept 1134
d. 12 Feb 1180

Hugh
b. 1 June 1140

Ysabel
b. 31 May 1143

=

Howell
b. 24 Dec 1158
=
Editha
b. 4 Apr 1161

Godric
b. 3 May 1153
d. 14 Nov 1190
=
Aeleis
b. 12 July 1165

Arthur
b. 22 Apr 1157
=
Isabella
b. 6 Mar 1160

Philomena
b. 4 Jan 1178

Jenna
b. 9 Sept 1177

Herbert
b. 8 Oct 1180

Eleanor
b. 3 Apr 1154
d. 24 Oct 1154

Josse
b. 10 Oct 1160

Yves
b. 15 Sept 1162
=
Marie
b. 1162

Patrice
b. 30 Nov 1163
=
Agnès
b. 1163

Honoré
b. 12 Mar 1165
=
Pascale
b. 1168

Acelin
b. 8 Aug 1166
=
Theophania
b. 1166

Auguste
b. 18 Feb 1185

Eleanor
b. 12 July 1187

William
b. 13 May 1190

Richard
b. 3 Dec 1184

Luke
b. 21 Apr 1182

Marie-Ida
b. 5 July 1184

Mathilde
b. 14 Oct 1185

Jean-Yves
b. 6 June 1187

Robert
b. 19 June 1189

Madoline
b. 15 Aug 1191

The spiteful wind of a bleak, icy February blasted down the muddy track and around the sparse huddle of buildings as if it hated the world and everything in it. There had been snow earlier in the day, but now it was too cold for further flakes to fall. Even if they had, they would have been blown halfway to the chilly sea before being allowed to settle. The wind was out of the north-east: it could as easily have come from the frozen Arctic wastes.

One of the buildings was a gaol. Inside one of its three cells, a young woman lay on the soiled stone floor. She had spent many hours trying feebly to discover which area of the dank stone was the least wet, but such meagre effort was now beyond her. The damp in part comprised melted snow that had found its way in through the cell's single, tiny window; too high to allow a view of the forgotten world outside, too small to permit the flow of fresh air, good only, it seemed, for letting in the fast-blown snow. In part, the moisture seemed to be a constant weeping from the very flags of the floor.

In part, too, it was the woman's own bodily waste. For there was no receptacle put out for her use, and she was now too weak to do anything but let the urine flow out of her where she lay.

She was feverish. She knew, in some part of her mind that retained a little lucidity, that the fearful wounds she had sustained had become infected. Even if the lash itself had not poisoned her flesh, then this filthy cell would have done so, probably the instant she had been flung inside it.

Musing to herself as if it were a matter of academic interest, she reflected on her faint surprise that her back should pain her

1

so much more than her brow. For they had but whipped her back
– twenty-five lashes, a lighter penalty because of her sex – whereas
her forehead had received the brand.

A letter, they said. Just that, a single letter. Burned into the
smooth skin of her forehead with a red-hot iron. A time of terrible
agony – she could still hear the echo of her own screams – but now,
nothing. It was as if whatever it was in the body that transmitted
pain had been excised. It was, she supposed, a blessing. Of a
sort . . .

Her eyes closed. Reality faded – another blessing – and she
slipped into a state somewhere between sleep and unconsciousness. Her mind, released from her desperate plight, took wing.
And her senses filled with the past.

She saw them, those beloved companions. Saw their smiles, their
love for her, for each other. She felt the warmth of their arms
as they embraced her. She smelt lavender, that scent forever
associated with the newcomers who had come from the south
bearing the great news. And she heard the joyous sound of their
voices raised in song.

The hallucination was so vivid that she thought they were there.
That, against all reason, all hope, they had come for her.

She raised her head from the foul sludge on the floor. She said,
'I'm here! I'm here!'

She believed herself to be shouting. But her voice emerged as
a croak, barely audible.

'Here I am!' she cried again. 'Oh, don't go without me! Don't
abandon me!'

She struggled to her feet, falling forward against the cell wall.
Gazing up at the window so far above, she beat her fists weakly
against the dripping stones. 'Here I am! Oh, why don't they
come?'

Perhaps they didn't want her any more! Aghast, she put a
blood- and dirt-stained hand to her mouth as if to stop the
terrible thought. But then, why *should* they want her, she who
had betrayed them, who, through her own passion and weakness,

had introduced the crack in their defences that had so swiftly and frighteningly led to the downfall of them all?

No.

She sank down to the floor. No, they will consider themselves well rid of me. I am alone. Quite alone.

She tried to pray for them, a prayer of beseeching: please, of thy great mercy, let them be safe. Keep them safe. A soft sob broke from her, but she did not recognise it as her own. Her head shot up, her senses alert.

Somebody is here! she thought wildly. There's someone – maybe several people – in one of the other cells! Oh, is it, can it be, *them*?

She got to her knees, leaning heavily against the wall. Holding on to the hinge of the stout door, she began to beat her fist against it. 'Are you there?' she called. 'Oh, please, answer me! Forgive me! Don't shun me now, when I have such need of you!'

No reply.

Reaching deep inside herself, she found a louder voice. Some strength with which to thump the door. '*Please!*' she cried.

After long moments of effort, she had an answer. But it was not the one she was so desperately hoping for.

Footsteps sounded along the passage outside. Heavy footfalls, from large feet in stout boots. The woman's heart filled with hope, and she raised herself so that her face was almost up to the small, mean grille let into the wood of the door. 'I'm here! Oh, thank you, thank you . . .'

The brilliant flame of a torch scorched across her dark-adapted eyes. Covering them with her hands, she was suddenly flung backwards into the cell as the door was unlocked and thrust open.

Hope dying, she raised her head.

Above her stood not a beloved companion but her gaoler. Even as she felt the chill of ultimate despair, he swung a bunched fist at her head and sent her reeling.

'Stop that bawling, else I'll give you something to bawl about!' he shouted, his harsh voice in the narrow cell hurting her ears.

'Oh, please!' she sobbed. 'Won't you let me see them? Won't you at the least tell them I am here?'

Her words seemed to puzzle the man. Most things did, for he was not employed for his reasoning powers, simply for his brute strength.

'Ah, enough!' he said. 'God alone knows what you're ranting about, *I* don't. Can't make out a word of it.' He made as if to retreat out of the cell. But then, staring down at her as she lay at his feet, he caught sight of a faint glimmer of pale, soft skin. The swell of a breast, white, rounded . . .

The woman's gown had been ripped from her back for the flogging. She had tried to fasten the torn pieces together but with little success, so that now they no longer decently covered her upper body.

It was to be her final undoing.

The gaoler forced the torch into a bracket high on the wall. Then he fell heavily to his knees and grabbed at her.

Knowing what was coming, she made one last effort. Slipping to one side, swift as a snake, she wriggled out of his grasp. Leaping to her feet – she was small and light, and possessed of the adrenalin-fed strength of desperate peril – she evaded him and made a lunge for the door.

She almost reached it.

But the gaoler had long arms – the crueller of his associates remarked that his knuckles grazed the ground as he walked – and he shot out a hand and grabbed her ankle. Then, with a smile of pure lust, he pushed his hand up her calf, her thigh, until his strong fingers pinched hard into her buttock.

'Now where d'you think you're going, my little beauty?' he crooned. 'Out into the cold night when you could be nice and warm with old Forin here?' His other hand was pulling at the front of her gown, reaching in and closing on her breast.

Wrestling, drawing on the last of her strength, she tried to push him away, spitting into his ugly, coarse face.

That was a mistake, for it angered him.

'Slut! Whore!' He shook her, so hard that her teeth clamped

together, painfully biting her tongue. 'Spit at me, would you?' He threw her down on to the floor and her head bounced against the stones with a loud crack. She went limp.

But the gaoler did not notice. Blood lust ran hot in him, and in seconds he had ripped away the remnants of her clothes and pulled down his breeches. Fiercely aroused by the fight she had put up, he was hard and more than ready. Forcing her legs apart, he thrust into her, savage strokes that tore at her; he was built like a bull, and not for nothing did the town whores evade him unless there was no choice.

His climax came quickly, for a man like him had no concept of self-control. Panting, he slumped on the woman. 'There, now,' he managed after a while, 'that weren't so bad, eh?' And – thinking that he might again have for free what he normally had to pay for – 'We might do that again, now, eh? Old Forin might come by again, maybe bring you . . .'

But whatever his unimaginative mind might have come up with as a suitable gift for a woman he had just raped was never to be expressed. For, belatedly, he had noticed his prisoner's unnatural stillness.

Rising up – he was kneeling between her wide-spread legs – he gazed down at her. There was blood on her thighs, and he wondered if he had just deflowered a virgin. Shame if so, he'd have made more of the moment if he'd known. Silly cow ought to have said.

Then he saw the other blood. Flowing from the back of her head, where she had hit the floor.

He thrust one hand into her long, dark hair, pooling around her head. He felt something warm and wet and, withdrawing his hand, he saw that it was covered in her blood.

He stared down at her small white breasts. Soft, they were, and nicely rounded. He put his hand on one, pinching the nipple hard; that'd wake her up if she was shamming.

She made not the slightest move.

He stared at her face. Her eyes were wide open, fixed; he could not bear to look into them. Leaning down over her, he listened for a hint of breath, watched for any rise and fall of her chest.

Nothing.

Standing up, pulling up his breeches and straightening his tunic, he said, in a low and somehow triumphant tone, 'She's dead, then. Aye, dead.'

He reached up for the torch and took it from the bracket. Then, leaving the cell door open – she certainly wasn't going anywhere now – he strolled off along the passage.

Dead. Ah well, it'd save the hangman a job.

# Part One

## Lewes and Hawkenlye Abbey

### Winter 1192–93

# 1

'King Richard a *prisoner*? Nonsense – this cannot be so. Someone must be having a wicked jest!'

Josse d'Acquin, house guest of his late mother's brother, Hugh of Lewes, heard his own heated words and belatedly remembered his manners. 'I apologise, Uncle,' he muttered. 'But, nonetheless, I am certain there can be no truth in this terrible story. Why, the King heads a great army!' Or at least he did three years ago, Josse added silently to himself, when he rode off with such proud pomp at the head of the vast crusading force. Since then, King Richard had suffered mixed fortunes. Moreover, of late the sparse news filtering back from Outremer with returning crusaders had been depressing.

And, for all that there were many tales that boasted of the King's bravery, prowess and deeds of outstanding daring, there were also the hushed voices that spoke of sickness. Of a recurrent fever. Of a wound. Of plotting between Richard's own brother, John, and the King of France, Richard's sworn enemy. There were even – God forbid! – whispers that said King Richard was dead.

Trying not to dwell on that frightful thought, Josse blustered on. 'How could it be that those whose sworn duty it is to guard the King would have allowed him to be taken?'

Hugh had waved the apology away. 'Oh, Josse, I understand your emotion and I too, on hearing the fell news, had the same reaction: there must be some foul trickery here.' His shocked eyes met Josse's. 'But not so. The reports flying around at court are, I deeply regret to say, absolutely true.' He glanced over his shoulder as if to ensure that they were not overheard, then, putting his mouth close to his nephew's ear, whispered, 'Editha has it from

Howell, who, as I believe we have told you, is kin to one of the secretaries of Walter of Coutances.' The whisper dropped to a still softer pitch as Hugh added, 'And it was Walter himself who broke the news to Queen Eleanor!'

'Aye,' Josse said distractedly. 'Aye, you have indeed spoken of Howell's important and influential cousin.' He refrained from adding that it was strange how Howell – married to Hugh's middle daughter Editha – managed to have distinguished relations whilst remaining unutterably dull and unremarkable himself. 'But how does Walter of Coutances come by the news? Is there not still room for hope that the report, wherever it comes from, may yet prove false?'

'I do not know, Josse.' Hugh gave a heavy sigh. 'I pray you are right, yet in my heart . . .' He did not continue with the remark. Then suddenly he burst out: 'I fear for England if Prince John rules us!'

Josse, too, had his misgivings concerning the Prince. He had encountered the man a matter of months previously, and knew better than many with what single-mindedness, even then, John's hungry ambition had been fixed on the throne of England.

Yet, indeed, with Richard gone, who else *was* there?

But Hugh was speaking again. Josse arrested his despairing thoughts and listened.

'Editha and Howell will be here again by and by,' Hugh said. 'Then we shall have fresh tidings, for they have been visiting Howell's family. I pray God the news is good.'

'Amen to that,' Josse agreed.

'Until then,' Hugh said, on another sigh, 'let us try to turn our thoughts to happier matters.' His face brightening, he managed a light laugh. 'A game of chess, perhaps? I believe you like to play?'

'Er – it is many years since I enjoyed a game, and I fear that what skills I once possessed may have deserted me. But I will take up the challenge, Uncle, if you issue it.'

Now Hugh's laughter was stronger. 'That I do, nephew, albeit on another's behalf. For if the guest whom we expect this afternoon can indeed spare the time to grace us with a visit, he will certainly not wish to pass up the chance of pitting his wits against a new opponent.'

His heart sinking – chess had never really been his game – Josse said, trying to put a note of polite enquiry into his voice, 'And who may this guest be, Uncle?'

'Why, Father Edgar!' Hugh exclaimed, as if Josse ought to have guessed. 'You remember, our priest!'

'Oh.'

Hugh wrapped an affectionate arm around Josse's shoulders, thumping the fist of his other hand against his nephew's broad chest for good measure. 'Ah, now, Father Edgar's a good fellow, Josse, with a wide-ranging mind and possessed of lively intelligence. You have not yet had occasion to assess the measure of the man.' Noting Josse's expression – which despite his best efforts must have remained sceptical – Hugh laughed again and said, 'Just wait! Just you wait!'

Josse had been the guest of his uncle and aunt throughout the Christmas season and the month of January. Aware that he had neglected them for far too long, he had not been entirely sure what sort of a welcome he would receive. His father's kin were from northern France, where Josse's four brothers lived with their wives and their children on the family lands of the d'Acquins. Josse's father Geoffroi, however, had married an Englishwoman, Ida, daughter of Herbert of Lewes with whom he had fought in the Second Crusade. As a boy, Josse had been despatched by his mother to visit his English relatives and he had kept warm, though faint, memories of Uncle Hugh, Aunt Ysabel and his three cousins, Isabella, the eldest (who was the same age as Josse), Editha and Aeleis. Until this Christmas, however, he had not seen any of them for more than twenty years.

Any misgivings that Josse might have entertained over how the family at Lewes would receive a kinsman who had stayed so long away dissipated as soon as he set foot across the threshold. Admittedly, it had been but three days before Christmas Day, and the household was already clearly feeling the jubilatory influence of the Lord of Misrule. However, whatever the reason, they had welcomed him in as if he were the one person whose presence was required to make the festivities perfect.

They had been quite a party. Most senior were Hugh, now a stout, balding man of more than fifty years, and his wife Ysabel, quiet and calm where her husband was loud and demonstrative, but clearly the mistress of the household. Although grown plump and breathless, the remnant of her former beauty was still there for those with eyes to see it. Then there were Isabella, Editha and Aeleis, the elder daughters accompanied by their husbands, Arthur and the dull-witted Howell, and by Isabella's and Editha's daughters. Isabella also had a son, called Herbert after his grand-father and always referred to in the family as Young Herbert. He, however, was not of the company since, having reached the age of twelve, he was squire in the household of another knight. Aeleis, the youngest of the sisters, had been widowed two years previously and was childless. She might secretly mourn the latter state – Josse did not know – but she gave no sign that she missed her late husband. He had been some twelve years older than Aeleis and, according to Editha, might as well have been his lively wife's senior by twenty or even thirty years. 'Better for both of them to have him snug in his grave,' Editha had murmured privately to Josse, 'that way he doesn't wear himself to a shadow fretting and fussing at her and she can breathe again.'

There had been nothing, Josse felt, which he could say by way of an answer to that remarkable statement, especially on such short reacquaintance. He had contented himself with going 'Hmm' earnestly and attempting to look wise. He guessed that Editha was not fooled for an instant because she had gone off giggling to report to her widowed sister and their combined laughter had rung up to the beams of the wide hall.

In addition to the immediate family, there had been cousins, relatives of the sons-in-law, friends of the children and all manner of sundry other folk who, it seemed, presented themselves in Hugh's hall and took advantage of his generosity for no better reason than that they happened to be passing. Nobody appeared to mind; there was plenty of food and drink and the entire family, Josse concluded, loved nothing better than to sit comfortably before a roaring fire and gossip away the short days and the long, dark, December nights.

But then January ushered in a new year and, after the twelve days, the Christmas celebrations at last came to an end with the Feast of Epiphany. Merrymakers sobered up, guests began to think about leaving, adult sons and daughters departed from their parents' homes and made for their own. Only Josse, still enjoying his uncle's company and in no hurry to depart, stayed on as the weeks of January slipped by and February blew in. Then, so far only for the ears of those with access to inner court circles, came the frightful news about the King.

The kinsman of Editha's husband Howell heard it. He was in fact one of the first among the common folk to do so, working as he did in the employ of the great Walter of Coutances. A King's man to his very bones, Walter led the Council of Regency appointed to act on Richard's behalf while he was away on Crusade. Desperately worried throughout the autumn of 1192 by the lack of tidings concerning the King, Walter had sent his spies across to the Continent to see what news could be gleaned. One of his men had infiltrated the court of King Philip of France, and it was he who sent his master Walter a copy of the very letter announcing to Philip the capture of his enemy, King Richard.

That the King was captive was all that was known, as yet, to anyone outside the closest of court circles. And in all conscience, Josse thought now as he tried to sharpen his wits for a game of chess with an unknown prelate, it was enough . . .

He was losing to Father Edgar when there came the sound of a horseman in the courtyard outside. The hour was late – Josse had been working on the principle that the right moves might miraculously occur to him if he took his time, and consequently he and the priest seemed to have been playing for hours – and Hugh hurried to the door in some surprise. But then, as a servant wrested it open and Hugh could see who had arrived, he called out loudly, 'Howell! We had all but given you up! Come in and warm yourself, and quickly – my lads will see to your horse. Editha is not with you, I see?'

Howell, trying to shrug off his heavy travelling cloak, rub some life back into his cold hands and embrace his father-in-law all at once, readily allowed himself to be led across to the fire. Josse and Father Edgar moved to make room for him, and the Father pushed his mug of warmed ale into Howell's hands.

'Ah, that's good.' Howell nodded his thanks. 'Dear God, it's cold enough to freeze a man's b— er, to freeze his legs to the saddle.'

'Quite so,' murmured the priest.

'Surprised you came so late,' Hugh said. 'As I said, we weren't really expecting to see you tonight – thought you'd leave the journey till the morrow.'

'Editha insisted,' Howell said with the faint air of resignation of a man used to doing what his wife said. 'She sends her love and says it's too cold for her to ride abroad and anyway Philomena's gone down with a bad chill and Editha's nursing her.' Having done his duty and delivered his wife's message, Howell gave himself up to the ale.

Only when he had drained the pewter mug did Hugh say, 'Howell, why did Editha insist that you came tonight? Is there – oh, my heart misgives me, but I must ask! Is there news of the King?'

Howell sank down on to the bench where Josse had been sitting, stretching his short, sturdy legs towards the fire. 'There's news, aye. And Editha said she had promised you would hear, soon as there was anything to tell. We've had the honour of entertaining my cousin William' – the fatigue miraculously left him as he swelled with the pride of being related to a man thrust into importance, even if it was only a temporary state – 'and he's revealed to us all that he is allowed to tell. It's secret, see.'

'Of course,' Hugh said, even as Josse said 'Naturally' and Father Edgar breathed 'But yes!'

Satisfied with these reassurances – he would, Josse thought briefly, have been satisfied with even less, so eager was he to regale them with his news – Howell took a deep breath, leaned confidingly forward and said, 'It's the Austrians, they've got him. Duke Leopold's men took him when he was sick and hiding out in a little village a few miles from Vienna – *was* it Vienna?' – he frowned – 'and now he's held captive in some great castle on that big river.'

'Which big river?' Hugh demanded.

'Er – I don't know.'

'The Rhine?' Josse suggested. His knowledge of the geography of Europe was no less hazy than the next man's, but he had an idea that both the Rhine and Austria were somewhere in the middle.

'No, it wasn't the Rhine.' Howell was scratching his head in an apparent effort to help his memory along. 'What *was* it, now?'

'The Danube,' Father Edgar said quietly. 'If you relate correctly what you were told and King Richard was indeed taken near to Vienna, then the river in question is undoubtedly the Danube.'

There were nods of satisfaction, quickly curtailed as the four men realised that knowing where the King was did not in fact do much to help him regain his freedom.

'What do they *want*?' Hugh burst out. 'I mean, I know there were stories that King Richard didn't always see eye to eye with the other captains of the West out there in Outremer, but to take him captive! As I say, why? What's it *for*?'

'Money,' Father Edgar said. 'I may be wrong, Howell, but I imagine there is – or there will be – a ransom demand.'

'I know nothing about a ransom,' Howell said stiffly, looking at the priest with an affronted expression as if the despicable idea had originated with him.

'But there will be a demand of some sort, I'm certain,' Josse said heatedly. 'That will be what those devils are after, that and the terrible humiliation they impose on the King of England by walling him up inside one of their foul dungeons!'

'Oh, it is not to be borne!' wailed Hugh. 'Dear God above, what are we to do? What is England to do?'

Josse, Hugh and Father Edgar all looked at Howell, who shrugged and, flushing, muttered, 'Don't ask me!'

There was a short silence as the four men reflected on the King's fate. Then, turning to Father Edgar, Josse said, 'I have an idea, Father, that this frightful action is in violation of the Truce of God?'

The priest nodded. 'My thoughts run to the same conclusion,' he agreed. 'Will these wretches stop at nothing?'

'What is this truce?' Howell asked.

Father Edgar explained. 'In essence, the Truce of God protects the person and property of a man whilst he is absent on crusade, and those who violate it run the grave risk of excommunication.'

'Excommunication!' someone – Howell or Hugh, Josse was not sure – breathed softly. Then there was utter, horrified silence as the men reflected on what that meant.

After some time, Hugh cleared his throat and said, 'The Queen will take this hard, God bless her.'

'Aye,' Josse agreed.

'She's not so young as she was,' Howell said lovingly. 'It fair tears at my heart, to think of her spending her Christmas alone at Westminster with all her loved ones far away. And oh, how I feel for her, that she must bear this new burden.'

'Old she may be,' the priest put in, 'but she still has her fortitude.'

'She'll be needing it,' Hugh muttered.

It was interesting, Josse thought, how all of them knew without asking that when Hugh had referred to the Queen, he meant Queen Eleanor, the King's mother, and not Berengaria, his wife. To be fair to Berengaria, she had not yet even set foot in the realm in which she was to reign as Richard's queen, so it was no reflection on her that the people took little notice of her. Eleanor, determined that a suitable bride be found for her favourite son, had fetched Berengaria from her native Navarre and hurried out to the Mediterranean in pursuit of the crusading bridegroom. She had caught up with him in Sicily, where Berengaria had ceremonially been handed over, and the royal couple's nuptials had subsequently been performed in Cyprus. Since then, Berengaria had been in Outremer with Richard; exactly where she was now was not certain. But she was not in England.

It was hardly surprising that Eleanor remained queen to the English; they had known her and loved her for almost forty years.

'She'll be suffering, aye, there can be no doubt of it,' Hugh sighed.

'She will take comfort, as always, in the help and the strong support of God,' Father Edgar said gently. 'He has seen her through many trials and will not desert her in this one.'

'Amen,' the others murmured.

But she knows what it is to be a prisoner, Josse thought. And, knowing Richard as she does, she will fully comprehend his suffering.

Poor soul.

Eleanor, Josse was recalling, had also borne the heavy burden of imprisonment. In her case, her captor had been her own husband, Henry II of England. Tiring at last of his wife's tendency to plot against him with his own sons, the late King had had her shut away under close guard, mainly at Winchester, on and off for fifteen years.

Aye. Queen Eleanor would likely suffer along with anyone wrongly imprisoned. What she must be feeling on her beloved son's account hardly bore thinking about.

Josse stirred from his reverie, realising that Howell was speaking once more.

' . . . said that she wanted to go and find him, straight away, like, only her sense of duty is such a force in her that she knew she couldn't. Who would guard England and Richard's throne if he were imprisoned and she went to fetch him home?'

'Thank God for a Queen who knows her duty,' Hugh said piously.

And, once more, the others all said, 'Amen.'

There was not a great deal more talk that night. Howell had run fairly quickly to the end of his real news; what followed was mainly conjecture and speculation, and the latter became increasingly wild as the night went on.

In the end, the priest had tactfully suggested that the others join him in prayer, and then they had gone their separate ways to bed.

Josse woke to a bright day, with a weak but determined February sun sparking flashes of light off the frost.

He knew where he would go that day. He had been dreaming of Queen Eleanor, and it seemed that he witnessed her distress. Then he became aware of another figure, although it remained in the shadows and he could not identify it.

His waking mind, however, knew who it was.

He thought of that person now, of how her kind heart and the forbidden pride that remained in her loved and treasured the special relationship with the Queen. How she would welcome the Queen when she visited, cosset her, listen to her, tentatively and tactfully offer what comfort she felt the Queen would accept.

Ah yes, but she would be needed now! For, if Eleanor could make the time, then this was one place to which she would surely go.

As he took the first meal of the day with Hugh and the household, Josse announced that today he must depart. When Ysabel asked if he would return to New Winnowlands, his manor in Kent, he said no, not straight away.

'I am bound for Hawkenlye Abbey,' he explained.

Where, he added silently to himself, I shall seek out the Abbess Helewise and indulge myself in the pleasure of a very long talk with her.

# 2

Hawkenlye Abbey, serene and quiet under the hard, pale blue sky, did not at first glance look like a place in which wild and destructive emotions were running free. The stone walls stood stout, protecting those within in a strong embrace, yet, by day at least, the wooden gates were always open and admission was offered to those who came to lay their burdens, their sickness of mind, body or soul, on the Abbey's patient and caring nuns and monks.

It was the winter season, and the trees whose branches protected the Abbey were bare. Nature was asleep and nothing grew; even the plants that thrived so well in the herb garden under Sister Tiphaine's experienced hands were little more than dry twigs.

Behind the Abbey, its perpetual dark backdrop, the great Wealden Forest brooded. Here too the trees were skeletal, the majority of leafless deciduous specimens interspersed with a smaller number of yew, juniper and holly that broke up the uniform greyness of bare branches with dots and splashes of deep green. The forest was a forbidding place, a secret world of myth and rumour; some said that the faint tracks that wound through it, twisting this way and that, had been made by the Romans seeking iron ore. Some said they had been made by people far more ancient than that, people who, it was whispered, were barely human . . .

Those who spent their lives within the Abbey's protecting walls spared scarcely a thought for their silent neighbour. The life of prayer and of service was hard, and nuns whose days began in the darkness before dawn and ended, exhausting hours later, with a very welcome sleep on a straw mattress, had few free moments in which to ponder on the nature of who, or what, might be found within the forest. Most of Hawkenlye's nuns and monks were content merely to accept that it was *there* and leave it at that.

Most of them.

The very few exceptions had the good sense to keep their thoughts – their wanderings – to themselves.

Totally in keeping with the Abbey's air of serenity was the absorbed figure of Sister Phillipa. Despite the cold, she sat in the meagre shelter afforded by a secluded corner of the cloister where, with fingerless mittens on her hands, she was engaged in painting an illuminated manuscript.

To be accurate, she was working on a practice piece. She had prepared an old scrap of parchment, a decent-sized cutting left over from someone else's earlier work, on which that same someone had tried out pigments and styles of lettering. Sister Phillipa was doing her very best work, the letters bold, stylish and even, the tiny painting – of a bramble, showing leaf, blossom, berry and prickle – delicate yet vivid. She knew she was on trial and, if she passed, that she might very well be granted the great honour of producing a herbal.

More than that she had not been told and did not dare to ask. It was not her place, a nun who had but six months ago taken her perpetual vows and was hence one of the youngest of the fully professed, to question anything that the great Abbess Helewise said. Or, in this case, did not say. What did it matter, anyway? The wonderful thing for Sister Phillipa was that, after so long – only three years, perhaps, but it felt like a lifetime! – she was once again engaged on the work she loved. And for which – yes, it was boastful, prideful, and she would have to confess and do penance but, despite all that, it was the *truth*! – she had a rare talent.

She had become aware of that talent at a young age. Perhaps been made aware of it expressed it better, for, isolated little girl that she had been, she had unthinkingly assumed that every small child drew and painted with the fluency given to her. It had been her father – gentle, learned, head-in-the-clouds Gwydo – who had lovingly pointed out the error: 'You're an artist, Philly, and no mistake. You've inherited what skills I possess, and to those you add something very special that belongs just to you.'

He had taught her everything he knew. With no wife – Phillipa's mother had died of the dreaded childbed fever a month after giving birth to her only child – his little daughter had been the sole recipient of his love. They had lived close in their little hut, father and daughter, each content in the other and in the beauty of the work at which both were so talented. Artist and visionary, Gwydo had tried to put his daydreams and his nightmares into his pictures. When pigment and parchment proved too small a vessel to contain his soaring imagination, he had been known to fling his materials against the wall of the hut in a fury that temporarily blinded him. Phillipa feared only for him when the ill humour took him; aware of the depths of his love for her, she knew him to be incapable of hurting her and so never feared for herself.

With growing dread, Phillipa had watched as Gwydo's health began to fail. A lifetime of poverty – his work was beautiful beyond compare, but what use was that if nobody knew of it and presented themselves with purses full of gold to buy it? – and of sitting hunched and cold over his work while his concave stomach burned and rolled with hunger had undermined him. When sickness came to the village, Gwydo nursed his feverish daughter with a tenderness that spoke deeply of his love for her. Succumbing himself just as she was returning, thanks to him, to strength and health, he had little in reserve with which to combat the disease.

He died two days later.

Phillipa, shocked, grieving, weeping and shaking, had nobody in the world to turn to. Gwydo had been her life and, so far as the future was concerned, she had vaguely imagined continuing to work alongside him and taking over when he could no longer work. Now he was gone, there was no money and nothing, other than her and Gwydo's materials, to sell. Since nobody in the village had any use for those, it looked as if Phillipa would starve.

They told her to go to Hawkenlye. Still deep in her mourning, she obeyed. Initially the nuns received her only as a patient, skilfully drawing her lost mind back as they healed her weak, half-starved body. The impulse to become one of them, to enter the Hawkenlye community as a postulant, had grown on her but slowly, at first dismissed as an emotional response that grew out of her gratitude. But then, praying with the sisters, lapping up the love and the care that they daily offered to her, she started to think it might be more than that. She understood – or thought she did – that their limitless devotion, pouring from them, used up yet constantly replenished, had a source: it came from God. After six months she had made up her mind and she entered the community the following week.

Postulants and novices were not allowed to do work of a specialist nature; before there could be any question of that, they had to learn what it was to be a nun. Phillipa did her share of cleaning, pot-scrubbing, bandage-washing, laundry, herb gathering, weeding, vegetable scraping and cooking. She also prayed, more frequently and at greater length than ever before, and as she did so, learned to love the peace and the power of the Abbey church and the presence of the Lord within it.

She took the first of her vows after a year, her perpetual vows two years after that. Then, at the interview with Abbess Helewise which all of the newly professed must face, she was asked that astonishing question: 'At what, Sister Phillipa, are you best? Where, would you say, do your talents lie?'

Closing her mouth, Phillipa had swallowed, taken a breath, decided to go for the truth and confessed. 'I love to paint and to letter,' she said. 'I know it is immodest to say so, but my father was a great artist and taught me well.' Then, folding her hands in her lap and dropping her eyes, she waited.

'A painter,' Abbess Helewise murmured. Then she added – or Phillipa thought she did – 'How very refreshing.'

In retrospect, it must surely have been a mistake. The Abbess was just not the sort of person to make such a remark, expressing as it did relief, of a sort, to have someone with artistic talent present herself in the community. Art was not nearly as worthy as, say, being good at sponging the befouled bodies of the sick, or possessing the endless kindness needed to cope with the aged who wandered in their minds, or having the patience to teach grubby and snotty-nosed little urchins not to drink filthy water, pick their scabs and noses and belabour each other with sticks. No. Phillipa must have misheard.

She had returned to the duty on which she had then been engaged: helping one of the infirmary nurses scrub out a curtained recess in which a patient had lately died of a plague of pus-filled, bloody boils. She had put all thought of her conversation with the Abbess right to the back of her mind.

But then, a few weeks after Christmas, Abbess Helewise had sent for her. And, wonder of wonders, told her to produce a piece of work. A painting and some lettering. When Phillipa had hesitatingly asked, 'What should I paint?' the Abbess had replied, 'Something that one might find within the pages of a herbal.'

So now, neither knowing nor caring why, that was precisely what Sister Phillipa was doing.

Sitting back, looking at her work and trying to see how it would look to another, she read what she had written.

> Blossom of the bramble is beneficial for fresh wounds. Lay fresh
> blossom of same direct on to the injured flesh and the flowers
> will heal the hurt.

Dipping her brush into the madder pigment, she added a blush of pink to the white petal of her bramble blossom. Then, hearing in her head Gwydo's oft-repeated reminder that a good artist knows when to leave well alone, she cleaned the brush and laid it down. I have done my best, she thought. Now it is up to the Abbess to make what use she wishes of my skills. If any, she added, superstitiously crossing her fingers against the unpleasant possibility that Abbess Helewise would make no use of her at all.

Sitting there in her chilly corner, a thought occurred to her. Slowly she uncrossed her fingers, muttering aloud a swift apology to God. Then she got up, carefully covered her work and made her way to the Abbey church. Some time spent on her knees was, she knew, a far more suitable way of asking for what she wanted than any amount of finger-crossing.

In another part of the Abbey, Abbess Helewise presented to her visitor an outward demeanour as serene as that of Sister Phillipa working at her lettering. However, in Helewise's case a smiling face and calmly folded hands hid an irritation that was swiftly escalating into anger.

She had been on her knees in the small room reserved for her own use, from which she conducted much of the day-to-day business of the Abbey, deep in thought and about to enter into a fervent prayer. The object of her thoughts had been an earlier visitor, one who was always welcome and whom Helewise wished would spare more time from her busy life to rest in Hawkenlye's peace . . .

Queen Eleanor was and always had been deeply involved with Hawkenlye Abbey. Its foundation had occurred at a time when Eleanor, newly married to Henry, had the power to exercise an influence over the determining of its nature. She had urged that it be based on the model of her beloved Fontevraud, the great abbey in the Loire region where nuns and monks served in the same community under the rule of an abbess. Eleanor had watched Hawkenlye grow, had engaged French stonemasons and a French architect to build it and, it was rumoured, had presented to the Abbey the jewel of its treasury: an English-made carving in walrus ivory of the dead Christ supported by Joseph of Arimathea. Her involvement did not cease once the Abbey was functioning. At the very least, she tried to be present each time a new abbess was elected, and she did her best to spend a night or two, or just a few hours, at Hawkenlye whenever practical.

She was particularly close to Abbess Helewise. It was not uncommon for the Queen to talk to the Abbess of matters close to her heart, and so Helewise had been delighted but not surprised when Eleanor had arrived, several weeks into the New Year, and unburdened herself of her fears for her captive son in the privacy of Helewise's little room.

Helewise had already heard a rumour of King Richard's fate. Hawkenlye was close to the road that ran from London to the coast and travellers calling in at the Abbey frequently brought news from the capital. But she would never have come to hear a detailed account of the business had it not been for the Queen.

Eleanor was on her way back to Westminster from Robertsbridge. Exhausted, the strain evident in her face, for once the Queen had looked her seventy years; Helewise had instantly ordered food and drink and, as the Queen took refreshment, had sat at her feet and listened to her speaking.

'I knew, Helewise, that something was amiss,' Eleanor sighed. 'There should have been news, you see – we knew he had set sail from Acre back in October, and there were reports that the *Franche-Nef* had put in at Cyprus and Corfu. The ship was sighted near Brindisi and we understood he was making for Marseilles. It seemed only a matter of weeks before he would be back – indeed, all of Normandy was making ready to welcome him home! But then, nothing.' She reached for her goblet of wine and drank deeply. Then: 'I feared for his realm.' There was no need for her to elaborate: Helewise knew full well what she meant. 'I ordered that the borders of Normandy be strengthened; one cannot be too careful.'

'No, my lady,' Helewise murmured.

'Then I received the letter.' Eleanor's voice was dull, almost expressionless. 'My good Walter of Coutances's man had fulfilled his mission – exceeded it, one might say – and managed to obtain a copy of Emperor Henry's letter to that vile cur, Philip of France. On 21st December, the letter said, the King of England – oh, Helewise, how they disparaged him, calling him "the enemy of our Empire and the disturber of your kingdom"! – was taken prisoner by Duke Leopold of Austria. Walter knew full well how this frightful news would affect me, for he enclosed a letter of his own exhorting me to bear up and be brave.'

'He is a man,' Helewise said softly, 'and has not a mother's heart.'

She felt the brief pressure of the Queen's hand on her shoulder. Although Eleanor did not speak, Helewise knew that, in that instant, both of them were thinking the same thing.

'What will happen now, my lady?' Helewise asked after a moment.

'I have sent the Abbot of Robertsbridge to Austria to search for the King. He is to be accompanied by the Abbot of Boxley. They are sound men and I know that they will do their utmost. But oh, how I yearn to be going myself! I would find him, I know it, and then let the piddling Duke Leopold and his scurrilous master the Emperor look to their defences! They would not understand what an enemy they had unleashed until I descended on them!'

The room rang with the echoes of the Queen's shout. Then, as silence fell, she said, 'Ah, well. I am an old woman, and I can do more good here in England.'

'You hearten us, as always, by your presence and by your brave example,' Helewise said. Her words were no empty flattery; she spoke from the heart.

The Queen, it seemed, knew it. 'Thank you.'

'What can we do, my lady?' Helewise asked. 'Anything that is in our power, you only have to command and it is done.'

'Will you pray for us, for my poor captive son and his grieving mother?'

'Yes! Oh, yes, of course we will!'

The Queen smiled. 'If you put such fervour into your prayers, Abbess Helewise, then surely God cannot help but hear.'

Helewise returned her smile. Then she asked, 'Would you care to pray with us, my lady, before you leave?'

'Yes. I should like that very much.'

The Queen had prayed that evening and again the next morning. Before she left, surrounded by her attendants and in haste to return to Westminster where there might be news, she took Helewise aside.

'I have asked my nuns at Fontevraud and at Amesbury also to pray for us,' she said quietly. 'Like you, they earnestly promise to comply.'

'I am quite sure—' Helewise began.

The Queen held up a hand. 'I know. What I wish to say, Abbess Helewise, is that Queen Eleanor does not ask a boon without giving something in return.'

'But there is no need—'

Again, the Queen stopped her words with an imperious gesture. 'I have for Hawkenlye a bag of gold,' she said. 'Put it to whatever use you see fit. My only stipulation is that whatever you do is done in the name of the King and of his mother.'

Helewise bowed low. 'You do us, as ever, too much honour.'

Eleanor put her hands on Helewise's shoulders, raising her up again. 'Not so. In Hawkenlye I am given support and rare comfort. Why should I not bestow upon the community a little of what I have in abundance?'

Then, to Helewise's amazement, the Queen leaned forward, embraced her and kissed her.

Clutching the bag of gold as she watched the royal party depart, Helewise had tears in her eyes.

That visit was now several days in the past and already Helewise had taken the first steps towards the spending of the Queen's unexpected bounty. A Hawkenlye Herbal, she thought, what better use could there be, for it would serve both as a permanent tribute to King Richard and his mother and also, because of its content, benefit healers both currently engaged at the Abbey and those that were to come. Sister Phillipa was even now engaged in preparing a demonstration of her skills, and Helewise had written out – although not yet despatched – an order for parchment, pigments, inks, brushes and quills.

She had retired to her room to go over in her mind the recent interview with the Queen and to pray for her. Then, just as she had settled on to her knees, the knock at the door had come. And

Sister Ursel, the porteress, had announced that Father Micah was outside and wished to speak to her.

'I have told him that it may not be convenient but—'

'But I insisted,' Father Micah interrupted, pushing Sister Ursel out of the way and entering the room. 'Your prayers must wait, my lady Abbess, for I need to speak to you urgently.'

Rising to her feet, Helewise had swallowed her annoyance and, with a smile, invited Father Micah to be seated.

Standing before him – he had ignored the stool which Helewise kept for visitors and sat himself down in the Abbess's own throne-like chair – she listened in growing incredulity as Father Micah divulged the nature of his urgent matter. Now, swallowing her growing anger, Helewise was finding it more and more of an effort to keep the smile on her face.

For Father Micah's discourteous interruption had been for nothing more grave than to inform her that he was in need of a housekeeper. 'One of your nuns will do,' he was saying with a wave of a long, bony hand. 'Get her to come in once or twice a day. There is cleaning to be done and, for all that my appearance belies it, I have a good appetite and I need a woman who can cook a decent meal.'

Helewise was speechless. Biting down the angry retort – that her nuns had their own duties, thank you very much, and it was up to Father Micah to see to his domestic arrangements – she reflected how very, very sorry she was that poor Father Gilbert had broken his ankle and dumped this ghastly replacement on the Hawkenlye community. For a moment Father Gilbert's kindly face swam into her mind; he had struggled down to the small pond near to his house to break the ice and allow the birds to drink. Then, turning to go back inside, he had fallen heavily on the rock-hard ground. As well as the broken ankle, he had given himself a severe concussion.

His benign image helped her to reply politely, 'My nuns have work enough here, Father Micah, but perhaps I can find someone in the neighbourhood who will be able to cook and clean for you—'

'I'm not having some slut of a girl with dirt under her fingernails and lust in her heart!'

'I would not recommend such a girl, even if I knew of one.' Helewise kept her tone level.

Father Micah was looking suspiciously at her. 'I don't want one of those whores you tend in your house of fallen women, either,' he went on, as if she had not spoken.

That idea was so inconceivable that Helewise almost laughed. 'Quite so, Father,' she murmured. 'It would not be suitable at all.'

'They are evil in God's sight,' the priest declaimed, 'and by their foul and unnatural behaviour they lead good men into sin!'

Helewise, who had always considered that it was at least as much the other way round, wisely kept her peace. It was not the moment – if moment there ever would be – to remind the Father that many women were driven to prostitution as the only alternative to death by starvation. Which, while it might be acceptable to a woman on her own, with only herself to worry about, was certainly not an option when she had a child or two to feed.

And, anyway, was mankind not taught that their God was a God of love, and that He forgave those who repented of their sins?

Listening to Father Micah – he had taken the opportunity to launch out into a vicious diatribe against women who turned men's eyes, heads and hearts from where they should be, rapt in the contemplation of the Lord – Helewise admitted to herself how much she disliked him.

And that, she well knew, was going to be very awkward since, all the time Father Gilbert lay incapacitated in his bed, Father Micah was her confessor.

Oh, dear Father Gilbert, she pleaded silently, come back to us soon! How am I to manage with this cold substitute, who stares at me as if he hates me and who is as likely to understand the particular problems of my position here as the stable cat?

Helewise and Father Gilbert had, over the years, established an excellent relationship. It was helped by the fact that they genuinely liked one another and were good friends. Although Father Gilbert took his responsibility for Helewise's soul far too seriously for there to be any question of leniency with her, nevertheless, once he had heard her confession and given her penance, he frequently managed to turn their subsequent conversation round to matters that caused her anxiety. There had been the time, for example, when Sister Euphemia, the infirmarer, had reported to Helewise that the daughter of a rich and influential merchant was not, as her fond father believed, suffering from a stomach upset but was in fact pregnant. The girl had quietly lost the baby and Helewise had not corrected the father when he said what a relief it was to see his girl over her sickness and with no harm done.

Having heard her confess her lie and awarded her penance, Father Gilbert had remarked gently that it was wise to ask oneself three things before answering a difficult question. Is my reply true? Is it necessary? Is it kind?

'And how should one act if only some of the answers are in the affirmative?' Helewise had asked.

Father Gilbert had given her his sweet smile. 'Abbess Helewise, I usually act on the principle that three out of three means I give the answer, no matter how difficult; two out of three means I may or may not, depending on the circumstances; and one out of three means I keep my mouth shut.'

Imagine, Helewise thought now, such a conversation with *this* dry fellow. She wondered absently just how long Father Micah was intending to go on haranguing her; already it felt as if he had been ranting away for hours. She began to pray quietly for a diversion.

Quite soon her prayer was answered. There was another tap on the door and, as soon as Helewise said, 'Come in!' Sister Ursel appeared once more and announced that Sir Josse d'Acquin had just ridden through the gates and, if it was not too much trouble, would like a few words with the Abbess.

Sir Josse, Sir Josse, how very fond I am of you! thought the Abbess.

With a carefully polite inclination of the head to Father Micah, she said, 'A shame that we cannot continue our conversation, Father, but I know how busy you are and I would not detain you longer.' Then, turning to the porteress, she added, 'Please, Sister Ursel, ask Sir Josse to come in.'

# 3

'They are an abomination in the sight of God. They must be cast into the purifying flames, every last man, woman and child.'

The thin priest's eyes, fixed on Josse, were dark and impenetrable. As black as the cloth of his robe, and reflecting as little light. As little life; it was difficult to believe that a human heart pumped within the narrow chest. That a human brain was contained within the pale, shaven skull.

Josse, the guest at the Abbey, waited to see if the Abbess would speak. But although her flushed face appeared to indicate a degree of indignation, she kept her peace. Josse was at a loss to understand what was going on. Having been ushered into the Abbess's room by a harried Sister Ursel, he had discovered that she was not alone, as he had expected, but stood stiff with outrage before a scrawny, white-faced priest who seemed to have taken up permanent residence in her chair.

And somehow the conversation had turned to the subject of heresy. The Father, it seemed, had been well into his stride when Josse entered the room; Josse had overheard some remark about those who abandoned the ways of righteousness not being worthy of consideration, and apparently the priest had cited heretics as a prime example.

With an apologetic glance at the Abbess, Josse said carefully, 'Are not heretics also the children of God, Father?'

Father Micah's deep eyes seemed to burn with fervour. He said, with the finality of the weigher of souls on Judgement Day, 'They forfeit that blessed right when they set their feet on the paths of sin.'

'Surely you overlook forgiveness?' Josse persisted. 'Did Our Lord not order us to forgive those who trespass against us?'

The expression on the Abbess's face should have warned him; she was frowning so hard that her brows almost collided. And she was right, Josse reflected; it was folly to have opened a debate on ecclesiastical philosophy with a fanatical cleric . . .

'But the trespass is not against us, is it, Sir Josse?' Father Micah's lean, pale cheeks had taken on a faint flush. 'The sin is against God Himself, from whom these wretches turn in their madness!' He paused, breathing deeply, and appeared to be waiting until he was calm once more before continuing. 'Any man – any woman or child also – who turns from the one True Church and from the knowledge of God commits treason,' he said eventually, his voice cool and distant. 'And the penalty for treason is known to all.'

'Death,' Josse whispered.

'Indeed.' Father Micah, whose virtually lipless mouth had briefly twisted into a sardonic smile, gave him a brisk nod of approbation, as if rewarding a dull child who had finally and against all expectation come up with the right answer. 'Death by burning.'

Josse, momentarily brought to a standstill by the horror of that sort of death, found he had nothing to say. The Abbess, as if she had been waiting for the chance, instantly spoke up. 'Father Micah, we have detained you far too long,' she said smoothly, moving as she spoke to go and open the door. 'I am quite sure you wish to be about your duties, a busy man such as you.'

At first Josse thought she must be making some sort of a joke and he half expected the priest to drop his frightening intensity and relax his ferocious face into a grin.

But he didn't. Getting to his feet with a swish of his long dark robe – which emitted, Josse noticed, a faint smell of old fish – Father Micah nodded curtly to him, gave the Abbess a glance that looked strangely like a sneer and swept out of the room.

The Abbess walked across the floor and sank into her chair. Josse, closing the door firmly, rested his broad shoulders against it just in case the Father decided to return for one last harangue. 'And exactly who,' he asked, 'is *that?*'

The Abbess had leaned her head against the back of her chair and closed her eyes. Josse watched her anxiously, concerned at the desperation he saw in her face. But then, at first very slowly, she began to smile. Opening her eyes, she looked at Josse and said, 'That, my dear Sir Josse, friend and deliverer, is our parish priest, the replacement for Father Gilbert.'

'Father Gilbert is . . . ?' Josse could not bring himself to ask the question.

'Oh, no, no, he's all right! Well, he's not, he has broken his ankle and given himself a nasty blow to the head, but he will recover. I pray he hurries up about it!'

'So you're landed with that cold fish?' Josse whistled softly. 'Oh, my lady, I *am* sorry for you.'

He had spoken in all sincerity, but to his discomfiture the Abbess began to laugh. 'Sir Josse, you must excuse me,' she said after a moment, merriment still lively in her face, 'but it amuses me that, after but a brief experience of the man, you judge so accurately that he and I are not destined to be friends.'

'To say the least,' Josse muttered.

'Ah, I am glad to see you!' She was still smiling widely.

'So it seems. Your deliverer, my lady? What did you mean?'

'I had been praying that someone would come and rescue me before Father Micah talked me into my grave.' She tried, and failed, to straighten her face. 'He had been lecturing me for some time on the irredeemable sins committed by fallen women and, I believe, gone on to the even greater sin of heresy, only I confess I had all but ceased to listen. Then in you came, and what more welcome rescuer could there be than you?'

They talked for a long time. Good friends that they were, they had not met since the previous autumn, and there was much to catch up on. Having covered the minutiae of both the Abbess's daily round and his own – in considerable detail, since each was well-versed in the doings of the other – the conversation eventually turned to the pressing matter of the moment.

Josse was immensely gratified that he had been right in his assumption that Queen Eleanor would have made the time for a visit to Hawkenlye Abbey. Listening intently to the Abbess's account of what had passed between the Queen and herself, he was pleased, for Queen Eleanor's sake, that she had found a kind and sympathetic ear at Hawkenlye.

When the Abbess told him about the Queen's gift and what she had in mind to do with it, he agreed that the concept of a Hawkenlye Herbal was a good one. 'And you have someone with the skill to do justice to such a book?' he asked.

'I believe so, Sir Josse. A young nun, one whom I do not think you have met, informs me that she is an artist. She is preparing an example of her work so that I may judge for myself. In fact' – she rose to her feet as she spoke – 'I think she may by now have finished. Will you accompany me while I go to see?'

'Gladly I will.'

He followed the Abbess as she led the way along the cloister and around a corner to a private spot that he did not think he had visited before. There was nobody there, but a tall desk and a stool indicated where the artist had sat. On top of the desk, a cloth had been carefully tucked round several objects to protect them. As Josse watched, the Abbess raised the cloth, revealing pots, paints, brushes, ink and a small piece of parchment.

The Abbess picked up the parchment. Josse waited. After a moment, she said, 'Sir Josse, I believe that my project's success is assured.' Then she passed the parchment to him.

He saw straight away that she was right. The unknown nun had captured the very essence of her subject; the blackberries looked so lifelike that they all but made his mouth water. And the text was inscribed in a bold, flowing hand that was both attractive and easy to read, although Josse, whose reading skills were not well developed, found he had to struggle a little with some of the words.

'It is exquisite, my lady.' He handed back the scrap of parchment.

'You think I would be right to go ahead and order the materials?' She looked at him anxiously. 'It is a lot of money . . .'

'Aye, I do,' he said firmly. 'Queen Eleanor, you say, wishes a permanent tribute to the King?'

'Yes. That was what she specified. To the King and his mother, in recognition of their grief and sorrow at this terrible time of the King's imprisonment.'

'Aye.' He sighed. The King's present condition was a fact that seemed to have taken up permanent residence in his mind, sometimes at the back, sometimes – as now – brought to the forefront. Turning back, not without effort, to the matter in hand, he said, 'Well, in your proposed herbal, it would seem, you have something both useful and decorative. What could be better?'

The Abbess appeared to think for a while longer. Then, her face clearing, she said, 'Thank you. Then I will arrange for the order to be sent without delay.'

'Er – might I ask to be allowed to meet your artist?' he ventured.

'Sir Josse, of course! I will send for her, and you shall be present when I tell her of the role she is to play in our great undertaking. But the meeting will have to wait until after Nones – will you come to pray with the community?'

Telling her that he would like nothing better, he walked beside her across the cloister to the Abbey church.

Back in the Abbess's room, Josse leaned against the wall as she settled herself in her chair. She had despatched a novice nun to go and find Sister Phillipa and tell her she was wanted in the Abbess's room and, after a short wait, there was a soft tap on the door.

In answer to the Abbess's quiet 'Come in' a young nun in the black veil and habit of the fully professed opened the door and advanced into the room. She was, Josse could see, very nervous; the oval face with its high cheekbones had a pink flush, and the clear blue eyes were very bright. Even with the severe, starched white wimple that concealed the jaw, neck and throat, and the forehead band that covered the hair, it was plain to see that this girl was a beauty. It pleased him to watch her graceful movements as, with a low bow to the Abbess, she straightened up and stood, head bent, hands folded in front of her, to wait for her superior to speak.

'Sister Phillipa, this is Sir Josse d'Acquin, a good man and a true friend to our community.' The Abbess indicated Josse, and Sister Phillipa turned and gave him a radiant smile. Temporarily bowled over by its intensity, Josse quickly decided that it was more a reflection of the young woman's nervous state than of any sudden rush of emotion towards him. They were, after all, total strangers. 'We have been looking at the example of your work,' the Abbess was continuing, 'and we are agreed that it seems right that you be given the task that I have in mind.' She paused, and Josse guessed she was weighing her next words. 'Hawkenlye Abbey has been asked, as have other foundations, to pray for our great King Richard, for he has need of our prayers. His lady mother, the Queen Eleanor, has been very generous and given us a gift of coin in recognition of our intercession on the King's and her own behalf. With this bounty, Hawkenlye will prepare a herbal, in the names of the King and his mother.'

Josse noticed that Sister Phillipa was trembling. Touched that the painting of the herbal meant so much to her, he wished he could see her expression. But she stood with her back to him, facing the Abbess.

'Sister Phillipa, will you make the Hawkenlye Herbal?' the Abbess asked gently.

And, with what sounded like a sob in her voice, Sister Phillipa said, 'Yes. Oh, *yes!*'

The short February daylight was almost over when Josse left the Abbess. They had shared a happy moment together after the blissful Sister Phillipa had departed; as the Abbess had remarked, it was a rare pleasure to give one of her community tidings that brought such joy.

Josse realised that it was too late to think of riding on to New Winnowlands tonight. So, having checked with Sister Martha that his horse would be well looked after – there was no need for such a check, but he always enjoyed exchanging a few remarks with the brawny nun who tended the stables – he took the path that led out from the rear of the Abbey and made his way down into the Vale.

In the Vale was situated the miraculous Holy Water spring that was the reason for the Abbey's having been sited where it was. The spring was housed in a simple little shrine, two of whose walls were formed from the rock out of which the magical waters ran. Beside the shrine was a rough and ready shelter where pilgrims who came to receive the waters could take their meals and, when necessary, put up for the night. A little way down the track was the dwelling where Hawkenlye's monks and lay brothers lived. It, too, was rudimentary, with few comforts other than a roof, four rather insubstantial walls and some thin old mattresses and blankets.

What the monks' dwelling lacked in amenities it made up for in the warmth of the brothers' welcome. In particular, that of the two lay brothers, Brother Saul and young Brother Augustus, who were Josse's particular friends. As Josse stuck his head in through the open doorway, Brother Saul saw him, got up and came over to embrace him, crying out, 'Sir Josse! It's good to see you! Come in, come in, and warm your toes by the fire!'

'A fire! Great heavens, Saul, you're getting soft in your old age!' Saul was no more than thirty, at most.

'Aye, we're lucky, Sir Josse, and indeed it is a rare luxury. Only it's been so cold, these last few nights, and' – he lowered his voice diplomatically – 'some of the older brothers do suffer so, and the Abbess, bless her good, kind heart, said we might light a blaze come evening.'

Josse smiled, giving Brother Saul a quick touch on the shoulder. 'It's a luxury that I shall enjoy to the utmost.'

He allowed himself to be led forward to a bench by the hearth.

He nodded to the monks whom he knew, exchanging a few words of greeting with Augustus and old Brother Firmin. Presently, he was brought a bowl of broth and a hunk of rough bread, both of which he ate enthusiastically. The soft hum of male voices around him lulled him into drowsiness and, before the night was very old, Saul made him up a bed in the corner and he was soon asleep.

He awoke to the sound of hammering.

Getting up – he seemed to be the last man still asleep inside the monks' dwelling – he went outside to see what was happening.

He noticed straight away that it was considerably colder this morning than yesterday. The sky looked . . . sort of *thin*, he decided, and the wind had dropped. The air, however, felt like solid ice.

A group of monks were standing in a rough semicircle around the doorway of the pilgrims' refuge. A large branch had fallen down from one of the chestnut trees in the grove that sheltered the Vale's buildings, and it had landed right on a corner of the refuge's roof. The flimsy construction was not designed to withstand the impact of heavy branches and it had partially collapsed.

Saul and Augustus were trying to get the weight of the branch off the roof before it did any more damage. Brother Erse, the Hawkenlye carpenter, had a mouth full of nails and a hammer in his hand and seemed to be attempting to fix a strengthening truss under the sagging roof. All three were, quite obviously, failing.

What they needed was another pair of hands. Josse rushed forward and added his strength to that of Saul and Augustus. With three of them pushing, the branch gave a little. Then a little more. Then they managed to roll it right off the roof and there was a great crack as the now-unsupported branch tore away from the chestnut tree and fell to the icy ground.

There was a ragged round of applause from the audience of monks. Turning to grin at them, Josse noticed how cold they looked; they were, he noticed with compassion, mostly elderly, thin and shivering. Brother Firmin's skinny old feet in the clumsy sandals were bare and rapidly turning blue.

He turned to Brother Saul, whom he had always considered the most sensible and wise of the Hawkenlye brethren. 'Shouldn't the old boys go back inside?' he whispered.

'I've been telling them so all morning, Sir Josse!' Saul protested. 'Only Brother Firmin, bless him, said they wanted to help.' He gave a kindly laugh. 'Help! Hardly likely, is it?'

'Shall I try?' Josse suggested.

'Oh, Sir Josse, I wish you would!'

Josse's powers of persuasion were clearly superior to those of Brother Saul, or perhaps the old monks had simply got too cold to persist; either way, they gave in without an argument and meekly shuffled back to their dwelling.

Saul watched them go with a smile, then turned back to the pilgrims' shelter. And, eyes widening, said, 'Dear Lord, but it's ruined!'

From within, Brother Erse called out, 'Not as bad as that, Saul. Not quite,' and Augustus, up on the roof, added, 'It's close, though!'

The four of them collected in front of the shelter. The roof had caved in on one side, where a supporting post had given way. The wooden planks of one wall had deep cracks in them; another wall had developed a worrying outward curve.

After some time, Brother Erse said lugubriously, 'Reckon we'll have to rebuild the whole thing. Won't be safe, else. We don't want the risk of it coming tumbling down on top of a gathering of pilgrims.' With a quick grin, he added, 'The poor souls come here to have their hurts mended, not be given a whole lot more.'

'Thank God nobody was inside last night,' Saul breathed.

And they all said, 'Amen.'

'How long do you think it will take?' Josse asked. He was thinking of Hawkenlye's visitors, the sick, the injured and the needy who came to take the healing waters and pray with the monks for relief from their afflictions. What were those poor folk to do if they arrived in this bitter weather to find no shelter, no comfort, nothing but the cold, hard ground?

Brother Erse was eyeing the collapsed shelter as if it were a dangerous animal, rubbing his chin absently with one square hand and swinging the hammer in the other. 'Won't be an easy job,' he remarked. 'Ain't no way we can ask the old 'uns to lend a hand – they'd be more of a liability than a help. Reckon a week, maybe more, with just the three of us.'

Several thoughts ran through Josse's head. He pictured some poor family with a sick child making the fraught winter journey to Hawkenlye and finding nowhere to shelter. He thought of the welcome that the monks and the nuns always gave to everyone, him included. And he thought how long it was since he had thrown himself into a satisfying job of manual work.

Making up his mind – not that it took long – he said, 'Not three of you, Erse. Four. If you're prepared to put me up a while longer, I'll stay and help.'

# 4

It was not long before Helewise heard about the new labourer working down in the Vale. Brother Firmin considered it his duty to inform her, which he did with his usual amount of conversational preamble. Was she in good health? Did she not find the very cold weather a trial? How good it was of her to permit the lighting of an evening-time fire in the monks' home.

Trying not to show her impatience – there were at least twenty tasks that she had promised herself she would complete before midday – she interrupted him with a gentle, 'How may I be of assistance, Brother Firmin?'

He had to scratch his head in thought before replying; even he, it seemed, had forgotten the purpose of his visit.

'Ah, yes!' he said after a moment. 'The pilgrims' shelter had been damaged, my lady Abbess. The branch of a tree fell on it, damaged, it is thought, by the hard frost. We are putting it – the damage, I mean – to rights. That is, Brother Saul, Brother Erse and Brother Augustus are. And Sir Josse has very kindly said he will help.'

'Has he, indeed?'

'Aye.' Brother Firmin nodded eagerly. 'We are, of course, offering him what hospitality we can, and he says he is well used to sleeping down in the Vale.'

'We are lucky in our friends, are we not, Brother Firmin?' she said quietly.

'Oh, yes, my lady. Yes. Er . . .'

'Yes?'

'We – that is, I was wondering . . . Might you spare a moment to

41

come down and see how work progresses? Your presence would, I am sure, spur our little workforce to yet greater efforts.'

'I will, Brother Firmin. And I will take the chance to thank Sir Josse.' She went on smiling at the old monk, feeling her cheeks begin to ache with the sustained effort. He went on smiling back. Finally she said kindly, 'Was there anything else? Only I am rather busy . . .'

Bowing, apologising and backing out of the room all at the same time, he wished her good day and left her.

Helewise eventually went down to the Vale as the short afternoon was ending. As she descended the path she saw with dismay that the pilgrims' shelter was all but demolished. Hastening her steps, she hurried towards the four black-clad figures working in its ruins.

Someone had found a monk's habit for Josse to work in. It was a little too short; she had a rather disconcerting sight of strong, muscular, hairy calves above firmly tendoned ankles. She had not appreciated how broad he was; in his usual garb of padded tunic, it was impossible to tell where the man ended and the garment began. But, dressed in the single black woollen garment – which, she now perceived, strained across Josse's shoulders as he worked – she saw just what a fine figure of a man he was.

Stop it, she ordered herself firmly. Stop looking at him like that.

Pausing to arrange her face into a suitably nun-like and innocent expression – none of the men had noticed her approach – she folded her hands in the opposite sleeves of her habit and glided up to the shelter.

'How goes the work, brothers?' she called.

Saul and Augustus were fixing the vertical planks of the outer wall to the horizontal supporting beams; Josse and Erse were working one each end of a large saw and appeared to be preparing more planks. All four men stopped what they were doing and, as best they could given that they were clutching either a large piece of wood or the end of a saw, gave her a courteous bow in greeting.

'We have strengthened the basic structure of the shelter, my lady,' Brother Erse said, panting from his recent exertions, 'and now we are replacing the walls.'

'You have all worked hard,' she observed. Appreciating, now that Erse had explained, just what a task they had set themselves, she thought that 'hard' understated the case. 'You must be exhausted!'

Josse wiped a hand across his brow. 'No, my lady. And the advantage is that the effort has kept us nice and warm!' He gave her a happy grin.

'We are in your debt, Sir Josse.' She returned his smile. 'Once again, you lend us your strength in our time of need.'

'I do so gladly,' he said simply. Then, the grin once more breaking out, 'I can't recall when I spent such a satisfying day!'

She was moved by him. By all of them, these four good men who threw themselves so honestly into this hard and exacting job. Not wanting her sudden emotion to show, she said brightly, 'How long until you finish?'

'We hope to have the new shelter built in another two or three days, my lady,' Brother Saul said. 'We're not receiving many visitors just now – too cold for travel – and those few who decide to make the journey and need a place to stay can come in the monks' house along with all of us. By the time this cold snap takes itself off, we'll be ready.'

'Good, good.' She nodded. She wondered what she could do to help; an idea occurred to her. With a private smile, she nodded again and bade them farewell.

As the monks, lay brothers and Josse settled down for a bite to eat before turning in, they were surprised – and very pleased – to receive, along with the soup and the bread, a large jug of hot, spiced wine. 'With the Abbess's compliments,' said the young cookhouse nun who brought it, 'and she hopes there's enough for the workers and the rest of you and all.'

Sleep, Josse reflected drowsily as he lay down on his straw mattress and arranged the blankets around him, came a good

deal more readily after a hard day's work, a hot meal and a mug
of good, strong wine . . .

Two days later, in the early afternoon, the shelter was all but
finished. Brother Erse was putting the final touches to the roof,
Brother Augustus was giving the beaten earth floor a good
sweeping, Saul and Josse were preparing the small amount of
furnishings, making them ready for being replaced in the shelter
as soon as it was ready. They had thoroughly scrubbed the rickety
table, and Erse had done what he could to make it a little less
rickety. They had given the long benches similar treatment, and
now were engaged in beating the dust and dirt of years from
the thin palliasses and the much-mended blankets. Augustus had
earlier taken the old, worn trenchers and mugs away and washed
them ready to be put back on the freshly scrubbed shelf where
they were habitually stored.

Folding the last of the blankets and adding it to the neat pile,
Saul said, 'You know, Sir Josse I reckon that there old branch did
us a favour. We've had to rebuild the shelter, aye, but in doing so
we've given it a clean and a tidy-out the like of which it hasn't
seen in years.'

Josse glanced at him, noting the smile of satisfaction. 'Aye,
Saul,' he agreed, 'a job well done, eh?'

'And a job completed just in time,' Augustus added, emerging
from the shelter and coming to stand beside them. 'There, if I'm
not mistaken, come the first occupants.'

Josse and Saul turned to look where he was pointing. A party
of five was making its way along the track that ran beside the lake,
frozen now into deep winter stillness. A man led the way, holding
the rein of a donkey. Perched on the animal was a woman holding
a small child in her arms, and walking along behind was an older
woman and a boy of about seven.

Someone inside the monks' dwelling must have been keeping
lookout. Three monks emerged, walking out to meet the visitors,
taking the donkey's rein from the man, helping the woman to
dismount and relieving her of her burden. There was the sound of

enquiring voices, tired answers. One of the monks turned to look towards the shelter; Saul called out, 'It's ready. Give us a moment and the visitors can come in and make themselves comfortable.'

Within an hour, the pilgrims had been fed, given hot drinks and were seated on the shelter's benches before a cheerful fire. There were two sick among them: the smaller child and the old woman. The child had a persistent cough, and Saul had already gone to fetch Sister Euphemia and ask for some of Sister Tiphaine's white horehound cough mixture. The old woman's trouble was less straightforward; she was complaining of a dragging feeling in her belly and Brother Firmin, who was overheard muttering about 'women's troubles', had announced it to be clearly a matter for the infirmarer.

In the meantime, the monks had taken the little family into the shrine for prayers and Brother Firmin had given them all a draught of the healing waters. By bedtime, all five were in much better spirits and already hopeful of recovery.

Sister Euphemia came down to see the old woman the next day. Josse had no idea what transpired during the consultation; the infirmarer had very firmly and pointedly closed the door of the newly rebuilt shelter and said that she wished for privacy. Whatever she did must have been effective; the old woman emerged with a smile on her face and a lightness of step that certainly had not been there when she arrived.

The family, once freed of their anxieties, proved to be entertaining guests. They had not come far; their village was no more than a short morning's walk away. They brought news of violent happenings: a few days ago, a sheriff's officer guarding the gaol just outside the village had been attacked and killed. The two prisoners who had been in his custody, a man and a youth, had disappeared. Nobody seemed to mourn the sheriff's officer, who, according to the younger woman, had been a 'right bastard, vicious and a bully an' all'. When Brother Firmin timidly asked if there was anything to fear from the escaped prisoners, the man of the party scratched his head, furrowed his brow in thought for a moment and finally said, 'Dunno.'

There was considerable fascinated speculation. Josse, listening, occasionally smiled to himself at some of the wilder conjectures. The talk was harmless, though, and understandable; the monks lived an isolated and monotonous life down in the Vale and exciting events reported from the outside world always generated a lot of gossip.

Among the chatter he suddenly heard his own name mentioned. Alert, he listened in to the conversation.

' . . . want to get Sir Josse here to investigate,' Brother Erse was saying to the man and the old woman.

'Eh? Sir what? Ain't he a monk?'

'No, indeed he is not. He's only dressed that way because he's been helping us to rebuild the shelter,' Erse explained in an all too audible whisper. Then, looking up and noticing that Josse was listening, he reddened faintly and said, 'They say there's a bit of a mystery, Sir Josse. The dead man was hit in the face, seemingly, only it wasn't such a blow as should have killed him. I was saying, you're a bit of an expert on such things and maybe you'd . . . ?' Apparently overcome by the daring nature of his proposal, Erse dropped his chin and shook his head in confusion. 'But there, I dare say you've more important things to do with your time,' he muttered.

Forestalling the old woman's remark – she began to protest that it *was* important, at least to the people of her village – Josse said, 'I will be happy to come, if that is what you wish?' He raised his eyebrows at the man.

'Well,' he replied slowly. 'Well, I don't know as if I should—'

'Never mind if you should!' his wife protested. 'There's a matter needs resolving and here's someone willing and, it appears, able to do just that.' Josse could not but admire her summing-up of the matter. 'Why not take advantage of him, that's what I say! If you're truly willing, sir knight?'

'Aye,' he replied, grinning at her. She smiled back, and her pretty mouth was only slightly marred by a missing tooth. 'I am. When you depart from here for home, I will accompany you.'

Josse went to see the Abbess in the morning. The family was planning to set out as soon as they had eaten and he wanted to be mounted and ready so as not to delay them.

He told her what he intended to do and she nodded. 'You do not need my permission, Sir Josse,' she reminded him gently.

'No, I know I don't. But I wanted you to be aware that the shelter is finished; I am not deserting one task in order to take up another that is more to my liking.'

'The thought had not entered my head.' She paused, then said, 'Sir Josse, is any more known of this family or of the officer who died other than these sparse facts that you present to me?'

'No, my lady.' He waited for her to enlarge and, soon, she did so.

'I am thinking that there may be grounds for suspicion.'

'Oh? How so?'

She hesitated, then said, 'Probably I see danger where none exists. But we speak of a death; for all that the officer seems only to have suffered a minor blow, yet it has killed him. I fear . . .' She did not say what she feared. Instead: 'Will you take Brother Augustus with you, Sir Josse? Simply so that you will have someone young, fit and capable to watch out for you?'

He would have liked to say no. To add that he could take care of himself and did not need a guardian. But the Abbess's words, he had to admit, echoed his own vague uneasiness; there was something strange about this matter. And who but a fool ventured alone into a mystery when he was offered a reliable companion?

'Thank you, my lady, for your consideration and your sense,' he said. 'Aye, I'll take young Augustus, if he's willing to come.'

'He will be,' the Abbess murmured. Then, in a louder voice, 'Tell him to take the old cob. The animal could do with some exercise; Sister Martha says he's getting far too fat and lazy.'

The sun came out to see the travellers on their way. As before, the man led the donkey with his wife and younger child – now almost free of his cough – riding on the animal's back. The older boy walked beside his mother. The older woman had been pushed and pulled astride the Abbey's cob, and Augustus walked at the stirrup. Chortling, she said she'd never had such a fine ride in all her life.

Josse rode at the rear. He had offered the older child a seat in front of him up on Horace's back, but the child, apparently frightened, had violently shaken his head. It was understandable; Horace was restless and kept rolling his eyes and pulling at the bit, a sight quite alarming enough to scare a child into keeping his distance. Josse guessed that Sister Martha had been spoiling the horse; she usually did when he was in her care. When they were clear of the frozen pond and the track widened out, Josse took Horace out in front and kicked him into a canter, riding him hard for a mile or so before reining in and trotting back to meet the rest of the party. Having got the playfulness out of him, Josse settled down for a quiet morning's ride.

He and Augustus saw the family safely back to their little dwelling and asked for directions to the building that housed the gaol. Then, bidding them farewell, they rode on.

The presence of a mule and a couple of horses indicated that the representatives of law and order were still inside the gaol building. Tethering their own mounts and going inside, Josse and Augustus heard raised voices. Two men were arguing, another plaintively interrupting.

Josse called out. 'Hallo there!' The dissenting voices abruptly ceased. Then, from some hidden place at the end of a passage, there came the sound of footsteps.

'I'm coming!' a man's voice panted. 'These cursed steps will be the death of me!' And into view came a short and very fat man in a leather tunic over saggy, soiled hose. 'Yes?'

Josse introduced Augustus and himself, saying where they were from and how they came to be there. 'I was informed,' he went on regally, 'that there was a dead man and some mystery as to how he met his death. I have some experience in these things and have come to offer my services.'

The fat man seemed to be amazed that anyone should bother. 'He weren't a well-liked fellow,' he said, face creasing in puzzlement. 'Reckon there ain't no more mystery than that one of his prisoners thumped him in the face and the pair of 'em – him and the other one – legged it.' He grinned.

'They were locked up?' Josse asked.

'Aye, course they were. This here's a *gaol*.' The faint sarcasm was evident.

'And the sheriff's officer would have entered the cell to take in food?'

'Nah, not him! There's a trap door in the wall, see, and he opens the flap, shoves the food in then locks it up again.'

'I see. Then how, do you imagine, did the prisoner manage to achieve the blow to the guard's face?'

'Oh. Er. Hm.' The fat man lifted the front of his jerkin and began an enthusiastic scratching of his crotch. 'Hm.'

'I should like to see the body.' Josse stood over the fat man, trying to awe him into obedience.

'Oh. Suppose you can if you want. Come with me.'

The fat man led the way along the passage and down a short flight of steep stone steps. Below, three small cells opened off a corridor. The doors to all three were open and the foul stench from within each cell made Josse want to retch.

The fat man went ahead of him into the end cell. 'Here.' He pointed. 'Here he is. Tab, Seth, out of the way.' He kicked at the two men crouching by the body and they leapt aside. The presence of a hurdle beside them on the wet and soiled floor suggested they had been about to put the dead man on to it and bear him away.

Josse looked down at the guard. He lay on his back and, as Josse had been told, had clearly suffered a fist in the face. The top lip was split and the nose squashed. Quite a sizeable fist, Josse thought, or else the assailant hit him more than once.

But he had to agree that the blow did not at first glance

look as if it had been fatal. Perhaps the man had fallen and cracked his skull on the hard stone floor. Lifting the head, Josse felt all over it for the presence of a wound. There was nothing.

But something had killed him.

Leaving aside the vague and unlikely possibility that the man had been sick and just happened to die at the very moment that he was punched and two prisoners broke out of his gaol, Josse proceeded to examine the rest of the body.

There was not a mark on it.

He sat back on his heels, thinking.

Then, spotting something, he said, 'Augustus?'

'Here,' came the lad's instant reply.

'Gus, can you get me a light?'

'Aye.' Augustus ran off, along the passage and up the stairs, quickly coming back again bearing a flaming torch. Good lad, that one, Josse thought. Keeps his eyes open. He must have noticed the torch when we were in the room upstairs.

By the light of the flame, Josse leaned forward and studied the dead man's throat. Yes. He had been right.

'Gus?'

In an instant the boy was crouching beside him. 'Sir Josse?'

'Look.' Josse pointed. To the left of the throat, up under the ear, where there was a faint, dark bruise. And to the right, in the same place, where there were four more.

He heard Augustus's sudden sharp gasp. And the boy said, 'Someone throttled him.'

'Aye,' Josse agreed. 'Gus, let's have your hand . . .'

Comprehending instantly, Augustus put his hand around the dead man's neck. His thumb and fingers, even at full stretch, came nowhere near the bruises. Josse then did the same. Although his hands were larger than Augustus's, he could not have made the marks either.

'He was a big man, this killer,' Augustus breathed into Josse's ear. 'Uncommon big.'

'Aye,' Josse muttered back. 'And there's something else,

Augustus.' He waited, almost believing that he could hear the lad's quick, intelligent brain at work.

Suddenly Augustus gave a sharp exclamation and swapped his hands over. Now his thumb was over the single bruise and his fingers a few inches short of the group of marks.

'Aye,' Josse whispered. 'When I asked you to stretch out your hand, instinctively you put out the right, because you're right-handed. But, as you have just realised, the killer used his left hand. Unless some circumstance prevented him from using his dominant hand – it was injured, or perhaps bound – then I think we can say we're looking for a left-hander.'

Augustus whistled softly. 'Aye,' he added, his awe-filled eyes meeting Josse's, 'and a bloody great big one.'

# 5

While Josse was away, Helewise received another visit from Father Micah. The priest informed her that he was dissatisfied with standards within the Abbey and Helewise, controlling with some difficulty her instinctive, outraged reaction, asked him meekly to elaborate.

'We will take a turn around the Abbey's various departments,' he said grandly. 'I shall point out those areas which are of most concern.' Rebellion seething under her quiet demeanour, Helewise fell into step beside him.

Within quite a short time, she had a good idea of what it was that formed the foundation of his complaint. In the small room behind the refectory where the cook nuns spent most of their working hours monotonously preparing large amounts of virtually the same few foods, Father Micah objected to the little songs some of the sisters sung and the occasional laughter-inducing pleasantry that helped to pass the long hours. In the infirmary anteroom, he objected to a weary young sister sitting down to roll bandages. The pain in her legs, which were swollen because she had spent much of the night on her feet caring for a very sick patient, should be, in Father Micah's opinion, offered to God in penance for her sins. She must henceforth stand to do her work.

Out in the chilly cloister, the priest stood for some time over Sister Phillipa, seated at her desk and engaged in illuminating a capital letter A. The work was beautiful, Helewise thought, but Father Micah complained that over-use of blue and gold smacked of luxury, not seemly in an order vowed to poverty. About to tell him that the Queen herself had bestowed the wherewithal for the purchase of those very pigments, Helewise changed her mind. She would not explain herself to this man.

He passed through Sister Bernadine's room without comment. Sister Bernadine was in charge of the Abbey's small collection of precious manuscripts. Something about her austere manner and her air of detachment, as if she silently communed with the angels, earned Father Micah's approval; with an all but imperceptible nod, he beckoned to the Abbess and left Sister Bernadine to her scripts.

Sister Emanuel, who had the care of the elderly in the small hostel that the Abbey ran for retired nuns and monks, also initially escaped without criticism. But then the retirement home was a quiet, devout place; aged men and women who were walking calmly and courageously towards their death and the hope of heaven tended not to sing and make jokes. When Sister Emanuel explained that she also helped the Abbess by taking over the keeping of the accounts ledger when Helewise was very busy, however, Father Micah fixed both nuns with an angry expression.

'This duty then interferes with the devotion you owe to your patients, Sister.'

It was an accusation that was, Helewise knew quite well, totally unfounded. She was on the point of saying so when, to her amazement, the priest turned to her. 'And, Abbess Helewise, you should not seek to ease your own burdens by increasing those of others.'

Helewise experienced the full range of emotions of the unjustly accused. Fury, resentment, humiliation and, yes, a certain amount of self-pity: she wanted to shout out, like a hurt and angry child, *it's not fair!*

Taking a calming breath – if she were to remonstrate with Father Micah in her own defence, to do so in front of the astonished Sister Emanuel was not the place – she inclined her head and walked out of the retirement home into the fresh, cold air outside.

Rather to her surprise, she found that Father Micah had followed her. Did it count as a minor victory, that, instead of waiting for him decide when he was ready to leave and lead the way out, she had pre-empted him?

Probably not, in his view. But it certainly did in hers.

Father Micah reserved the greater part of his spleen for the home for fallen women. Unfortunately, this was the area of her responsibility in which Helewise felt the most satisfaction; during her time as Abbess of Hawkenlye, the Abbey had earned a reputation as a humane, instructive and encouraging place for those deemed by society to be outcasts. Yes, some of the older women were too set in their ways to heed the call back to the path of righteousness. But even they, whom the nuns knew would make their way straight back to the dark corners where they plied their trade and earned their crust, were given help when they asked for it and sent on their way with a good meal inside them. Their unwanted babies were loved and cherished in exactly the same manner as the legitimate offspring of the richest nobleman.

Younger women, some of them resorting to prostitution in desperation, some the victims of assault, some fooled by young men promising everlasting love and marriage if they would but give in just this once, came in shame to Hawkenlye and found there the answer to their prayers. The nuns cared for them in their pregnancies and, in return, they performed what tasks were set them usually without protest. They were encouraged – an encouragement that had the force of an order – to attend services in the Abbey church and to pray for the strength to amend their lives. Their babies were delivered under the watchful eyes of the infirmarer or one of her midwives and afterwards, when mother and child were strong enough, the nuns did their best to find them homes. Sometimes a reluctant father could, with a little pressure, be persuaded to take the mother of his child to wife and give her baby a home. Sometimes a baby would be adopted by some childless couple as their own. Sometimes the nuns themselves would keep the child in their care while the mother left and returned to her former life.

Few women presented themselves again at the Abbey for

the same reason, which alone made Helewise believe that the Hawkenlye method was the right one.

Father Micah, it was immediately apparent, did not agree. The home was fairly quiet just then and, as he stalked into the low room, divided into one section for those who were pregnant and another for those who had given birth, only five women and two babies looked up to watch him.

'Come to lead us in our prayers, Father?' one of the recently delivered women asked cheerfully. She was a street woman from Tonbridge, known to the nuns because she had earlier brought a younger colleague to Hawkenlye. They had been surprised to see her present herself into their care; as Sister Tiphaine had remarked, she had been engaged in her trade for so long without mishap that they had imagined she could take care of herself.

Now, a first-time mother at the advanced age of twenty-nine, she held up her chubby and gurgling baby girl for the priest to bless.

He did no such thing. Instead, drawing his robes aside as if he feared that contact with a whore would pollute them, he said, 'Begone from my sight, harlot! And take that spawn of Satan with you.'

Then he spun round and marched out of the room.

Helewise heard the noisy sobs of the woman, the angry cries of her fellow-patients and, as an inevitable aftermath, the crying of their babies, frightened and upset by the disturbance. Above the babble a single female voice shouted out, making a suggestion as to what Father Micah ought to do with himself that was highly imaginative, if biologically impossible.

Helewise hardly heard. Racing after the priest, she caught up with him on the threshold.

'Father Micah, I must protest!' she said, as quietly as she could manage. 'In the name of Christ and his charity, I—'

He turned on her a face like thunder. 'Do not dare to speak Our Lord's name in such a context!' he commanded. 'That woman is shameless! *Shameless!* Holding up her bastard to receive the blessing of a man of God, with her cronies simpering around her, displaying their foul flesh, polluting God's pure air with the stench of their rottenness, the smell of the disgusting, putrid substance that seeps from their swollen breasts! How *dare* she! They should be flogged, the lot of them, aye, and branded with the mark of their shame!'

His thin face had turned almost purple in his fury. His breathing came very fast and small bubbles of sweat were appearing on his brow and upper lip.

Helewise, observing him, feared for his health. And, in the midst of that detached thought, she suddenly felt sorry for him.

'Let us return to my room,' she said calmly. 'Perhaps you will take a restorative glass of cool water, Father.'

He turned on her. 'Not from you,' he replied rudely. 'I shall visit the holy brethren in the Vale.'

'As you wish.' She kept her tone neutral.

'I expect there to be changes here.' He was gazing out towards the Abbey church. 'I want to see less flippancy and wasteful profligacy and more evidence of devotion.' He turned to stare at Helewise. 'And those filthy whores are to be gone when next I visit.'

He is mad, Helewise thought as she watched him stride away. That, surely, is the only answer. Walking back to the precious sanctuary of her little room, she wondered what on earth she was to do.

Some time later, there was a timid knock on her door and Brother Firmin came in. He was in tears. Father Micah, he said, had ordered him to stop being so generous with the Holy Water and to be sure to give it only to those who led a devout life and prayed several times a day for forgiveness. 'But how am I to *tell*, my lady?' the old monk sobbed. 'He didn't think to explain that!'

Trying to comfort him – which was not easy – Helewise told him to continue as he had always done for the time being, and promised that she would take the matter up with Father Gilbert.

'He said he would be back,' Brother Firmin said dully. 'He told us he had other calls to make – he mentioned some noble lord who has to be reminded of God's law and he said something about banishing lost souls to the eternal fires. But he'll be back, my lady.'

His tear-reddened eyes met Helewise's, and her heart turned over with pity.

'Try not to worry, Brother Firmin,' she said kindly. 'Return to the Vale and to ministering to your pilgrims. Leave Father Micah to me.'

She saw, with relief, that her words seemed to bring some comfort to Brother Firmin. She wished, as she watched him shuffle away, that she could say the same for herself.

Josse's return later in the day brought a very welcome distraction. Putting aside her own concerns, she asked him what he had discovered about the dead gaoler. Listening to his deep voice as he told her of the marks on the dead man's throat, gratefully she turned her mind to the mystery.

'Is it any way possible, Sir Josse, that one of the prisoners could have reached out through this trap door you speak of, where food is put into the cell?'

'I think not, my lady. And, in any case, neither prisoner had noticeably large hands, apparently. One was an adult man, but short and slight, the other but a youth.'

'And the cell door had not been forced?'

'No. Opened with a key.'

'The dead man's own key?'

'His colleagues believe so. But, my lady, they are a sorry lot and, I would guess, singularly dull-witted and unobservant.'

'Hmm. I conclude, Sir Josse, as I am certain you do too, that the assailant came from outside, struck down the guard, took his key and released the prisoners.'

'Quite so.'

'But why? Who were they, Sir Josse? Were you able to discover?'

'The other guards had little to offer on the matter.' He sighed, and she could sense his frustration. 'I dignify the three of them with the title of guard, but indeed two seemed to have been recruited merely to serve as bearers; they were on the point of removing the body when Augustus and I arrived. He's a good lad, Augustus,' he added. 'Uses his head.'

'I agree,' she said quietly. Then: 'You were saying, Sir Josse, that the guards had little to say?'

'Aye, aye.' He sighed again. 'One of them reported that the prisoners were strangers. Foreign, he said. His friend the dead man had complained that they kept shouting out and he couldn't make out what they wanted. Not that it would have made any difference, I imagine, since I'm sure he wouldn't have given them what they were asking for even if he had understood what it was.'

He was, Helewise observed, looking uncharacteristically dejected. 'What is it, my friend?' she asked gently. 'What is bothering you?'

'Oh – I'm being soft,' he said, rousing himself to a brief smile. 'It is entirely possible that those two prisoners were justly jailed, that they were guilty of some crime which deserved harsh treatment. But, my lady, you and I would not keep an animal in such conditions as I found in those cells, let alone a human being.'

'I do not think that your compassion earns you the accusation of being soft,' she said. 'If, indeed, such is a matter of accusation. But, Sir Josse, could you gain no idea of what their crime was?'

'No. The gaolers didn't seem to know and, when Gus and I tried making a few enquiries among the villagers, they wouldn't talk to us. They seemed afraid.'

'Of the gaolers?'

'Funny that you should ask, but no, I don't think that was it. There was someone else they feared. One woman Gus spoke to kept looking over her shoulder as if she feared the Devil himself was going to leap out at her. And a small child broke out in sobs and said something about the black man.'

'The black man? Black-skinned, do you think?'

'Aye, maybe.'

'Could these foreign prisoners have been dark-skinned?' Eager now, she pursued the idea. 'Perhaps a really tall, broad, black man came to rescue his friends, killing the gaoler with a huge hand and scaring all the villagers with his very size!'

Josse looked indulgently at her. 'I don't know, my lady. But it's as good a guess as any I've managed to come up with.'

★  ★  ★

In the morning, Helewise went to Prime with a heavy heart. She had slept badly, overcome with anxiety concerning what she was to do about Father Micah. Kneeling, she thanked God for that gift of pity for the priest, without which she would have been well on the way to hating him. 'He needs help, dear Lord,' she whispered, 'for surely something is seriously amiss with him . . .'

As the office began, she gave herself to her devotions. Peace began to settle around her, as it always did, and she felt the inestimable help of a strong energy supporting her. Some time later, heartened, she went out to face the day.

The first of the dramas came in the middle of the morning, when Helewise was seated at her wide oak table studying a list of outstanding rents owed by some of the tenants who farmed the Abbey's lands. Her concentration was broken by the faint sounds of someone outside her door. There was no knock, but she heard a quiet, suppressed cough and the sound of soft footfalls, as if someone were walking up and down the cloister.

Once she had noticed the noises, she found it impossible to ignore them. It seemed likely that, if she managed to do so and get back to work, whoever it was would instantly make up their mind that they really had to see her and tap on the door.

Helewise got up, went over to the door and opened it. Outside, her hand raised as if about to knock, was Sister Bernadine.

'Sister Bernadine!' Helewise said. 'You wish to see me?'

'Yes, my lady. That is, I am not sure – it is probably nothing, just my imagination, but although I keep telling myself so, I am still perturbed.'

It was quite a long speech for the usually reserved Sister Bernadine. 'Come in,' Helewise said, 'and tell me what it is that worries you.'

Sister Bernadine looked pale, Helewise thought, even more so than usual. And the smooth-skinned hands that were normally tucked neatly away in the opposite sleeves of the nun's habit were restless and fluttering.

Helewise guided Sister Bernadine to her own chair. 'You do indeed appear anxious,' she said. 'Here, take some sips of water . . .' – she held out a cup to Sister Bernadine's pale lips – 'there, that's better. Now, what has happened?'

Sister Bernadine turned wide, fatigue-shadowed eyes up to her superior. Not a woman to waste words, even when she was upset, she said, 'I went to the script room after Tierce. When we were there yesterday with Father Micah I had noticed that there were fingerprints on the lid of the book chest. I was relieved that the Father did not see them for I should have been ashamed had I given him the opportunity for a reprimand.'

'Quite,' Helewise murmured. The Father, she thought, had issued quite enough reprimands as it was.

'When I knelt down on the floor and began to polish the lid of the chest, something prompted me to look inside. I fetched the key from where it hangs in the window embrasure and opened the chest. And – oh, my lady Abbess, I cannot swear to it but I believe that somebody has been through the precious manuscripts.'

Helewise kept her voice calm. 'Is anything missing, Sister?'

'I don't know. My first swift glance inferred that about the right number of scripts were there, but I did not stop for a proper look. I thought it better to come straight to you, my lady.'

'Quite right, Sister Bernadine,' Helewise said stoutly. 'Now, we shall go back together and you will look more closely.'

'But—' Sister Bernadine, still very pale, closed her eyes.

'But what?'

Opening her eyes, she raised them to Helewise's. 'Supposing the thief – if, that is, there *is* a thief – is still there? Hiding behind the door, waiting to jump out on us?'

'It is not very likely, now, is it?' Helewise said briskly. 'Even if this hypothetical someone was there when you entered the room just now' – Sister Bernadine gave a low moan at the very thought – 'then they surely will not have remained there to be discovered.'

'But—'

'Come along.' Helewise made her tone purposeful. 'The sooner we have a good look, the sooner we shall know what we are faced with.'

She marched out of her room, Sister Bernadine at her side.

They walked around the cloister to the small room that was Sister Bernadine's domain and, silently, the pale nun pointed to the wooden book cupboard, a wide, shallow structure that stood roughly knee-high on six stout legs. Its front panel was decorated with a series of arches.

Helewise knelt down in front of it. She did not often look into the book chest and she had never gone right through it to inspect every script in detail, so she had little idea of what in fact she was looking for. She was about to make a remark to this effect when suddenly Sister Bernadine let out a wail.

'Oh, I have not checked that the missal is still here!' She hurried forward, knelt down beside Helewise and leaned into the chest. 'Oh, I pray that it is!'

'The missal, Sister?'

Sister Bernadine was carefully going through the scripts at one end of the chest. 'The St Albans missal, my lady, one of our most precious documents, presented to us by His Grace the Bishop . . . oh, thank God! Here it is!' She held up some sheets of parchment bound together, a smile of relief on her pale face. Helewise caught a glimpse of a page of careful lettering illustrated with three large and vivid illuminated capital letters before, with the care of a mother tucking up her infant child, Sister Bernadine tenderly replaced the missal in the book chest.

Looking around her, Helewise said, after a moment, 'I do not believe that I can be of help, Sister Bernadine. Because I am not familiar with the usual arrangement of the manuscripts, I cannot tell whether any have been removed. Is this chest the only repository for our manuscripts?'

'No, there is also the book cupboard let into the wall over there.' Sister Bernadine pointed. Getting up, she went to inspect the cupboard's wooden door. 'It may have been opened,' she said, 'I do not know.' She peered inside the cupboard then, with a sigh, said, 'I *think* that all is in order. But, as with the chest, something does not seem quite right.' She frowned, biting her lip in her anxiety. 'I am sorry, my lady, that I cannot be more explicit. It is merely that I know what the chest and the cupboard usually look like, and today – today—'

'They look different,' Helewise finished for her.

Sister Bernadine shot her a grateful glance. 'Precisely.'

'And you cannot yet say whether anything is missing?'

Sister Bernadine gave a helpless shrug. 'No, my lady. I am sorry, but no.'

'Very well.' Helewise spoke decisively. 'I suggest, then, that you now go through the full contents of the book chest and the cupboard and sort through the contents. I will send Sister Phillipa to assist you; between you, it should be possible to list what is here and compare it to the inventory. Take your time; I will not press you. Come and see me when you are able to say whether there has indeed been theft or whether somebody has merely been mischievous.'

Sister Bernadine, absorbed already in her task, muttered, 'Yes, my lady. Of course,' and gave Helewise a very brief bow. Then she began lifting manuscripts one by one from the chest, studying them and dusting off each one with a long white hand as if the possible indignity they had suffered, of somebody interfering with them who had no right to do so, could be stroked away.

And Helewise left her to her absorption and walked slowly back to her room.

She had decided that, regarding Father Micah, she must pay a visit to Father Gilbert. As a first step, in any case, for Father Gilbert might have knowledge of his replacement that could help Helewise in her dealings with him. She could also enquire tentatively how long it would be before Father Gilbert was up and about again.

If Father Gilbert could not help, then Helewise would have to appeal to a higher authority. Father Micah's superior first and, if all else failed, then to Queen Eleanor herself.

Whatever it took, Helewise vowed to herself, she had no intention of doing what Father Micah said and turning her fallen women out on the dubious mercy of the world.

*Whatever* it took.

★   ★   ★

By the time she returned to the Abbey church for Vespers, Helewise was feeling considerably more optimistic. As always, her mood was improved by having thought about her problems and taken the first steps towards solving them. Full resolution might be some way off still – Sister Bernadine and Sister Phillipa had as yet only scratched the surface of their task, and the difficult matter of Father Micah still seemed all but insurmountable – but at least, Helewise told herself, she knew what she intended to do. Closing her eyes and bending her head, humbly she asked God to spare the time to consider the priest. *Please, Lord,* she begged, *help him out of his distress. Help me, too. Please save the Hawkenlye community and those we serve from his wrath and his narrow-mindedness.*

The voices of her sisters rose into the still air, and Helewise gave herself up to the sweet sound of their chanting.

The alarm went up before dawn the next day.

A pedlar with a heavy load had set out early for Tonbridge market, knowing that his burden would make his progress slower than usual and wanting not to be late and risk losing his habitual spot in the market place.

On a dark stretch of the track up above Castle Hill, where an outcrop of the Great Forest cast even deeper shadows across the night's gloom, the pedlar noticed what he thought was a large sack lying half on the track, half in the ditch. Reasoning that it might very well have dropped off the cart of some other early riser making for market – Tonbridge was now only some five miles or so distant – the pedlar put down his own pack and went to see if he could find anything to his advantage.

He put his hands down to feel around what he thought was the neck of the sack; it certainly seemed, in the darkness, to be the narrowest point. And indeed it *was* a neck, of sorts; a human neck, broken, from which lolled a shaven head.

The pedlar did not wait to investigate further. Abandoning his pack – only extreme terror could have made him do that – he ran as fast as he could down the track to the place where it branched, one way going on down the hill to Tonbridge, the other skirting the forest and leading to Hawkenlye.

Banging on the Abbey's wooden gates, yelling himself hoarse, the pedlar attracted the attention of the community as it prepared to rise for Matins. Two of the lay brothers, Brother Saul and Brother Michael, were summoned from the Vale and Josse came with them. The three of them accompanied the pedlar back to his gruesome find.

The pedlar was right, Josse instantly determined; the body was quite dead.

And, although it was difficult in the darkness to be absolutely sure, he had a good idea of its identity.

Agreeing with the pedlar's repeated claim that he had done all he could, all you could reasonably ask an ordinary man to do, Josse said he could go on down to market; the pedlar had recovered by now and was once again preoccupied with his day's trading. When Brother Michael asked in a whisper if it was wise to let him go, Josse replied that the pedlar could hardly be a murder suspect since only a fool would kill a man, unseen, unsuspected, in the middle of the night and far from human habitation and then go and confess to an abbey full of nuns that he had done so.

'Oh,' said Brother Michael. 'Oh, I suppose so.'

Between the three of them they rolled the body on to a hurdle and, having first covered the head and face with a piece of sacking somewhat grudgingly given by the pedlar, bore it back to Hawkenlye.

The Abbess was waiting.

She accompanied the three men into the infirmary. Under Sister Euphemia's direction, they carried the corpse to a curtained-off recess and placed the hurdle on a trestle. Then, holding a light, Sister Euphemia leaned down, removed the sacking and inspected the dead face.

Straightening up, eyes wide with shock, she stared at the Abbess. Who had also seen who the dead man was.

In a voice that shook, the Abbess said, 'Dear God, it's Father Micah.'

# 6

'But how did he come to be lying out there?' the Abbess asked for the third time. 'What was he *doing*?'

Josse, bending over the corpse with Sister Euphemia beside him, felt a moment's annoyance; it was not like the Abbess, he thought, to stand wringing her hands in distress.

'We cannot yet know, my lady,' he said. 'The first thing is to determine how he died.'

'I thought you said his neck was broken!'

'Aye, it is.' Josse sensed rather than heard the infirmarer's irritation with her uncharacteristically nervous superior. Turning to the Abbess, he said, forcing what he hoped was a reassuring smile, 'Why not leave this to Sister Euphemia and me? When we're ready to start finding out what the Father's movements were yesterday, I'll come and find you to discuss how we might best go about it.'

'Oh.' She frowned. 'But I—' Then abruptly she nodded, turned swiftly and strode out of the infirmary.

'Something's worrying her,' Sister Euphemia muttered. 'But we won't dwell on what it is at the moment, eh, Sir Josse?'

'No,' he agreed. He gave her a grin. 'More important things to do.'

They returned to the task of inspecting Father Micah's dead body. As the infirmarer began carefully to unfasten and remove his garments, she said, 'Sir Josse, this robe feels like the laundry when it's been left out in the frost. It's stiff as a board.'

'Aye, Sister, you're right. Which suggests he was lying out there for quite some time.'

They worked in silence for a while. Then Josse said, 'Sister, would it be in order if we sent for Brother Augustus?'

She raised her head from removing the priest's sandals. 'You think we could do with another pair of sharp eyes?'

He chuckled. 'Well, you and I have managed reasonably efficiently on our own before now. But I'm thinking it would be good for the lad to give him some more experience in something for which he already shows an aptitude.'

'I agree,' she said. 'Aye, Sir Josse, you send for our Gus.'

Brother Augustus arrived from the Vale a little while later, panting. 'There was no need to hurry, lad,' Josse remarked. 'The Father here isn't going anywhere.'

'It is true, then, what they told me?' Augustus was advancing wide-eyed towards the trestle and its burden.

'Depends what you've been told,' Josse replied. 'What's true is that Father Micah was found on the track above Castle Hill early this morning. It seems that he was lying there all night. His neck is broken.'

'Did he have a fall? An accident?' Augustus asked. His eyes, Josse noticed, had gone straight to the dead man's throat.

'I already checked that,' Josse murmured to him. 'They're not there. No bruises on this one's neck.'

Sister Euphemia wrenched off the last of the priest's meagre undergarments. He lay, pale, thin and still, naked before the three of them. It was Augustus who muttered a quiet prayer; Sister Euphemia met Josse's eye and gave him a faint smile, jerking her head in Augustus's direction as if to say, nice lad, isn't he?

Josse wondered if the infirmarer had shared the Abbess's antipathy towards the dead priest. On balance, it seemed likely.

Augustus finished his prayer and opened his eyes. He looked faintly accusingly at Josse and the infirmarer, both of whom muttered belated and sheepish amens.

'Now then,' Sister Euphemia said, 'let's see if there is any information to be gained from this poor wretch's corpse.'

And then for some time there was quiet in the little recess as the three of them put their various emotions aside and got on with their task.

'His body bears no obvious injury,' Josse reported to the Abbess in the middle of the morning, 'other than a bruise on the chin and, of course, his broken neck. That appears to have been done from the front. As if, for example, he had run into a beam, hitting it hard with his chin so that his head was thrown violently backwards.'

'But there are no beams out on the track,' the Abbess said.

Josse wondered why her customary intelligence appeared to have deserted her. 'Quite so, my lady. I only cited the beam as an illustration. He could, perhaps, have slipped and hit his chin on the low branch of a tree.'

'A tree. Ah, yes.' Her grey eyes were vague and unfocused. Then, looking up and seeing him watching her, she appeared to make an effort. 'Or I suppose he might have died elsewhere – where there *were* beams – and then been dumped on the track.'

'He could, aye,' Josse said slowly. 'But that would make it murder, my lady, since a man whose neck is broken does not get up and walk somewhere else.'

To his consternation, she flushed deep pink and shouted, 'Well *I* didn't kill him!'

He said instantly, 'My lady, I did not imagine for one moment that you did!'

But she could hardly have heard. She was weeping, her head lowered on to her arms folded on top of her table. He went round to stand at her side, putting out a tentative hand to touch her shoulder. 'There, there,' he said, thinking even as he did so what an inane, inadequate utterance it was.

After a moment, one of her hands came up and clasped his in a quick, hard squeeze. He flinched slightly; she had strong hands. Then she raised her head, wiped her eyes and said, in almost her normal voice, 'I am sorry, Sir Josse, for that outburst. I did not sleep well, for my conscience is uneasy concerning Father Micah.' She turned her head so that she was looking up at him. 'I feared, in the first shock of receiving the news, that his death was my fault. I prayed to God last night at Vespers that Father Micah be helped out of his distress. I also asked that we at Hawkenlye be saved from his wrath and his bigotry.'

Josse perched on the edge of her table, a liberty he would not normally have taken. 'And you thought that God had answered your plea by kindly breaking the Father's neck for you?' She nodded. 'Oh, Helewise!' he whispered.

For a moment her eyes on his were full of emotion. Then she lowered them and began an earnest and concentrated examination of her folded hands.

He got off her table and went round to the other side of it, taking up his usual position just inside the door. From that slight distance, it was easier to get his own feelings under control. After a moment – which he could not help but think she needed as much as he did – he cleared his throat and said, 'I have indeed been wondering, in fact, if somebody attacked him. Not that there is any certainty of that – Sister Euphemia, Brother Augustus and I found no evidence for or against. It is equally possible that he had a fatal accident.'

'The putative branch,' she said. She still did not meet his eyes. 'Quite so.'

'We now have to look into how the Father spent his day yesterday,' Josse went on. This was easier, he was finding, if they kept their minds on the business in hand. 'He was here in the Abbey early in the day, I believe, my lady?'

'He was.' At last she raised her head and looked up at him. 'He insisted on my escorting him all around the various departments so that he could point out where we were going wrong. He was particularly vociferous in his condemnation of our work with the fallen women. He made a vicious comment to one of our newly delivered mothers and either she or one of her friends gave him an equally savage reply.'

'Indeed? Do you know which woman?'

'No, Sir Josse.' She gave a very faint smile, quickly gone. 'And even if I did, I am not sure that I would tell you. The idea that a heavily pregnant woman or a recently delivered mother would creep out of the Abbey, locate Father Micah out on the road and break his neck is, as I am sure you will agree, unlikely.'

'Aye,' he said softly. 'But women have men friends, do they not?'

'If they bear a baby then yes, they must have had on one occasion at least,' she replied tartly. 'So now we have an outraged expectant or new father murdering a priest because he insulted the man's woman? Really, Sir Josse! I think not.'

'Nevertheless, my lady, I must have your permission to ask the women in the hostel a few questions.' She did not answer. 'I will be gentle with them, you have my word.'

Her anger seemed to vanish as quickly as it had arisen. 'I know,' she said quietly. 'I know, too, that you understand the ways of the world a little better than poor Father Micah did. That you are well aware of the lives those women lead and you realise that to spend them in vice and sin is not necessarily their choice.'

He bowed his head. 'Aye, I do. And thank you.'

Somehow, he thought, the interview had become emotional again. Casting around for a simple question with no dangerous undercurrents whatsoever, he said, 'Do you know what Father Micah did after leaving you?'

'He went to see the brethren in the Vale,' she answered. 'I know that because later Brother Firmin came to see me in some distress. He, too, had been the recipient of a tongue whipping.' With a sudden flash of her usual smile, she said, 'But I don't suppose dear old Firmin broke Father Micah's neck any more than I did.'

'No.' He grinned back. 'Even less likely a candidate, I should imagine.' He thought – but managed not to say – that the old monk's hands were nowhere near as strong as hers.

'Oh!' she exclaimed suddenly. 'Sir Josse, I've just remembered something! You'll have to seek out Brother Firmin for the full story, but he – Firmin – told me where Father Micah was going next. I don't in fact know if he meant straight away or some time in the next few days, but Brother Firmin said that the Father spoke of calls he had to make, one to a nobleman or something, one to—'

She frowned as she tried to recall. 'No, it's gone. It was something rather horrible, I seem to remember . . . Something that made me recoil and think, oh, yes, that sounds like Father Micah.' There was silence for a moment as she tried to bring the details to mind. 'No. I'm sorry, Sir Josse, you'll have to ask Brother Firmin.'

He was already opening the door. 'I will,' he said. 'As soon as I've called in on the women in the hostel. Thank you, my lady,' he added belatedly. 'You have been very helpful.'

Then he closed the door and, breaking into a sprint, headed off along the cloister.

He was not sure what he had expected to find, but Hawkenlye's home for fallen women quite surprised him. For one thing, it was tidy and spotlessly clean; I am prejudiced, he told himself sternly, I believe squalor and filth to be the natural state of prostitutes rather than conditions brought about by abject poverty. For another thing, there was a decided air of happiness, of joy, about the hostel. He could hear soft female voices talking quietly and then someone laughed. He caught the gentle strains of a lullaby; one of the new mothers must be rocking her baby to sleep.

Standing just inside the door, he attracted the eye of a young, plump nun and raised his eyebrows in enquiry. She came gliding up to him across the polished flagstones. 'Yes?'

'I am Josse d'Acquin,' he said. 'May I speak to your – er, the women?'

'It'll be about that priest that's upped and died,' the young nun said sagely. 'Because we wear the habit of obedience and love of God, I cannot but pray for him. But in truth, Sir Josse, I—'

She managed to swallow the remark she was about to make. Studying her flushed face and the way in which she had tightened her generous lips, as if to hold the words in by force, Josse guessed that it took quite an effort.

'Father Micah visited the women yesterday, I am told,' he said. 'I would like to ask them what happened.'

'Of course. Follow me.'

He did as he was bid. The nun took him through an area

of the room where there were six beds, only three of which showed evidence of present occupancy. They then went through an archway into a second area where there were more beds and more space around them. 'This,' the nun said, 'is where the mothers and babies are cared for.'

'How many are here at present, Sister – er, I do not know your name.'

'I am Sister Clare. We've three pregnant women, although one I believe to be in labour. It is her first confinement and she is very nervous' – Sister Clare's voice had dropped to a whisper – 'so it may be merely anxiety that is making her think she feels her pains.'

'Ah.' He really could think of no fuller response.

'And we have two newly delivered mothers,' Sister Clare went on. 'Come and meet them.'

There followed an extraordinary spell. Josse was introduced to Gemma, Bertha and Belle, all round and slow in advanced pregnancy, to Jehane, cradling a sleeping baby, and to Alisoun, calmly feeding a robust-looking infant as she talked. They were all eager to tell their visitor about Father Micah and to repeat the dreadful things he had said. Repeating them brought tears to the eyes of young Belle and she had to be led away and comforted by Sister Clare.

'It's her time,' Alisoun confided to Josse. 'She's scared, see, and that foul-mouthed bastard of a priest didn't help her.'

'The man is dead,' Josse reminded her quietly.

'Good riddance,' Alisoun flashed back. Her baby, apparently picking up her mother's anger and disliking it, detached her perfect, pink mouth from the milky nipple and let out a wail of protest. Alisoun, love in her face and tenderness in her large, rough hands, replaced her nipple with infinite gentleness and the child resumed her suckling.

What am I doing here? Josse wondered. It is surely impossible that any of these women was abroad last night intent on waylaying Father Micah and breaking his neck. But, having made the effort to come to talk to them, it made sense to see it through.

'Er – you were all here in the hostel last night?' He felt a fool even as he asked.

Alisoun laughed. Jehane said, 'Aye, that we were. We did wonder if Gemma here might chase after the priest and attempt to carry out what she suggested he do to himself, but she decided after all to stay here in the warm.'

He knew he shouldn't, but he asked anyway. 'And what was that suggestion?'

There was quite a lot more laughter and, as Gemma told him, he joined in. Turning to her, he said, still chuckling, 'I believe that lets you out, Gemma. He certainly wasn't killed like *that*.'

There was one thing he still had to ask. It was, he thought, trying to find the right words, even more tricky than asking if any of them had left the hostel last night.

'You have – er, that is, do you receive visits from your – er, the babies' fathers? Or other men?'

More laughter. Then Alisoun said, her expression deceptively innocent, 'We wouldn't mind, sir knight, only the nuns don't take kindly to us keeping company in here.' Dropping to a whisper, she added, 'They're trying to cure us of earning our bread on our backs, see, not encourage it.'

Again, he joined in the merriment. Then, as the laughter subsided, he said, 'I am afraid, though, that I have to pursue this. Did any of you tell anyone on the outside about Father Micah's visit? He was unforgivably rude, I know, and I just wondered if . . .'

'If one of us told some strong, handsome, honourable fellow who took it into his head to avenge the insults and the curses and attack the Father?' Jehane finished for him. 'Oh, no, sir knight. If any of us had a man of that quality, do you reckon we'd be in here?'

He looked at her face, oval, with a full-lipped mouth and hazel eyes. She must have been very pretty, he thought compassionately, before the hardships and the dangers of her profession ruined her. Now her hair was thin and straw-like, her skin bore the scars of the pox and the expression in her eyes was

72

world-weary and cynical. Her words were, he was quite sure, the absolute truth.

'No, Jehane,' he said quietly. 'No, I don't suppose you would. I am sorry I had to ask.'

She gave him a smile that, despite everything, still managed to be very sweet. 'It's all right,' she replied. 'We understand.'

He found Brother Firmin in the Vale's little shrine. He was with some other old monks and they were praying earnestly for the soul of Father Micah.

Unable to prevent the thought that, from all he had heard, the late priest had hardly been worthy of such fervour, Josse waited patiently outside in the cold for them to finish.

Brother Firmin was the last to leave. 'Sir Josse!' he said, his face creasing into a happy smile. 'My, but it does me good to see you this sad morning!' He took Josse's arm affectionately. 'You're cold!' he exclaimed. 'Come with me and I will give you a mug of something to put that right and send some warmth through your bones.'

He led the way to the monks' shelter where he set water on to the fire to heat, putting into it generous pinches of various powdered herbs. Then he set two coarse pottery mugs ready. When the water began to steam, a deliciously warming, sweet, spicy smell filled the room. Brother Firmin let the liquid boil gently for a short while, then he removed the vessel from the heat and poured the concoction into the mugs.

'Here,' Brother Firmin held out one of the mugs, 'try this. Don't ask me what it is, for I have no idea. Sister Tiphaine gives the herbs to me because she knows how I feel the cold. She is a good woman,' he said emphatically, as if Josse had said she wasn't, 'for all that she keeps one foot in the pagan past.' He tutted and shook his head. 'Ah well, that is a matter between her and God.' He sipped at his mug, smacking his lips in satisfaction. 'And, by, she makes a good potion!'

Josse listened to the old monk rambling on for some time. Then, when he could get a word in, he said, 'Brother Firmin, the Abbess said that you spoke to Father Micah yesterday and that he informed you he was going to make other visits. Do you remember to whom?'

'Ooh, you're tracking his movements, are you?' Brother Firmin looked as if the idea greatly excited him. 'Well, let me see, yes, he *did* say . . .'

The old face creased as Brother Firmin tried to remember. Josse's heart began to sink as the silence extended. Ah, well, it had always been unlikely, but worth a try at least—

'He was going to see a noble lord who had forgotten God's law and some lost souls who were to be banished to the eternal flames,' Brother Firmin suddenly said, making Josse jump. 'Perhaps not his exact words, but close enough.' The old monk beamed his pleasure at having done what Josse asked.

'Thank you, Brother Firmin,' Josse said heartily. 'You have been most helpful. Er – I don't suppose the Father mentioned any names?'

'Oh, dear – no, I'm afraid he didn't.' Firmin's delight turned swiftly to dismay.

'Never mind!' Josse said quickly. 'You have given me quite enough to be getting on with, Brother. And thank you for the drink, too – I now feel aglow from my head to my toes.' He rose to his feet as he spoke, reaching down to pat the elderly monk on his bony shoulder.

'Drop by and tell me how you get on!' Brother Firmin called out as Josse strode out of the door. 'Any time . . . !'

A nobleman who had forgotten God's law. Not much of a description, Josse thought as he marched back up to the Abbey to collect Horace. Besides which, it could apply to the majority of noble lords of Josse's acquaintance.

There was, however, one person who might know to whom the words applied in this case; the priest who usually tended the flock in Hawkenlye and the surrounding area. Quickly putting saddle and bridle on his horse, Josse called out to Sister Martha to ask if she would kindly give him directions to Father Gilbert's house.

★   ★   ★

The priest lived in a small, ill-furnished but scrupulously clean dwelling slightly separated from the small hamlet of Hawkenlye. When Josse put his head round the door and called out, 'Father Gilbert? Are you in there?' a faint voice replied from within, 'Yes! Who is it?'

Josse advanced into the house, closing the door behind him. It was a bitterly cold morning and Josse's first impression was that the inside of the house was no warmer than the outside, making his careful door-closing a fairly pointless gesture. He crossed a tiny scullery where a used trencher and mug lay beside a jug of water; ice had formed on the surface of the water. In the next room he found Father Gilbert, lying on a low bed and huddled into a variety of thin, insubstantial blankets. The priest appeared to be wearing every garment he possessed, which did not amount to very many.

Seeing who had come to visit him, he said joyfully, 'Sir Josse! It's glad I am to see you. Please, if you can spare the time, would you make up the fire?'

Turning, Josse noticed the hearth, in which two large logs were smouldering gently, giving out quite a lot of smoke but no discernible heat.

'Of course! Er – where's your wood supply, Father? Outside somewhere?'

'Out of the door, down the path and on the right.' The Father was already looking more cheerful, obviously anticipating the pleasure of some warmth.

Josse followed his directions and located the woodpile. It consisted of five or six cut and split logs and several large rounds cut, Josse thought, from an oak tree. Rolling up his sleeves and spitting on his hands, he picked up the heavy axe that had been stuck into the chopping block and set to work.

Some time later he had cut and split sufficient firewood to last for a day or two; he made a mental note to ask the Abbess if one of the Hawkenlye lay brothers could be sent each day to replenish the log supply. Then, bearing in his arms as much wood as he could carry, he went back inside.

As he relaid and lit the fire, chatting inconsequentially to Father Gilbert, it suddenly occurred to him that the priest did not know of Father Micah's death. Indeed, how could he, bed-bound as he was, unless somebody from the Abbey had already been to see him today? And if that were the case, then surely Father Gilbert would not be lying there making feeble but courageous jokes about the icicle on the end of his nose melting at last?

Josse gave the fire another poke – the blaze was roaring away now and the room was actually starting to feel warmer – and then stood up. Approaching Father Gilbert's bed, he said, 'Father, I have some bad tidings. It's Father Micah.'

To Josse's surprise, the priest's face fell and he said, 'Oh, Sir Josse, not more trouble! I do not wish to appear to moan, but, really, Father Micah is only doing his job in the best way he can, according to his own beliefs, and I do think that people might—'

'Father, I'm afraid it is a little more serious than that,' Josse said gently. 'There has been an accident. I'm sorry to have to tell you, but Father Micah is dead.'

'Dead!'

After the one word, muttered in a shocked whisper, Father Gilbert acted exactly as Augustus had done: he began to pray.

After quite a long time, he opened his eyes and asked quietly, 'How did he die?'

Josse told him.

'And you believe this was as a result of an accident? That Father Micah slipped, perhaps, on the icy track and fell?'

Josse hesitated. 'It's possible, aye.'

'Yet you believe it could equally have happened another way?'

In pain, cold and alone the priest might be, Josse thought, but there was nothing wrong with his powers of observation. 'I cannot ignore the possibility.'

With admirable brevity, Father Gilbert said, 'You will want to know of his recent concerns. I cannot tell you exactly what he did yesterday but I know that he intended to visit the Abbey. He was also deeply anxious about the Lord of the High Weald

76

and the woman to whom Father Micah insisted on referring as his Lordship's mistress.'

'The Lord of . . . who?'

Father Gilbert gave a swift smile. 'I see you have not come across him.'

'No.'

'He has made his home at Saxonbury. It is an ancient fort on the ridge to the south of us. Rumours about it abound, but I suspect that it was an old iron working. People believe it to be haunted, which suits the Lord since it keeps the curious away. He lives there with his family. His kinfolk appear to come and go but usually there seem to be some fifteen or so people living there.' Father Gilbert shifted under his blankets, winced, then said, 'Father Micah believed them to be godless. He expressed the intention of making a nuisance of himself up at Saxonbury until the Lord did what the Father told him.' He glanced up at Josse. 'His words, not mine,' he added. 'Father Micah did not care how much of a nuisance he was when he was about God's work.'

'So I'm beginning to understand,' Josse muttered.

Father Gilbert was still watching him closely. 'You intend to visit Lord Saxonbury?'

'Is that his title? Aye, I do.'

'It is how he styles himself, although whether or nor he has a right to it I cannot say. Have a care,' the priest added warningly. 'They do not take kindly to strangers.'

'I will.' Josse took the priest's outstretched hand. 'How do I get to Saxonbury? Will you tell me, Father?'

'I will, if you are resolved on going there.'

'I am.'

With a sigh, the priest gave directions. They seemed simple enough and Josse did not anticipate having any difficulty in following them.

'Is there anything I can do for you before I go?' He looked about him but there seemed no comforts he could offer. 'What about your food?'

'Oh, one of the village women brings me my meals.' Father Gilbert gave a wan smile. 'Not that I have much appetite.'

'I'll come again,' Josse said impulsively, 'if I may?'

'Of course!' Father Gilbert looked pleased.

I'll bring him something to cheer him up, Josse promised himself, a pot of good, hot stew, a flagon of wine . . .

But Father Gilbert was saying something: 'You will want something in return for your charity.' He smiled as if to make sure that Josse appreciated he spoke in jest. 'I will think, as I lie here, about Father Micah and ponder who, if anybody, might have wished him ill.'

Josse, suppressing the thought that such a task could surely not be difficult, gave him a brief bow. 'Thank you, Father. That would indeed be helpful. I'll be back soon.'

# 7

The ride up to Saxonbury took Josse around the edge of the Great Forest. Bare limbs of beech, birch, oak and hazel raised naked branches up to the pale grey sky and, interspersed with their quiet, misty shades, there were patches of deep, dark green where the holly and yew trees grew. Soaring high above the forest canopy were the needle-clad branches of the pines, at the very top of their long, bare trunks. There were tracks leading off under the trees that might have afforded a more direct route to Saxonbury, but Josse knew better than to go into the forest unless he had to. He had ventured into the forest before and understood, as well as any outsider could, that it held its own perils and was best left alone. In any case, Father Gilbert's directions had specified this path, and to divert from it might mean that Josse missed Saxonbury altogether.

The journey was not long: four, perhaps five miles, according to Father Gilbert. Nor was it arduous, for although the track dipped into occasional valleys and climbed out again, the slopes were quite gentle. In the main, however, the path kept to the higher ground and Josse surmised that it was one of the old dry ridge tracks. Had it not been for the extreme cold and the fact that he had not eaten since early morning, he would have enjoyed the ride.

He did not see a soul. He was hardly aware of another living being, come to that, although he did think he heard the distant howl of a hungry wolf. Packs of wolves were not unknown in the area, although they usually gave human beings and their habitations a wide berth. Passing the tiny settlement of Fernthe, he saw a thin plume of smoke rising up from one of the thatched wooden huts. Someone had recently repaired the fence surrounding the little hamlet; perhaps that person, too, had heard the wolf.

The track took another dip into a shallow valley. As it rose up again, Josse began to look out for the turning on the right that the priest had told him about. 'An ancient way, I believe,' Father Gilbert had said, 'for the footsteps of the ages have carved it deep into the ground and banks rise high on either side.'

Aye. There it was. And it looked dark and forbidding, going in there beneath the trees . . .

'Come on, Horace,' Josse said loudly. Horace twitched back his ears. 'The sooner we get on, the sooner we can turn for home.'

Horace's hooves fell on the hollow way with a dull thud, as if even ordinary sounds were muffled and strange in this lonely place. The tall trees on either side stood still, their bare branches untouched by the slightest breeze. The banks were rust-coloured with dead bracken and the track was black with the fallen leaves of hundreds of years. Nothing stirred. Nothing, it seemed, lived.

Climbing the increasingly steep gradient towards the summit of the ridge, Josse had the peculiar idea that this track went on for ever. That it would take him into some strange faery world where a few minutes passed would be an aeon in the outside world, so that when he returned it would be to find that all that he knew was dead and buried in the far-distant past.

He was approaching what looked like the vestiges of a ditch, on the far side of which a bank had been raised. The track went over the ditch on a crumbling earthwork. Crossing over, Josse thought of old legends of ditches and dykes, said, so the tales went, to be the devil's work. Overhead, some evergreen tree spread its thick, heavy branches. It was very dark . . .

Beyond the bank there was a dry-stone wall. It appeared to be in quite a good state of repair, and Josse felt a sense of relief. If someone were looking after the walls, then perhaps this place was still the abode of humans after all. In places the wall was supplemented by sections of paling fence, in one of which there were wooden gates. They were closed.

Josse rode up to the gates and shouted out, 'Halloa! Is any-one there?'

Somebody must have been on guard within. Instantly a deep voice called back, 'Who is enquiring?'

'I am Josse d'Acquin, and I come from Hawkenlye Abbey on a mission concerning Father Micah.'

'If you've come on that wretch's business, then you'll not receive a welcome at Saxonbury,' the unseen guard answered. 'Turn back, Josse d'Acquin, and tell them at Hawkenlye that each of their priest's emissaries will receive the same answer.'

'It is not Church business that brings me here.' Josse tried to think how best to plead his case; he was reluctant to break the news of Father Micah's death to a guard whom he could not even see. 'I wish to speak to Lord Saxonbury,' he announced, with more bravado that he was actually feeling. 'Is he within?'

'Wait.'

After the curt order there was silence for some time. Then Josse heard the sound of the heavy bar that secured the gates being drawn back and, a few moments later, he was riding into Saxonbury.

The guard was waiting for him inside the gates. He was short, stocky and wore an expression of extreme suspicion. He said, 'Follow me,' and led Josse across an open space of rough ground. Beyond it high walls rose up and, as the guard led him through an arched opening halfway along one of them, he saw the dwellings that were hidden away within their protection.

There were several, although none was large. Each appeared to have its own entrance and consisted of perhaps one large room at ground level with another positioned above to act as a sleeping platform. Some of the buildings appeared to be stables and storehouses; one was clearly a cookhouse. Beside it was a well, covered with a little roof of thatch.

Although Josse could see nobody inside the dwellings, all the same he was quite certain he was observed from within them. It was an uncomfortable feeling, to be aware of people closely observing him whom he could not see.

But one man at least was visible. Standing in the middle of the space enclosed within the walls was a very tall, broad-shouldered man with reddish-blond hair that was in the process of turning white. He was bearded, the long tangle of his facial hair falling on to a knee-length padded tunic that had once been a beautiful garment but was now stained with the mementoes of very many meals. Around his hips he wore a wide leather belt from which hung a broadsword in a scuffed scabbard. Thrust into the other side of the belt was a double-headed axe.

The man said in a strong voice, 'I am the Lord of the High Weald and this is my dwelling place. What do you want of me, Josse d'Acquin?'

Josse had slipped from Horace's back. Standing on this giant's land, it seemed prudent to remember his manners, so he made a low bow. 'Thank you for receiving me,' he said.

'I am told that your mission concerns Father Micah.' The tone was neutral.

'Aye.' Deciding that here was a situation when the only option was the truth, Josse said, 'The Father is dead. He was found on the track above Castle Hill early this morning with a broken neck. I am in the service of the Abbess of Hawkenlye, who has charged me with discovering what I can of the Father's recent movements, and I am told that he may have visited you.'

There was what seemed to Josse to be a very long silence while the bright blue eyes of the Lord of the High Weald considered him. Then the giant said, 'Come inside. I'll have someone see to your horse while we take refreshments together and I tell you exactly what Father Micah wanted with me.'

Then he turned and led the way up a shallow flight of stone steps into the largest of the dwellings. Josse, following, looked around him with interest; the long, low room was timber-built, its line of sturdy posts filled in with wattle and daub. At the far end there was a stone hearth in which a fire was blazing. Several people were sitting round the fire; two middle-aged men, a youth and a quartet of young women. Quite a lot of them seemed to be red-haired. With a wave of his hand, the Lord shooed them away.

'My family are well trained,' he remarked to Josse. 'Although they have their own firesides, they prefer to congregate around mine. However, they know when I want to be left in peace.'

'Your family,' Josse repeated.

'Aye. My sons and daughters live here with their spouses and their children, and their children marry and bring their new husbands and wives to Saxonbury in their turn. I am the patriarch.' He flung out his impressive chest. 'Now, ale.' He reached down for a large pewter jug that stood on a bench and poured some of the contents into two mugs, handing one to Josse. He tasted, smacked his lips appreciatively – the ale was malty and slightly sweet – and drank down several mouthfuls, at which the Lord quickly refilled his mug.

Waving Josse to a bench pulled up in front of the hearth, the Lord settled himself opposite and said, 'We are instructed not to speak ill of the dead, and so you must excuse me, Sir Josse, because I am about to do just that.' He paused. Then, surprisingly, he asked, 'Are you pressed for time?'

'No, not really.' It was not far back to the Abbey and there must remain several hours of daylight.

'Then, if you will hear it, I shall tell you my story.'

'I shall be glad to hear it.'

The Lord poured out more ale and then, cutting off a hunk of bread and a thick slice of venison, thrust them at Josse and began his tale. 'I was a soldier of the Crusade,' he announced, 'and I went to Jerusalem with my brother, who was of the company of the Templar Knights. In the assault on the Turks of Damascus many lives were lost, including that of my brother.'

'I am sorry for your loss,' Josse said quietly. 'My own maternal grandfather died at Damascus and my father too was there in the midst of the fighting.'

'Was he, indeed?' The Lord looked with interest at Josse. 'It seems I was right to trust to my instincts and allow you admission,' he murmured. 'I was gravely wounded,' – he picked up his narrative – 'and believed that my hour had come. But I was rescued from the field of battle and nursed back to health by a young and very beautiful woman, to whom I gave my heart. When I was fully recovered, we were wed and she consented to leave her home and return with me to mine. She bore me three sons and two daughters and has been, in every respect, the most satisfactory wife a man could wish for.'

'She lives still?' If she became a wife more than forty-five years ago, Josse was calculating, then she must be sixty, surely, at the least. As must this man who sat in front of him, even though he did not look it.

'Indeed she does, but sadly she is frail,' the Lord said. 'In body, at least, although not in mind, for it is her indomitable will that rules here at Saxonbury, Sir Josse. She lies most of the day snug and comfortable in her chamber, yet her word is law.' He smiled affectionately.

'A woman to admire,' Josse murmured.

'Precisely!' The Lord's eyes lit up. 'I am glad that you perceive this, for that damnable priest did not.' He leaned forward, his face earnest, and, speaking urgently as if it were imperative that his guest fully understand him, said, 'You see, my wife is a Muslim woman. She is of Turkish blood and, naturally, of foreign appearance and habits. A strange creature indeed to one such as Father Micah, and he made no attempt to disguise his distaste for what he could not understand. The problem, of course, for such a man was that my wife is not a Christian and, for all that we were wed according to her faith, I would not force her to make vows according to mine. You see, Sir Josse,' – he put a hand like a shallow basket on to Josse's leg – 'I felt that I had already asked enough of my beloved in bringing her here and commanding her to make her home so far from her own people. If she chose to keep her own faith and not convert to mine, what did it matter?'

Treating the question as rhetorical, Josse merely nodded.

'And shall I tell you what that evil man said when he discovered that I live with a Muslim woman in a marriage that, to his blinkered eyes, does not exist?'

'What?'

The Lord paused for dramatic effect and then said softly, 'He said that my wife – my frail, ageing, devoted wife – must be whipped. That this was the only way to drive the Devil from her and make her ready to receive the blessing of Jesus Christ.'

It was shocking in its savagery. But to Josse, for whom each new fact learned about the late priest merely served to enhance the impression he had received from the first, it came as no surprise. Meeting the hurt and furious eyes of the giant sitting before him, he said, 'The man was twisted, mad. It must be so, for what other explanation can there be for a priest who had devoted his life to the service of a loving God to advocate such cruelty?'

'Mad?' The Lord raised his massive shoulders. 'I cannot say.' The blue eyes turned away from Josse and then, slyly, looked back. 'But I am glad that Father Micah is dead for, when last he visited us here, he swore that he would be back. And for the life of me, Sir Josse, I do not know how I would have received him.'

Then as Josse watched, the slyness left the brilliant eyes to be replaced with a look of such menace, such palpable violence, that Josse could not prevent himself from pulling back.

'What would *you* have done?' the giant asked softly. 'Ask yourself this, before you rush to judge me. Suppose that it was your own elderly mother, let us say, who was threatened with this extreme measure. Would you allow it?'

Josse's mother was dead. He had loved her dearly and knew that he could not have stood back to see her abused. No, he would have defended her, whatever the cost to himself. Meeting the Lord's eyes, he said, 'No. I would not.'

'Thank you for your honesty,' the Lord said. Then he gave a short and, it seemed to Josse, rueful laugh, cutting through the tension in the hall. 'More ale?' He offered the jug.

Josse, whose head was already feeling muzzy, said, 'Thank you, but no.' He was wondering how on earth he was to go about ascertaining where the men of the Lord's household had been last night – even knowing how many of them there were would be a good start – and intoxication was not going to help.

Possibly the Lord had also realised that, because he leaned down and refilled Josse's mug anyway.

Absently sipping from it, Josse said, 'Father Gilbert told me where to find you. He said that your community here numbered some fifteen people.'

'Did he?' The Lord, it appeared, was neither going to confirm nor deny the priest's information. Instead he said, 'Not a bad fellow, Father Gilbert. Wider-minded than Father Micah, but then that, I would say, applies to almost everybody. How is he? Father Gilbert, I mean?'

'I have just come from him. He is mending, I believe, although slowly. The cold weather works against him. His house was ice-cold when I arrived.'

'I see.' The blue eyes watched Josse steadily and he had the impression he was being assessed. Then: 'No doubt you cut wood for him and built up his fire.'

'Er – aye.' For some reason Josse felt embarrassed, as if he had performed the act of kindness purely to make people think well of him. From some distant past conversation he seemed to hear the Abbess's voice: *True charity is that which is known only to God.*

'It's what I would have expected from what I hear tell of you, Josse d'Acquin.' The Lord was still staring at him.

Who had spoken to this man of him? Josse could not imagine. Father Gilbert, perhaps? It did not seem likely, for the Father barely knew Josse. But who else could it be?

'And I hear good things of Hawkenlye Abbey,' the Lord was saying. 'Do not think that, because I dislike one man of the Church, it follows that I feel the same about every other man and woman in holy orders. That Abbess, now, they say she is a fine, fierce woman.'

'She didn't like Father Micah either.' The admission was out before Josse could ask himself if it was truly wise to make it. 'That is, of course she's terribly upset that he's dead—'

'Oh, terribly.' There was clear irony in the Lord's voice.

'—and there will be prayers for his soul at the Abbey, I know, and a deal of grieving.'

'Come, now, Sir Josse, that really *is* an unlikely exaggeration.' Again, the Lord gave his short laugh.

Josse gave a half-hearted grin. 'Very well. Not very much grieving. Just the natural shocked reaction to sudden death.'

'Sudden *accidental* death, think you?' The question was put so subtly that Josse, increasingly fuddled, did not immediately understand its importance.

'I cannot yet say.' He went to take another sip of ale but found to his vague surprise that he had once more emptied his mug. 'He could have slipped on the icy track and slammed his face hard against something that did not give but, on the other hand, someone could have forced his head backwards.' Absently he upturned his mug. 'I do not know.'

There was silence in the hall. A log settled in the hearth, giving out a soft sound like a sigh. From somewhere quite near at hand Josse heard voices; a woman's voice and, in one short, terse sentence, a man's. He tried to make out the words but could not, which was surprising because they were clearly audible. Then through the fog in his head he realised. The woman was speaking in an unknown language. There was a sudden cry of distress, of pain, and a high, strained voice cried out briefly, abruptly silenced. Of course, Josse thought, the Lord of the High Weald's wife was foreign. What did he say? Turkish? Aye. Something like that. And, poor soul, some quality of the frailty and sickness that kept her in her bed must give her pain. Poor woman.

Unreasonably pleased to have solved the little mystery of those overheard words in a foreign tongue, Josse beamed at the Lord. 'It is good to have met you,' he exclaimed.

'And you.' The Lord's expression was amused.

With some effort, Josse stood up. 'I must go,' he announced. 'It is not far to Hawkenlye, where I lodge tonight, but I would like to be back before dark.'

'You are welcome to stay here. We eat well in my hall.'

I am sure you do, Josse thought, if the quality of your ale and your venison is anything to go by. Venison. The thought suddenly struck him. The deer could only have been shot in the Great Forest, which made it poaching. And the penalty for that was almost as bad as that for living outside Christian wedlock with someone of a different faith.

About to make some remark to that effect, Josse opened his mouth. Then the Lord also rose to his feet. He towered over

Josse who, having taken into consideration that this huge man had a household of sons and grandsons who were probably equally huge, decided that the wise option was to keep quiet. If anybody asks me, he told himself sternly, I shall say, venison? What venison?

'Thank you for your hospitality.' He made a bow to the Lord, who returned it.

'Thank you for coming to see me,' he replied. Then, as if granting a great favour, he added, 'You may come again. I shall inform those who guard my land that you are welcome here.'

Josse was helped out to the courtyard, where the guard who had admitted him stood holding Horace. The Lord tried to get him into the saddle but it proved too much of a challenge, even for such a big man. The guard was fully occupied in holding on to a frisky Horace and so the Lord called out to someone else – whose name, Josse thought, was Morcar – to come and help.

Another man quickly emerged from one of the dwellings. He resembled the Lord too much to be other than his son and he was nearly his father's equal in size. Josse, at last safely mounted, touched his cap in thanks.

Then the gates were dragged open and he rode away.

He realised how drunk he was as he left the deep track leading down from Saxonbury and turned on to the path that skirted the forest. I was a fool, he thought; I allowed my host to refill my mug far too frequently. I should have stayed alert. I was there on official business, and what have I to report? Very little, other than that the Lord of the High Weald had good reason to loathe Father Micah and that he has a family of men quite capable of killing a man by breaking his neck.

But somehow – and the reasoning entirely escaped him – Josse did not believe that Father Micah's murderer was of the Saxonbury household. If indeed there *was* a murderer.

'Accident or murder?' Josse wondered aloud as he jogged along.

And he knew that, even had he not been suffering the after-effects of the Lord's ale, there was not going to be an easy answer.

# 8

During the afternoon Helewise received a visitor. Sister Ursel had announced that the Sheriff had arrived and wished to speak with her and Helewise, heart sinking, had prepared herself for a meeting with the odious and not very bright Sheriff Pelham.

But to her surprise it was a very different sort of a man who was shown into her room. He was smartly dressed, of a little above average height, slim and, she had to admit, handsome, with well-cut and smoothly dressed brown hair and light-green eyes. Bowing gracefully, he said, 'I am grateful, my lady Abbess, that you have found the time to see me. I am Gervase de Gifford.'

Accepting his greeting with an inclination of her head, she said, 'I understood that Harry Pelham held the office of Sheriff.'

'He may have given that impression,' Gervase de Gifford said easily. 'The de Clares have use for such men, but it is a mistake to give a man more authority than that with which he is equipped to cope.'

Wondering whether that amounted to a yes or a no, Helewise said, 'Won't you sit? There is a stool beside the door there.'

He looked where she pointed. Apparently he took in instantly the fact that, once seated on the low stool, he would be at a considerably lower level than she, sitting on her throne-like chair. He said courteously, 'Thank you, my lady, but I prefer to stand.'

'As you wish. Now, you said you wished to speak to me?'

'Yes, my lady. Concerning the dead priest, Father Micah. My lord, Richard FitzRoger de Clare, has asked me to discover what details are known of the death.'

'Very few. I have despatched Sir Josse d'Acquin, who is a friend of the Abbey, to find out more.'

'Sir Josse d'Acquin,' de Gifford murmured. 'Yes. The man is known to us.'

Wondering just who he meant by 'us', Helewise asked, 'You are tasked with bringing to justice anybody who may be implicated in the Father's death?'

'I am.' Gervase de Gifford gave her a smooth smile.

'You may call again,' she said, sounding grand even in her own ears, 'and discuss the matter with Sir Josse, once he has returned.'

'You think, my lady, that he will bring information?'

'I know he will.'

She met de Gifford's gaze calmly. She wanted to say, he will do better in his enquiries than some fashionably dressed servant of the grand family at Tonbridge Castle, but she held her peace.

'You will tell Sir Josse that I called.' In the mouth of de Gifford, it sounded more like an order than a request.

She said, 'Yes.'

Then, taking the hint, he bowed again and left the room.

She was still thinking about Gervase de Gifford when Josse came to see her after Vespers. He instantly apologised for coming so late. 'I was entertained too well up at Saxonbury,' he confessed, 'and I had to sleep it off.'

Disarmed by his frankness, she said, 'Saxonbury?'

He told her that he had visited Father Gilbert and gone on to see someone calling himself the Lord of the High Weald because Father Micah was known to have been there the day before he was found dead. She listened intently as he described his conversation with the Lord.

'It would seem,' she observed, 'that this Lord Saxonbury had good reason to ply you with strong drink. Do you think, Sir Josse, that he has something to hide?'

Josse scratched his chin. 'I believe him to be a powerful man, with good reason for antagonism towards the Father. I do not see him as a murderer, although there are things about the Saxonbury household that strike me as odd.'

'Such as?'

Now the chin scratching developed into a vigorous face rubbing. From behind his hands Josse said, 'My lady, I cannot now recall. I know full well that there were matters concerning which I told myself to take note, but what they were I have no idea.' As if to exonerate himself he added, 'Tiny things, you know. The sort that make you say to yourself, now why does that seem important?'

'The sort of things that are so elusive that they can all too easily vanish,' she said sympathetically.

'Especially after too many mugs of ale,' he added dully.

'Do not distress yourself, Sir Josse. Why not go to bed and have a good night's sleep?' she suggested. 'Perhaps your memory will serve you better by morning.'

'Good advice,' he muttered. 'And I am of no use to you, me or anyone else tonight.'

As he bade her goodnight she remembered that she had not told him about Gervase de Gifford. Ah well, tomorrow would do.

But the next day brought its own troubles. Helewise forgot all about Gervase de Gifford, and whatever it was that Josse had been trying to bring to mind concerning Saxonbury was driven out altogether.

Very early in the morning, while it was still dark and as the Hawkenlye community was leaving the Abbey church after Prime, there came a loud beating at the gates and a deep male voice called out, 'Hoa, Abbey! Help! Help!'

Sister Ursel rushed to climb up the short flight of steps to the spyhole in the wall beside the gates. As she opened it and peered out, Brothers Saul, Michael and Augustus sprinted to join her. 'Who's there?' she cried. 'What do you want of us?'

Helewise joined the gathering crowd of nuns and monks and they stood back respectfully to let her through. 'Who is out there, Sister Ursel?' she demanded.

'It's a man – he's carrying someone – a woman, I think, she appears to be slight and quite small,' Sister Ursel replied quietly. Then, raising her voice, she repeated, 'What do you want?'

But the man merely said again, 'Help!'

Helewise said, 'Sister Ursel, let me look.' As the porteress got out of the way, Helewise stepped up to the spyhole. Her instinct was to open the gates immediately; there had been a note of anguish in the man's repeated cry that persuaded her his need was genuine. But as Abbess she was responsible for the safety of her community, and there were ruffians abroad in the night who might try to gain entry to the Abbey by subterfuge.

She stared down at the short, broad-shouldered, barrel-chested man who stood outside. He raised his head and stared back. In the thin dawn light she saw the despair in his expression. She also saw that the front of his shirt was covered in blood. Judging by the way in which he carried the woman in his arms, it appeared to be hers.

Deciding, she stepped down from the spyhole. 'Sister Ursel, open the gates,' she ordered. 'Brothers, stand by in case of any disturbance.' She did not elaborate; meeting Brother Saul's eyes, she knew she did not need to.

The gates opened and the man came straight in. He gasped out something – it might have been 'Thank you' – and Sister Euphemia took hold of his arm.

Her eyes on the limp figure that he carried, she said, 'Come with me. I will look after her.'

Initially, the most difficult part of the infirmarer's task was in getting the man to relinquish his hold on the woman. His broad arms supporting her seemed to have locked into position and his eyes were fixed on her white face; he ignored the presence of anyone else.

Sister Euphemia had commanded Sister Caliste to prepare a bed in one of the infirmary's small curtained-off recesses. Having done so, Sister Caliste now stood ready, and the infirmarer noticed that the young nun, good nurse that she was, had set out a bowl of steaming water, wash cloths and bandaging materials. With the curtain drawn to keep curious eyes off the drama, all that now remained was for the man to lay the woman down and allow the nurses to do their job.

'Please, won't you put her down?' Sister Euphemia asked the man in a gentle tone. He turned, looked at her blankly, then went back to gazing at the woman in his arms.

Suddenly Sister Calise spoke. 'Sister, he doesn't understand!' she whispered. 'May I try?'

'Aye, do.' The infirmarer's tone was terse.

Sister Caliste stepped forward so that the man could see her. Then she mimed holding something and laying it down carefully on the clean white sheet of the prepared bed. She stared at him, nodding encouragingly and smiling, and after a moment an answering smile broke across his large face. With infinite tenderness, he laid the woman down on the bed.

'At last!' breathed the infirmarer. 'Now, Sister, weave a little more of your magic and get him to stand back; I can't work properly with him right at my elbow breathing down my neck like an exhausted ox!'

Sister Caliste reached for a little stool and placed it a few paces back from the bed, pointing to it and then to the man. Comprehending, he shuffled over and sat heavily down.

'Now, Sister, your assistance if you please,' the infirmarer commanded.

Sister Caliste went to join her at the bedside. Seeing at last the woman's injuries, she gave out a small gasp.

Sister Euphemia glanced across at her. 'Aye, it's not pretty, is it? And, unless I'm very much mistaken, there's more.' Carefully raising the woman's right shoulder as she spoke and pulling back the cloak in which she was wrapped, she stared down at the torn robe and the lacerated, bleeding, suppurating flesh beneath. 'Aye. It is as I thought. She's taken a beating.'

Sister Caliste said softly, 'Which do we attend to first, Sister? Her back or her poor face?'

'Her back. We'll just give the wounds on her cheek and her forehead a lavender wash to clean them' – instantly Sister Caliste put lavender into the bowl of hot water and, squeezing out a cloth, handed it to the infirmarer – 'then we'll do what we can to make her back less painful so that she can lie more comfortably.'

The two of them worked in silence. They were very aware of the man sitting watching them; from time to time he let out soft, low sounds, like an animal in pain, but he did not interrupt them. He appeared to understand that they were doing their best and seemed content to let them get on with it. They turned the woman gently over on to her side and Sister Euphemia soaked the tattered remains of the robe to remove the thick crust of blood and pus sticking it to the flesh. As she peeled away the cloth, Sister Caliste began to cleanse the wounds. There were twenty-five of them, evenly spaced down the woman's narrow back. Whoever had flogged her had done so with a practised hand.

Soon Sister Caliste had done all that she could. Some of the wounds were now bleeding cleanly but some had become badly infected and were surrounded by tight, bright-red skin that felt hot to the touch.

'A poultice of dried herbs – fresh ingredients where we've got them, Sister – that's what we need now,' the infirmarer said. 'Greater burdock leaves for the inflammation, wood avens root to control that bleeding and a good helping of feverfew and white willow for the pain.'

'Wood avens?'

'Herb Bennet.'

'Ah, yes. Of course, Sister.'

'Make up a hot, moist mash, spread it between two pieces of flannel and bring it here. We'll fix it to her back and let the good, healing herbs draw out the poison and give her relief.'

As Sister Caliste hurried to obey, she heard the soft, steady and infinitely comforting sound of the infirmarer's prayers.

When the poultice was in place, the two nuns laid the woman carefully on to her back. 'She'll drain better like that,' the infirmarer said. 'It may hurt her more than lying on her belly or her side, but we don't want that poison pooling inside her wounds.' Then she pushed back the thick, curly brown hair from the woman's face and she and Sister Caliste studied the wounds to the forehead and the cheek.

Now that it had been bathed, the cut on the right cheek was revealed to be not very serious. Sister Euphemia cut a square of flannel, soaked it in lavender oil and pressed it to the wound. 'We'll need to check it regularly,' she said, 'but I do not believe it will leave a scar. Not like this foul thing.'

Then the two of them stood staring down at what had been done to the woman's brow. Into the pale, smooth skin, someone had burned a mark. It was quite hard to tell, because of the swelling and infection affecting the whole of the forehead, but it looked as if it were meant to be a letter. Just the one letter.

'What is it?' Sister Caliste whispered.

'I don't know.' Sister Euphemia frowned. 'An A? Or an H? Perhaps even a B, for the right-hand side has a sort of curve.'

'But why?'

Sister Euphemia turned to look at her, compassion and a world-weary cynicism in her expression. 'I've seen the letter A branded on a woman before now,' she said. 'It was in my noviciate. There was this nobleman, a proud man he was, ambitious for his son, for whom he'd arranged a splendid marriage. Trouble was, the lad didn't love his cold, grand wife and he took up with one of his father's serving maids. When the father found out, he cast the lass out. But before he did so, he had her branded with an A.'

'A?'

Now the infirmarer's glance was pitying. 'Adulteress. Isn't that just typical? The lad was as guilty as the lassie, yet she was punished and thrown out to starve while he escaped unhurt.'

'He lost his love,' Sister Caliste pointed out.

'Aye, aye.' Sister Euphemia sighed heavily. 'I suppose he did.' Then, shaking herself out of her thoughts and her memories, she said, 'Another poultice, please, Sister Caliste. This time moisten it particularly well with lavender oil. I have remarked that it helps to lessen scarring, and this poor soul won't want that great mark on her brow for the rest of her life.'

Her hands already busy, Sister Caliste felt her heart lift. 'You think, then, Sister, that she will live?'

'Course she will!' Sister Euphemia exclaimed robustly. 'Nasty wounds, I grant you, but not enough to take her life. Not now she's here and in our care.'

Happy for the first time since she had entered the infirmary, Sister Caliste turned her head in the direction of the man on the stool. He was still staring intently at the two nuns, his expression as anxious and grief-stricken as ever.

'I think, then,' Sister Caliste said quietly, 'that we had better find a way of telling *him* the good news.'

Some time later, Helewise received the expected visit from the infirmarer. Sister Euphemia told her quickly and economically what had been done to the woman, how they had cared for her and that she would live. After expressing her relief and her appreciation of the infirmarer's skills – which Sister Euphemia dismissed with a toss of her head and the firm insistence that Sister Caliste had done as much if not more – Helewise asked, 'And what of the man who brought her here? Is he injured too?'

Sister Euphemia frowned. 'Do you know, my lady, we never thought to ask? I will put that right, soon as I'm back in the infirmary. Trouble is,' she added, 'he doesn't understand us. He's maybe a deaf mute. He only said those few words, didn't he, when he came a-knocking at the gates?'

'Yes. Does he not respond when spoken to?'

'No. He sort of fixes you with those agonised brown eyes, as if he knows you're talking to him but can't hear.'

'Or can't understand. Perhaps he is a foreigner and does not speak our tongue.'

Sister Euphemia was nodding. 'Aye, that's likely. Anyway, deaf or foreign, Sister Caliste and I reckon he's slow of understanding. A bit soft in the head.'

'I see.'

'Nothing wrong with his heart, however. He loves that woman like his own child. Never takes his eyes off her.'

'Perhaps she is his own child.'

The infirmarer considered for a moment. Then: 'He'd have had to be a mighty young father, if so. I reckon she's thirty, maybe a little older, and he's only ten years or so more. Ah well, I'll get Sister Caliste on to it.'

Helewise was puzzled. 'In what way?'

The infirmarer smiled fondly. 'It was a good day for the Abbey when that little one decided she was called to join us,' she said. 'As well as being a devoted and efficient nurse, a kind ear to those in trouble and a tireless worker, Sister Caliste has a talent for acting. She's been miming questions and requests to our poor softhead, and, bless him, he understands her. I'll be making my way back, my lady, if you'll excuse me,' – she was already heading for the door – 'to get her to ask him where they come from, who they are and who hurt that poor woman so grievously.'

Sister Caliste had begun to enjoy her task the moment she had managed to explain to the dumb man that the woman would live. As comprehension had dawned, he clasped Sister Caliste's hands in his and, beaming his joy, began to cry. Patting him on his broad shoulder, she murmured soft words until he was calm again.

Later, when Sister Euphemia returned from the Abbess's room and said that Caliste was to try to elicit information from the man, she took him out of the infirmary and found a quiet spot in a corner of the chapter house, at present empty of all but one of the Abbey's cats, who slunk away as human beings entered what she regarded as her domain. They sat down side by side on a bench, which creaked ominously as the man lowered his weight on to it, and then, pointing firmly to her own chest, Caliste said, 'Caliste. My name is Caliste.' Then, pointing the same hand at him: 'Name? What is *your* name?'

He frowned. He was muttering something; it sounded as if he were repeating *name, your name.*

Just as Caliste was concluding that he might well be slow-witted, foreign or even deaf but he did not seem to be dumb, the man suddenly shouted, 'Aah, *nome!* My – name – Benedetto!'

'Benedetto!' Caliste exclaimed, delighted. 'And the woman?' She mimed cradling someone in her arms, then indicated her own forehead and made a sorrowful face.

'Aurelia.'

At first Caliste did not grasp what he was saying; he made the word sound strange. He repeated it a few times.

'Aurelia?' Caliste tried.

'*Sì*. Aurelia.'

'And she is—' Caliste tried to think how to ask if the woman were his wife. Pointing to the third finger of her left hand, she raised her eyebrows in enquiry.

'No, no.' He frowned hard. 'No my wife. My – *fren*. All are my frens. I—' The frown intensified. 'I care. I guard.'

His friend? Was he saying that the woman was his friend? And he *cared*, he *guarded*. What did he mean by that?

'Thank you, Benedetto,' she said gravely.

He muttered something in response, giving her as he did so a small but graceful bow.

She was thinking, her mind racing. He had definitely said *all are my frens*. Friends, presumably. Was he the bodyguard of some travelling group of foreigners who had been attacked while journeying? While coming to Hawkenlye, perhaps? If he were, it might explain why he had been so devoted. Why it had been so difficult to make him put down the woman he had brought to them. And it would also explain why he was so badly affected by the whole thing; he would feel that, as their bodyguard, he should have saved them from attack.

Very carefully she said, 'There are more of you?' No – she could see that he had not understood. So, counting on her fingers, she said, 'Benedetto, Aurelia . . . ?' then, holding a third finger, raised her eyebrows.

'Aah!' He beamed his comprehension. Then his smile vanished. Dropping his face into one large hand, he let out a groan, thumping a fist down on his thigh.

There must be more, Caliste thought swiftly. And they are in some trouble. 'Benedetto?' she prompted gently. 'The others?'

But he had risen abruptly from the bench and was stalking away across the room.

There was, Caliste thought, little point in following him. He was clearly very upset and it did not seem prudent to pursue a large man in a bad mood. Instead she left the chapter house and went along the cloister to speak to the Abbess.

Helewise was in the middle of telling Josse about the events of the early morning when Sister Caliste tapped on her door. As she called out 'Come in!' and the young sister entered the room, Helewise could not help noticing Josse's broad smile of welcome. Yes, she thought, he always did have a soft spot for our Caliste. Answering Caliste's request to speak with a nod of encouragement, Helewise sat back to listen to what she had come to report.

' . . . and I really think that there must definitely be more of his party somewhere out there,' Sister Caliste concluded a short time later. 'They're definitely foreign, at least, Benedetto is. I suppose English travellers might well employ a foreign bodyguard.'

'Benedetto sounds like a name from southern lands,' Josse mused. 'Do you recall any words or phrases that he used, Sister Caliste?'

'He said *si* for yes,' she replied promptly. 'And there was a word he used when I thanked him for something, only I can't remember what it was.'

'They say *si* in the southern lands,' Josse said. 'At least, I believe they do. In Spain, for example.'

'Hmm.' Helewise, whose knowledge of other languages was limited, had nothing to offer on that question. But there was something that she wanted to say. 'There seems to be an error in this assumption that the man's party was attacked,' she observed. 'Sister Euphemia reports that the woman in the infirmary has been flogged and branded, neither of which are injuries one might expect from someone who was the victim of an assault out on the open road. Surely these are the wounds of punishment.'

Josse, eyes fixed on hers, slowly nodded. 'Aye,' he breathed. 'Aye.'

Sister Caliste was watching him wide-eyed. Helewise, who had an idea that more was to come, also watched and waited.

Then Josse shook his head. 'There's something niggling at me,' he confessed. 'I feel as if the puzzle of all this ought to fit together, if only I could *think*.' He hit the side of his head with his open palm.

Helewise and Sister Caliste waited a moment longer.

Then, with a rueful grin, Josse said, 'It's no good, it won't come and I can't force it. I will tell you one thing, though, ladies.' He glanced quickly at Sister Caliste and then back at Helewise. 'I would bet my boots that this has something to do with Father Micah. It *smells* of him, and no mistake!'

# 9

The Abbess asked, as he might have known she would, 'How can you be so sure, Sir Josse?

'Because of what he was threatening to do to the wife of the Lord of the High Weald!' he cried. 'I told you, my lady, he was going to have her flogged, for no better reason than that she was of another faith and, in Father Micah's eyes, living outside holy matrimony.'

'And what has that to do with a foreign woman brought here to us for succour?' Her grey eyes on his were cool to the point of chilliness, as if she thought he were making wild assumptions and did not approve.

'Well, he could have met the woman and the rest of her group on the road. Perhaps he got into conversation with them, as travellers do, and they told him they weren't Christians and he – the Father – thought, if they're not Christians then they're not really married, so I'll flog the woman and brand her for her sins.'

The Abbess was not even trying to disguise her scepticism. He didn't blame her; it sounded pretty feeble an explanation, even to him. 'On the other hand, perhaps not,' he finished lamely.

She smiled at him. 'It is important always to set up a hypothesis, Sir Josse,' she said kindly. 'From sometimes wild ideas, a kernel of truth may emerge.'

Ah, he thought, but she's a generous woman.

'May I speak?' Sister Caliste asked.

The Abbess turned to her. 'Of course.'

'Sister Euphemia says that once before she saw a woman branded. It was with an A because she had been the lover of a married man.' The young nun glanced at Josse. 'So perhaps there's something in what Sir Josse says.' She dropped her head, as if ashamed to support a scenario that her Abbess had just dismissed.

Josse watched the Abbess. After a short pause, she said, 'Thank you, Sister Caliste. Perhaps, then, we should conclude that the woman in the infirmary—'

'Her name is Aurelia,' put in Sister Caliste.

'—that Aurelia may indeed have suffered the wrath of Father Micah, but for some other reason and not because she came across him in the course of her journey and impulsively confessed to being of an alien faith. Yes?' She looked first at Josse and then at Sister Caliste who, after giving each other a swift glance, both nodded their agreement.

The Abbess muttered under her breath – it sounded to Josse something about hair-splitting details – and then, with a radiant smile that indicated, to he who knew her so well, that she was having trouble holding on to her patience and didn't want them to realise, said, 'In that case, let us propose that.'

'Where, then?' Sister Caliste asked timidly after a moment.

'Where?' The Abbess glared at her.

'Where did Father Micah meet Aurelia? And how did he find out she was an adulteress and had to be punished?'

Josse suppressed a smile. They were fair questions, and he was sure the Abbess would think so too, were she not so irritated. He was equally sure that she would not have an answer to either; he certainly could not think of one.

'We cannot possibly expect to know these things at present,' she said majestically. 'There is a great deal more that we must find out before we understand what has happened. Sir Josse!'

She had turned to him so quickly that he was unprepared. Wiping the amusement from his face, he said, 'My lady?'

'If indeed this was a Church matter, and the punishment was meted out on Father Micah's orders, then it is highly likely that Father Gilbert knows something of the matter.' Glancing at Sister Caliste, she went on, 'If Sister Caliste is right in her suspicion that this Benedetto was bodyguard to a group of travellers, then there may be news of the others. I had intended to visit Father Gilbert in any case, and I propose to do so straight away. Sufficient daylight remains, I would judge, to ride to his house and back before night closes in.' She hesitated for an instant, then said, quite meekly for her, 'I should be grateful for your company, if you would consent to ride with me.'

Now he smiled openly, pleased that she had asked. 'Aye, that I will, and gladly.'

They set out from Hawkenlye riding silently side by side. Josse was glad of the chance to give Horace some exercise. The Abbess rode a dainty pale chestnut mare, an elegant animal whose breeding was evident in her lines. Josse, after the first quick glance, had looked away and tried to think about something else.

The mare was called Honey, and she belonged to a young woman called Joanna de Courtenay. Josse had encountered Joanna when she was on the run from her cousin, who had a future mapped out for Joanna's young son that his mother found intolerable. Joanna had sought refuge with Mag Hobson, a woman who had cared for her when she was a child, then living in the depths of the forest and earning a reputation as a wise woman. Mag was now dead and Joanna, or so they said, lived out there in the wise woman's hut. Some also said that she was taking up old Mag's work.

Joanna had left her beautiful horse at Hawkenlye Abbey where, in exchange for the mare's keep, the nuns were permitted to use her when they needed to. As, today, the Abbess was doing. Josse had loved Joanna, and he was not entirely sure but thought possibly he still did.

Which made it painful to see the Abbess riding Joanna's horse.

He wanted very much to speak to her of Joanna. But, despite their closeness, Joanna remained one subject that was never discussed between them.

Perhaps it was just as well.

Breaking into his poignant thoughts, the Abbess suddenly said, 'I forgot to tell you, Sir Josse, in the flurry of everything else that has happened today, but yesterday I had a visit from one Gervase de Gifford, who describes himself as Sheriff and who is apparently a de Clare man.'

'Oh?' Quite relieved to be jerked out of his reverie, Josse said, 'What happened to Harry Pelham?'

'That's what I asked. De Gifford did not really answer, save to imply that Pelham had been promoted above his capabilities.'

'We already knew that.'

'Quite.'

'What did he want?' Josse was intrigued.

'He said he had come because of Father Micah. He intends to visit again so that he can speak to you.'

'To be told what I have discovered.'

'Yes, that's right.'

Josse snorted. 'The answer to that is nothing. Nothing that was not known from the first.'

'Come, Sir Josse!' she encouraged him. 'You have a strong instinct that Father Micah was somehow involved in the punishment of that poor woman in the infirmary!'

'Instinct, my lady! You use the word well, for there is no proof of the Father's hand in that.'

'But what of the Lord of the High Weald's tale?' She seemed quite determined to rid him of his pessimism. 'It is surely more than coincidence that you hear of a priest's threat to a woman he believes to be a sinner and the very next day you come across a woman who has been punished in exactly the way that was described.'

She was right, he supposed. But, all the same, it was not something he would have liked to put before this de Gifford. 'When does he intend to return?' he asked.

'He did not say.'

'Well, I'll just have to make sure I have something more definite to report when he does.' Filled with purpose, he gave the ambling

Horace a kick and said, 'Come on! Let's get on to Father Gilbert and see what he has to tell us!'

He thought he saw her smile briefly. Satisfaction at an end achieved? It looked remarkably like it.

Inside the priest's house, Josse noticed immediately that the temperature was considerably warmer than on his previous visit. There was a large stack of neatly split logs piled up a safe distance from the hearth and Father Gilbert, sitting up in bed and looking quite perky, was now covered with a thick, handsome fur rug and had consequently shed a few layers of clothing.

'My lady Abbess!' he cried as she preceded Josse into the little room. 'And Sir Josse! What a pleasure to see you both.'

'You've had another visitor,' Josse said, pointing to the logs and to the rug. 'One who, I would say, spent some time with you.'

'Yes indeed. Lord Saxonbury's son Morcar arrived this morning saying that he had heard I was in need of firewood. He also brought me this splendid fur, a dish of stew, which he heated up for me on the trivet, and a jug of ale.'

No wonder, Josse though, the priest's pale face was flooded with colour.

'Those were kindly deeds,' the Abbess was saying. 'They are good, Christian people up at Saxonbury, then, Father?'

'Christian, perhaps. Good, undoubtedly,' Father Gilbert said.

'You know about his wife, I believe?' Josse asked. 'When I was last here you said something about the woman whom Father Micah referred to as the Lord's mistress.'

'Yes, yes, I know.' Father Gilbert's hands were fretting with his blankets, tangled beneath the fur rug. 'Father Micah did not recognise any marriage to be lawful in the eyes of God other than one conducted by a priest. A priest of the Christian faith,' he added firmly. 'Since the Lord's wife is a Muslim woman and their marriage was celebrated in her faith, Father Micah considered them to be fornicators.'

'He was planning to flog her,' Josse said neutrally.

Father Gilbert's alcoholic flush faded. 'Was he?' he whispered.

'Aye.'

Josse and the Abbess stood side by side looking down at the priest in his bed. After a moment, Father Gilbert broke the accusatory silence.

'He would have been within his rights,' he said. 'The Church says that—'

'That an elderly, frail woman can be dragged from her sickbed and whipped?' Josse interrupted. He felt the Abbess's cautionary touch on his sleeve but ignored it. 'The Lord asked me, Father, what I would have done had it been my mother about to be flogged.'

Father Gilbert looked miserable. 'I understand your emotion, Sir Josse. Father Micah was – that is, sometimes he—' He shrugged. 'We each serve God in our own way,' he finished weakly.

'Father, may I ask a question?' the Abbess said, respect in her tone.

He turned gratefully to her. 'Of course, my lady.'

'Do you think that Father Micah was capable of flogging someone? Of, say, giving a delicate, slender woman twenty-five lashes?'

There was a long pause while the priest considered the question. It appeared to Josse that he was struggling with whether to save his late fellow-priest's reputation or to tell the truth. Finally he said, so quietly that Josse barely heard, 'Yes. I know he was. I know he *did*.'

The Abbess said, 'We have such a woman in our care at Hawkenlye. Was she, do you think, Father Micah's victim?'

Father Gilbert raised moist eyes to her. 'I cannot say, my lady, but I fear it may be so.'

'In God's merciful name,' Josse burst out, 'what had she *done*? She's also got a brand on her brow, Father, which looks like the letter A. Was she another woman whose marriage Father Micah refused to recognise, who slept with a man without the Church's sanction?'

Father Gilbert rubbed at his eyes with his hands. 'Father Micah believed he was doing God's work by such means,' he said wearily. 'Sinners are doomed to the eternal fires, Sir Josse.' He removed his hands and stared fiercely up at Josse, the priest taking over from the guilt-ridden, compassionate man. 'Do not forget that! Is it not better to suffer a little temporary pain here on Earth while the sin is burned away than to be condemned to damnation for the rest of time?'

'A little temporary pain!' Josse began, his voice strident with anger.

But the Abbess had hold of his sleeve again. More firmly now; her fist was clenched in the fabric like an iron clamp. She pulled him back towards the door. 'Sir Josse will wait for me outside,' she announced. Turning to him, he saw understanding in her eyes; she said under her breath, 'He is sick and in pain, Sir Josse. Do not shout at him because of something that is not his fault.'

'But—'

*'Josse!'*

Not for nothing was she Abbess of one of the largest communities in the south of England; the habit of command was strong in her, and meekly he did as she ordered.

Outside, the icy air hit him as if someone had thrown a bucket of cold water over him. As his fast breathing slowed and grew quiet, he strained to hear what was being said within. But, except for the low, soothing tones of the Abbess and the occasional deeper rumble of the priest's interjections, he could hear nothing.

After some time she came out, carefully fastening the door behind her. Immediately she came to stand beside him and said, 'Sir Josse, forgive me for ordering you from the room. I have no more right to command you than you to command me. But I did genuinely fear for him, in pain as he is, and in addition I thought that perhaps he would speak more openly to me.'

He acknowledged her apology with a grunt. 'And did he?'

'Not really.' She kicked at a stone frozen into the path. 'One thing, though, that may be of use to us – he said that Father Micah had been gravely preoccupied of late with the problem of how to bring some souls back to the faith. He—'

'Brother Firmin!' Josse exclaimed. 'He said that Father Micah mentioned two missions he had to pursue: one concerned a lord who had forgotten God's ways, which, we can be fairly sure, meant the Lord Saxonbury. The other involved some lost souls who were destined for burning in the flames.'

'Lost souls,' she repeated dreamily. Then, eyes wide, 'Sir Josse, what a frightful, haunting description! Oh, whatever it took, was not Father Micah right to try to bring the lost back into the love of God?'

'My lady, think of that poor woman in the infirmary! Was that right, what he did to her?'

'We cannot know that it was he!'

He smacked his hand against his forehead in exasperation. 'You are thinking with your heart, not your head!' he exclaimed. 'First you suggest that Father Micah was right to flog a woman twenty-five times, then you say, oh, but it might not have been him! Do you approve or not, my lady?'

She kicked the stone again, more forcefully this time so that it was dislodged and rolled away. Following it, she kicked it again. Then she said quietly, 'No.'

He knew better than to react in any way that might smack of triumph. Instead he said, 'It's time we were heading back. I'll fetch the horses.'

He saw her back to her room and there bade her goodnight; it would soon be time for Vespers and he did not expect to see her again that day. As he turned to go, she said, 'Sir Josse?'

'My lady?'

'I think that I should send for Gervase de Gifford. It seems very likely that Father Micah was responsible for the flogging of the woman in the infirmary, even if he did not himself wield the whip. If that is so, and it is also correct that she had companions, then one of them had a reason to harm the Father. We should, I believe, share this information with de Gifford.'

'Aye, I agree.' He paused; he was reluctant to say what was on his mind.

'What is it?' she asked.

'I was just thinking that what you just said equally applies to our large friend Benedetto. I wonder if we should at least question him?'

She nodded slowly. 'Yes, I see. And perhaps find some way of confining him until de Gifford arrives? If Benedetto is innocent it will do no harm, and if guilty, we shall have restrained him so that he may face justice.'

Thinking that she seemed to be placing a great deal of trust in this de Gifford's ability to know guilt from innocence, Josse said, 'May I speak to him first before there is any question of confinement? It is merely that I do not like to think that we might send a man to trial who was guilty of nothing more than devotion to his mistress.'

'And you have no proof of de Gifford's efficiency as an official of the law,' she added. 'Yes, Sir Josse. Please, go and speak to Benedetto now. I will be guided by you as to whether or not we should then turn him over to de Gifford.'

'Thank you, my lady. Shall I report to you after the office?'

'Yes. Please do.'

But he was back before she had even set out for the Abbey church.

He went to the infirmary, expecting to find Benedetto sitting in vigil with the woman, Aurelia. He was not there; Sister Caliste, preoccupied with tending her patient, trying to dress the wound on her forehead while the semi-conscious Aurelia writhed and moaned in pain, said that she thought he might have gone off to pray for her. But Benedetto was not in the church, nor, when Josse ran down to check, in the shrine in the Vale. He was not in the pilgrims' shelter, nor anywhere else in the Vale.

Racing now, feeling his heart pumping hard, Josse explored the entire Abbey. With the exception of the small leper house – which was a separate, isolated unit within the foundation and which nobody entered if they expected to leave again – he looked everywhere. He even searched the curtained cubicles of the nuns' long dormitory. Apart from the simple beds and some small personal effects, nothing.

Unless Benedetto had made himself so small that he could creep into a tiny, hidden corner, which hardly seemed likely, then there was only one conclusion: he had gone.

Feeling as if he were the bringer of very bad news, Josse went to find the Abbess.

# 10

In the middle of the morning of the next day, Helewise sat at her table and studied Josse and Gervase de Gifford as they took one another's measure. They were, she thought irreverently, like two large dogs in the market place, each suspecting the other of invasion of personal territory.

Despite the wariness, however, she sensed a similarity between the two men. Not a physical one; Josse was brown-eyed and dark, tall, broad-framed and, despite his rough-featured face, he habitually wore an expression that suggested he expected to like people rather than condemn them. Gervase de Gifford on the other hand was slim and elegant, and his green eyes had a look of detachment and slight amusement. No. The likeness between him and Josse was merely that they shared a sort of power, an indefinable something that sat on them like a garment. It was as if both had been put to the test, survived and consequently believed in themselves and their own ability to cope with whatever life might subsequently throw at them.

She became aware that de Gifford was speaking to her.

' . . . thank you for summoning me here, my lady.'

'It is my duty,' she said piously. 'Besides, I promised that you should be informed of any intelligence that Sir Josse managed to glean concerning the late Father Micah.'

'Indeed you did,' de Gifford said blandly. 'As Sir Josse has just been explaining, it is nothing definite, but every small pointer can be of use. Is it not so, Sir Josse?'

'Aye.' Josse, she noticed, was not yet ready to waste more than the basic civilities on this newcomer.

'To recapitulate,' de Gifford said, turning to Helewise to include her in his summation, 'you suspect that the woman Aurelia, brought here to your care gravely injured, may have been the victim of Father Micah's religious zeal. You think this because her wounds are similar to those with which the Father threatened another woman, the wife of this Lord of the High Weald. Yes?'

'Yes,' Helewise said, adding, 'It is, as you just implied, rather vague and we really should be trying harder to discover the truth but—'

'My lady,' de Gifford interrupted with an apologetic smile, 'I believe you may be accusing yourselves falsely. You have here someone who may have been flogged by Father Micah and, through Sir Josse's good offices, you have come to hear of someone who would have been a possible future candidate for the same treatment. It may interest you to hear that I know of others.'

'Really?' Helewise sat up straighter in her chair. Josse, she noticed, was scowling at de Gifford in concentration.

'Really,' de Gifford echoed. 'I am not certain where the boundaries of the Father's influence were set; he was a replacement for your Father Gilbert, I am aware, and Father Gilbert made but rare visits down to us in the Medway valley. He had his own concerns up here and, besides, our souls are adequately catered for by our own Father Henry. But, whether or not Father Micah *should* have been carrying out his mission of salvation in our vicinity, the fact remains that he was.' He studied Helewise for a moment, as if deciding whether he should proceed with what he was about to say. Apparently deciding that he would, he added, 'Father Henry understands our – er, our ways. Father Micah did not. We did not welcome him and Father Henry, I believe, resented him. Neither reaction had the least effect in keeping Father Micah away.'

Helewise was not sure what he was trying to imply. 'Your ways?' she said. 'Surely there is only one way for a godly man, Sir Gervase? Does not your Father Henry appreciate this?'

De Gifford gave her a charming smile. 'Naturally so, my lady Abbess, and reminds us all of our duty at every possible opportunity. I merely meant to make the point that priests may vary in the methods that they employ to keep their flock within the fold.'

'Hmm.' She was not convinced. She had observed an occasional exchange of glances between de Gifford and Josse – or rather, she corrected herself, glances from de Gifford directed at Josse – as if the Sheriff were trying to recruit Josse as an ally. Two laymen together facing a woman of the Church.

Josse said, 'Who else did the Father order to be flogged?'

'He did not merely order,' de Gifford corrected. 'He made it a rule to carry out himself any sentence that he imposed. A variant, I suppose, on the good commander's maxim: never order your troops to do something you are not also prepared to do. In answer to your question, Sir Josse, Father Micah flogged another woman, somewhat younger than Aurelia. She had been convicted of a crime by a Church court and she was to be handed over to the secular arm for punishment. However, Father Micah overruled that and said he would do it himself, which he duly did. Then he allowed her to be hauled away by a couple of guards and thrown into some filthy prison cell.'

'What became of her?' Helewise, to her distress, heard her own voice emerge as little more than a whisper. But she did not think there was anything that she could have done about it; de Gifford told his affecting tale simply but with quiet force, so that, for an instant, it had almost seemed that the poor beaten woman, dragged away to prison, was there in the room with them.

De Gifford was gazing at her, cool eyes briefly filled with pity. 'She died, my lady. Her gaoler decided to compound her various agonies by raping her. In doing so, it appears she hit her head on the stone floor of her cell, and it was a hard enough blow to kill her.'

'And what of the gaoler?' Now her voice was shaking.

De Gifford shrugged. 'What of him? Still a gaoler.'

'But he assaulted his prisoner!'

'She was to die in any case, my lady,' de Gifford said gently. 'They did not believe that her repentance was sincere, for they said she intended to revert to her wickedness as soon as she was able.'

Helewise was about to ask what form the woman's wickedness had taken – another adulteress? Surely not! – when Josse interrupted.

'I investigated the case of two men who escaped from a gaol,' he said. 'My own involvement began but three days ago, although I believe that the men fled some days earlier. A pilgrim family who came here for the Holy Water cure told us how someone had attacked the guard. He only appeared to have been hit once, or perhaps twice, in the face, yet he died. When one of the Abbey's brothers and I went to look at the body, we discovered marks on his throat that suggested he had been throttled.'

'Yes, I heard about him,' de Gifford said.

'And what about the men who escaped? Do you know anything of them?' Josse, Helewise noticed, looked eager, straining towards de Gifford as if he expected answers to all his questions suddenly to materialise.

De Gifford studied him for a moment. Then he said, 'No.'

I am almost certain, Helewise told herself, that his last statement was a lie. Josse met her eyes briefly, and she saw that he had had the same thought.

'I asked around in the village where the gaol was,' Josse said casually, as if it were a mere aside. 'Nobody there knew anything of the men, either. Or they *said* not, anyway.' He eyed de Gifford. 'Which I thought strange, since I was almost certain that they did. They were afraid, you see, de Gifford. To a man – and to a woman – they scarcely waited to hear me ask my question before they began shaking their heads and denying all knowledge. One old woman started to tremble, repeating over and over again that she didn't want any trouble and that she hadn't seen anything, didn't know anything, may God strike her down if she told a lie. I thought her statement was quite foolhardy, since she had undoubtedly just done exactly that. And a little child who was with her – he was a boy, no more than about five, too young to know how to keep a secret – said that he was frightened that the black man would come back and get him while he lay in his bed at night.'

De Gifford looked as if he were about to speak. Then, seeming to change his mind, shook his head slightly.

'I'll tell you another thing,' Josse went on. 'The prison guards reckoned that the men who escaped were foreign. One of their number had complained that he didn't understand a word the prisoners said. Now it's possible that the prisoners were well-educated men whose speech was not comprehended by the ruffians we employ in our gaols, or that the guard was singularly hard of hearing or dull of wit. But I believe it's much more likely that the guard didn't understand because the men cried out to him in another tongue. What d'you think, de Gifford? Do I reason rightly?'

Again, de Gifford appeared to go through the same process of deciding whether or not to confide his thoughts. But this time he made a different decision. With a gesture of squaring his shoulders, he said, 'My lady Abbess, Sir Josse, there is a limit to what I may tell you. But you are right – I do know something about these prisoners and of the woman who died in gaol. And, indeed, of the one now lying in your infirmary. Or so I believe.'

'You can't have her!' Helewise cried. 'She is under our protection and if you try to arrest her I will have her taken into the Abbey church where she may claim sanctuary!'

De Gifford turned his clear eyes on to her. 'My lady, you misunderstand, and I cannot blame you for that when I have perforce been so very reticent.' He frowned. 'On my honour, I am glad that Aurelia is here. What was done to her was vilely cruel and I would have brought her to Hawkenlye myself had I known where to find her. As it is, I shall ensure that nobody who wishes her ill shall learn from me where she is. Keep her here, help her to heal. When she is ready to go, then – but no. It is not yet time to speak of that.'

Feeling weak as the high emotion drained from her, Helewise leaned against the back of her chair.

Josse said, 'You were saying, de Gifford, that you know the identities of the two escaped prisoners.'

'I cannot be sure, for the tally of people we refer to here is but four – the woman who died in gaol, Aurelia and the two men who fled – whereas the group of which I heard tell numbered seven.'

Not four but five, Helewise thought. The two men, Aurelia,

the poor woman who died, and Benedetto. But if de Gifford did not know about Benedetto, then she was not yet ready to tell him. Nor, from the glance he sent her, was Josse. De Gifford, it seemed, had assumed that Aurelia had been brought to Hawkenlye by some Good Samaritan who came across her on the road.

'Four people?' Josse now said. 'Foreigners?'

'Er – yes. Some from the Low Countries, some from the far south. So I believe.'

'And why are they in England?' Josse demanded. 'Were they making for Hawkenlye?'

'No, not as far as I know.' De Gifford twisted his face in mock anguish. 'Sir Josse, please do not push me so hard. I am telling you all that I may, and even this much is more than I should. I can reveal nothing else about the travellers and I shall not do so, no matter how much you scowl at me. What I will say is that I am aware that Father Micah was on their trail. As I have told you, he was responsible for beating and imprisoning Frieda.'

'Frieda,' Helewise repeated softly. 'The woman who was raped and killed.'

'Yes, my lady.' De Gifford looked at her. 'It is better, is it not, to have a name for her? So that we may remember her as a real woman and not merely a faceless, unidentifiable prisoner?'

'It is,' Helewise agreed. 'We shall say a mass for her soul.'

'I do not think—' de Gifford began. Then, abruptly breaking off, he bowed briefly and murmured, 'A charitable thought.'

'Go on, now,' Josse urged. 'Father Micah brought about this Frieda's downfall. What else?'

'He was also responsible for the imprisonment of the two men, and he was beside himself in his rage when he learned that they had escaped. He went through that village with the force of an attack of the pestilence, cursing them for their evil ways, telling them that they were Satan's own and in league with the Evil One, that they should have kept their accursed eyes open and prevented two of the devil's minions from escaping.'

'If the villagers were Satan's own and the prisoners were his minions, then they were on the same side and it's no wonder the men were allowed to escape,' Josse observed.

'Quite so,' de Gifford agreed. 'But then Father Micah was never strong on logical thought, especially when he was in a thundering rage and about God's work.'

'You speak of a priest,' Helewise said coldly. 'Whatever his faults, Father Micah did his duty to God as he saw it. His methods should not be open to the criticism of ordinary people.'

'No?' De Gifford's tone was soft. 'Well, my lady, if you will excuse me, I must disagree. The Father's methods included burning down the houses of those he suspected of contravening the Church's edicts, and he did not care whether the inhabitants were inside or not. He also confiscated the meagre food of the poor in order to ensure that they fasted when he ordered them to, and he had been known to beat a man so badly that the poor fellow never worked again. That man had five children.'

Helewise opened her mouth, found she had nothing to say and closed it again.

De Gifford turned to Josse. 'You spoke just now of a little boy in the village who was terrified of the black man, Sir Josse,' he said. 'Did you have any idea who he meant?'

'I wondered if some friend of the prisoners had got them out,' Josse said, 'and I thought that he might have been foreign, like them, perhaps from the lands of the distant south and with a black skin.'

De Gifford smiled, shaking his head. 'Fanciful but inaccurate,' he said. 'The Black Man has become known to quite a lot of folk around here by now. He was feared wherever he went because he had a violent temper and he descended on the poor and the weak like a fury against which they were powerless.'

He looked from Josse to Helewise, making sure he had her full attention. Then, once more addressing Josse, he said, 'The Black Man is what they called Father Micah.'

While the Abbess, de Gifford and Josse were preoccupied with the drama of the Sheriff's account, Sister Phillipa sat by herself in the small, peaceful room that housed the manuscripts. She had been steadily working through the precious documents on and off for the last three days, slipping away to her pleasant and undemanding task whenever she was not required for other duties. To begin with, Sister Bernadine had helped her, but the two women had found that checking each script off against the inventory and inspecting it for damage was a job that one person could perform quite well alone. Sister Bernadine appeared to find the task stressful; Sister Phillipa guessed that she went in constant fear of discovering that something valuable had been stolen and of the punishment she might receive for her carelessness if this were so. The younger nun had kindly offered to proceed with the inventory alone, and Sister Bernadine gratefully accepted.

'But I must know if you find – if you find—' She had been unable to put the cause of her distress into words.

'If I discover that anything at all is missing or damaged, then I shall report first to you,' Sister Phillipa promised.

To her surprise, tears had welled up in Sister Bernadine's eyes. She had muttered something about Sister Phillipa being a good, kind girl, then hurried away.

Now, the only slight drawback to the work was that it kept Sister Phillipa from her herbal. At first she had itched to return to her painting and her lettering; they were deeply absorbing in themselves but, in addition, there was the thrill of the new knowledge of herbs and their uses that she was learning from Sister Tiphaine and Sister Euphemia. Both nuns were natural and gifted teachers and, even when very busy in their own departments, always strove diligently to make quite sure that Sister Phillipa understood exactly what they were telling her and would not make a mistake. However, regret for time lost for her herbal had gradually faded; as she had thrown herself into her careful examination of the Abbey's precious manuscripts, she had soon realised that this task in fact provided a lucky and perfectly timed opportunity for her to study the work of some of England's greatest artists and craftsmen.

This morning she was so happy that she hummed softly as she worked.

★   ★   ★

She found it just before the summons to Sext called her away.

She had been staring intently at a page in a glossed Bible; the page had an extract from the Book of Leviticus and the writing hand was so beautiful, so even, that it quite took Sister Phillipa's breath away. Putting it carefully back – I have a job to do, she reminded herself, and I ought not to waste time in rapture over another's fine penmanship – she noticed something bright lying on the base of the book chest.

It was pure chance that the small patch of colour caught her eye. Had she not had to push two scripts carefully aside to make room for the Bible pages, it would have remained hidden. She took out several scripts and placed them carefully on the floor. Now, in the much larger gap that she had made, she could see that another document had been placed on the floor of the chest. Once all the other scripts had been replaced upright on top of it, it had been totally hidden.

Now what, she wondered, removing the script, is this doing down there?

She studied it. The letters appeared to make words, but she did not know what they were. They were not in Latin nor, she thought, in Greek. Leaving aside the writing for a moment, she looked at the first page of illustrations.

She realised instantly that they were like nothing she had ever seen before. There was a wonderfully vivid, affecting little painting of a group of people with their hands held aloft and their ecstatic faces raised to the sky, out of which there shone a fiery sun with orange, yellow and gold rays. There were strange animals gambolling around the people, arranged like a sort of living frieze. Sister Phillipa did not recognise any of the beasts; she wondered if they might be symbolic, like the winged lion representing St Mark and the eagle St John, but of whom or what she did not know.

The second illustration was of a golden, bejewelled cross. But it did not look like the familiar cross that Sister Phillipa knew and loved; there was something strange about it, something unfamiliar.

Getting up, she went to check on the inventory to see what this alien document might be.

There was no mention of it.

She read through the inventory again, but the strange manuscript was not on it.

In a flash of insight Sister Phillipa realised what had happened. She called to mind why she was doing this exacting task: she was meant to be checking whether or not anything was missing from the chest or the cupboard. So far – and she had almost finished – nothing was. None of the manuscripts had been taken.

Instead, one had been added.

Josse walked with de Gifford out to where Sister Martha was looking after the Sheriff's horse. They had stayed only a little longer with the Abbess. Josse had perceived her struggle between standing up for Father Micah because he was a man of the Church and joining in with their condemnation because he was also cruel, perverted, narrow-minded and took advantage of the weak and the powerless, and he had opted for a swift departure so as not to prolong her suffering.

'She's a good woman,' Josse said when they were out of earshot of the few people out and about in the Abbey on that chilly morning. 'She has—'

De Gifford put up a slim hand, on to which he had just put a beautifully fitting cream kid glove embroidered with reddish-brown stones that matched the braid on his tunic. 'Please, Sir Josse, there is no need,' he said. 'Although I have had but two brief meetings with the Abbess Helewise and not the advantage of a long acquaintance such as yours, I feel that I have already taken some of the lady's measure. And, indeed, I ask myself how I would behave, were I in her position. To be called on to defend the indefensible is testing to us all, even more so to a woman to whom the truth clearly matters so very much.'

'She likes to see things as they really are,' Josse agreed, 'and is ever at pains to strip away the sort of concealing, self-deluding devices that most of us use to disguise unpalatable facts.'

'And now she has to cope with the aftermath of Father Micah,' de Gifford murmured. 'Poor lady. I do not envy her.'

'It is—' Josse paused delicately. 'I believe, de Gifford, that it is easier for us. We are laymen, after all, and we may criticise – that is, we can—'

'We are at liberty to say that Father Micah was an insult to the cloth he wore if we feel like it,' de Gifford finished smoothly. 'As, indeed, we do. I do, anyway.'

'And I,' Josse agreed. He checked again that they were not overheard, then said in a low voice, 'I wonder, then, since we are agreed on that, if you feel that you could be more forthcoming with me than with the Abbess. Not that I'm trying to learn secrets that you would rather not divulge.'

'Yes, you are,' de Gifford said easily. 'That is exactly what you are doing, and I can't say I blame you.'

'*Is* there anything else that you can reveal to somebody who is not bound by their very profession to support that dead priest?' Josse urged.

De Gifford studied him. 'It is true that in part my reticence stems from my fear that the Abbess of Hawkenlye is likely to reflect the attitude exhibited by Father Micah. We speak of a delicate business, Sir Josse,' he exclaimed as Josse made to protest, 'concerning which neither I nor, I suspect, you, can say how the Abbess will react.'

'Unless my silence compromises another, I will respect any confidence you make to me,' Josse said. 'Of that you have my word.'

De Gifford, still staring into Josse's eyes, frowned. Then he said, 'I believe you. And, let me say, it would be a relief to speak frankly.' He looked around, noticed a deserted corner where the end wall of the stable block rose up above the herb garden and said, 'Let us go over there into the small shelter provided by the wall, and I will tell you what I can.'

They walked quickly to the spot. A weak sun shone down on it and the temperature felt quite pleasantly warm. Again de Gifford checked that they were alone, then he said, 'The party I spoke of seek a place of sanctuary. Their leader, whose name is Arnulf, is from the Low Countries and he leads a group whose nationalities are varied. One is a fellow countryman of Arnulf's named Alexius, and these two are the men who escaped from the prison. They have a big man with them who is from the south, from Verona I believe. I think it is possible that it was he who killed the prison guard; they say he is exceptionally strong and he is doubtless capable of throttling a man with one hand.'

'The man who killed the guard choked him with his left hand,' Josse said.

'Indeed? I do not know if the man of whom I speak favours his left or his right hand.'

'You said seven people,' Josse prompted.

'Yes. Originally there were four men and three women. The fourth man is one Guiscard, who is from the Midi. Toulouse, Albi, I do not know for sure. Also in the group were Frieda, who was killed by her gaoler, Aurelia whom I believe is the woman who is safe here at Hawkenlye, and one other. Her name is Utta.'

'And where is she?'

'I have no idea.'

Josse, taken aback by de Gifford's willingness to talk, felt he ought to repay the confidences with one of his own. 'The strong man is called Benedetto,' he said. 'It was he who brought Aurelia here.'

'Was it?' The bright eyes went instantly to Josse's. 'I imagine he is no longer here?'

'No.'

'And nobody knows where he is now?'

'No.'

'The whereabouts of five, then, are or have been known,' de Gifford went on, more to himself than to Josse. 'Arnulf and Alexius were imprisoned but escaped, probably helped by Benedetto. Frieda was also imprisoned but she is dead. Aurelia was flogged but presumably Benedetto got her away before, like Frieda, she was thrown into prison. Guiscard and Utta we know nothing about.' He frowned.

De Gifford might have been frank about the party, Josse thought, but his frankness in itself revealed very little. 'Under whose orders were they beaten and imprisoned?' he asked. 'Father Micah's?'

De Gifford turned to him. 'They were apprehended on the road north of Tonbridge and given over to the Church authority, which tried them and imposed the punishment. As I told you earlier, it is usual for those of us in the secular arm then to take over, administering whatever measures the Church feels necessary and then arranging for the criminals' imprisonment, unless they're to be executed. In which case the lay authorities usually do that too. But, as I said, Father Micah liked to take his involvement a little further.'

Taking all that in, Josse said, 'I suppose someone found out what was going on in the group. I must say I find it hard to see how; they must have been very indiscreet. You'd have thought they could have kept that sort of thing hidden, wouldn't you?'

De Gifford was looking at him curiously. 'Well, no, not really. I mean, the whole point of their being here is surely because they want to win people over to their cause. After all, the more followers they have, the more formidable they will become.'

'Their cause?' Josse sounded incredulous. 'What cause? They were punished for adultery!'

'Adultery?' De Gifford gave a short bark of laughter, quickly suppressed. 'Sir Josse, what an extraordinary picture you paint, of the seven of them all fornicating with one another's husbands and wives – none of them is married, in fact, I am almost certain of that, not in the sense that we understand marriage – and of Father Micah coming across them in the midst of their frolicking and instantly putting them under arrest!'

'But Aurelia has a brand mark on her forehead,' Josse persisted. 'It looks like an A, which must mean that she was punished because of adultery!'

De Gifford was shaking his head. 'Whoever made the mark cannot have had a steady hand,' he said soberly. 'It isn't a letter A, Sir Josse. It is a letter H.'

Josse stared at him. 'H?'

'Yes. They're heretics.'

# Part Two

## The Great Forest

February 1192 – February 1193

# 11

Joanna had lived in the Wealden Forest for a little under a year when she was taken to attend her first Great Festival. From that time on, her new identity was assured.

She had few regrets over leaving behind the realm of the Outworlders, as her new people referred to them. The outside world, the one that was ruled by the Church and by men for the good of the Church and men, had not treated her well. It did not suit her. Moreover, she could not put her faith in a religion that was ruled over by a male deity and that denied and denigrated all that was female.

Her new people knew better.

Joanna knew, even before Lora, wisest of teachers, had instructed her, that Samhain was one of the Great Festivals. The forest people always gathered for such occasions, not always in the same place but at some hidden location within Britain's vast tracts of forest that was as yet undiscovered and unexplored by the Outworlders. Until Joanna attended one of these festivals herself, it had puzzled her how everyone knew where to go. She had not been able to attend the Samhain rites – she had been giving birth to her daughter Margaret – and Lora had deemed her not ready for the Yule celebrations, when their people honoured the Midwinter Solstice and welcomed the returning Sun. 'You're all the world to this little 'un now,' Lora had said, stroking Margaret's dark hair with long, gentle fingers. 'She's taking the essence of you into herself as she draws on your milk and you're aware of her every breath. You've nothing to spare for anything else, specially not something that requires so much intense concentration. You're in no state for your first festival, my girl.'

But, as Joanna had sat alone in the forest clearing in front of the hut, staring into her own little fire and singing a soft chant to the Sun as he turned in his path and began the long, slow journey north again, her new people had not forgotten her. Margaret – Meggie, as Joanna had started to call her – was sound asleep inside the hut, well fed, snug and warm in her fur-lined cradle. There was a deep sense of peace in the glade. Joanna, breathing deeply of the smoke from the herbs she had cast on to her fire, had felt her eyelids growing heavy.

Then she sensed that someone was watching her.

Over on the far side of the clearing, in the thicket of hazel and brambles beyond Joanna's herb bed, she could make out a dim shape. Tall – taller than most men – and broad. Dark – the whole of him was dark.

She opened her eyes wide, then looked slightly to the side, a trick she had learned to help with night vision. The figure was still vague, but now it seemed that she could make out two deep, dark eyes watching her. And she thought she heard a low, rumbling growl.

She was not afraid. Awe-struck – for she believed that she knew what this strange creature was – but not afraid. Very slowly and carefully she got to her feet and stood up straight, shoulders squared, to await his approach.

He came on out of the shadow of the trees, a dark being made, it seemed to her entranced eyes, of the very substance of the secret forest. The black, pointed muzzle was raised as he sniffed at her, the small ears erect on the rounded head. He was, she realised, taking her in with all his senses.

One great forepaw was raised, as if in greeting. With stirrings of real alarm, she saw the five long, sharp, curved claws. There is nothing to fear, she told herself. He is not what he seems, and he will not hurt me.

Then it seemed that the man animal smiled at her, with a human mouth. Perhaps he picked up both her moment of apprehension and the fortitude that followed, for now his approach was swift and suddenly he was right in front of her, between her and the light of her fire.

She said very softly, 'Welcome to my hearth. You honour me with your presence.' Then, prompted by something too profound, too ancient for her to comprehend, she gave him a deep bow.

She felt hands – hands? Clawed paws? – on her shoulders as he raised her up. She made herself stare up into the strange face that was sometimes a muzzle thickly covered in dark brown fur, sometimes the features of a man with delight in his dark eyes that sparkled with firelight.

Which was peculiar, she thought afterwards, since he had stood with his back to the flames.

A voice said, speaking directly inside her head, *This is your place, child of Anu*. And, spreading throughout her whole being, she felt such a joy that she had never dreamed existed. Weak with longing – for what, she did not know – she leaned towards him and smelt on him the scent of the forest, of greenery that never died, of the deep Earth that received back into herself every living thing that gave up its life beneath the trees.

She thought she heard him laugh, a rich, stirring sound that made her want to laugh too. Swaying against him, she felt the thick pelt brush her arm. She stood like that for some time, as if frozen inside a moment. Then she was aware that he had gone.

In the morning she would have thought it was a dream, the wonderful, generous gift of a very special trance because she was on her own and could not celebrate with the others. But, as she raked up the ashes of her fire and set the hearthstones ready for the next time, she found something on the ground.

It was a claw.

It is his gift, she thought, holding it in her hands and feeling its essence enter through her skin. He left it here for me, that I should keep a very small part of him with me.

Later, when Meggie had been fed, bathed, comforted, cuddled, told a story – Joanna did not think it mattered that her daughter did not understand the words; she certainly understood the love behind them – Joanna put her back into her cradle and carefully closed the door of the hut. The babe would soon be asleep, she knew, and would not miss her mother's presence for a little while. Then Joanna took her knife, her flint, her chalice and a short, thin length of hide that she had recently cured and went down to the brook that ran close to her glade.

She followed it back upstream until she came to the spring that bubbled out from a large sandstone outcrop. Here the water was as clear as light, icy-cold and smelling faintly of the Earth from which it issued. Joanna rinsed out her chalice and filled it with fresh water, then washed her knife and the length of hide. Finding a reasonably flat piece of ground, she put the chalice down and, beside it, heaped up a handful of moss, some dead, dry leaves and some twigs for a small fire. She lit the kindling with her flint and when the little fire was burning to her satisfaction, she dried her knife by holding it in the flames and then cut off a length of hide, long enough to slip over her head when knotted. Then, picking up the claw, she put it into the chalice.

There was flesh on the thick end of the claw. It was fresh; as it lay in the water, some blood flowed out of it, staining the water red. Joanna began to chant; a long string of words that seemed to come to her lips at another's prompting. Some time later, she took the clean claw out of the water and dried it in the flames.

Then she tied the leather thong tightly around the thick end of the claw, winding it round several times and tying it with a knot. She was good at knots; Mag had taught her well. Mag had had a knot for every occasion and they did not come undone.

Joanna put the claw on its cord around her neck.

There were, she had been told, silversmiths among her people, great craftsmen who understood the nature of the metal and worked it with rare skill. If ever she had the good fortune to meet one, she vowed, she would ask him to set her claw in a silver mount and make her a silver chain. Whatever he asked in return, she would gladly give it.

She emptied the blooded water from her chalice on to the

ground, returning both blood and water to the Earth. She gave
heartfelt thanks for her gift as she did so.

When the forest people came back from their Yule feasting,
Joanna told Lora about the encounter. 'It was a gesture of great
kindness,' she told the older woman, 'for him to have left the
festival just to come and see me. I hope he wasn't away from the
celebrations for long – I should not like to think that he missed
anything for my sake. And his bear mask and cloak were really
wonderful – he even *smelt* like a bear!'

   Lora barely answered. Instead she gave Joanna a long, considering look and what appeared to be a brief nod, as if something she
had suspected might happen had just in fact occurred. Allowing
Joanna no time to ponder on this, she had straight away said,
'Come on, my girl, we've got work to do – if you're to be ready
for the next festival, there's much you still have to learn.'

Throughout December and much of January, Joanna had learned
herb lore, charms, simples and the treatment of wounds until her
head seemed so packed that it ought to burst. She learned the ways
of her people, their beliefs, their relationship with the deity. Not
everything was new, for both her old friend Mag and, latterly, Lora
had already taught her much. She worked tirelessly, for she knew
that Lora, as the person presenting her to the people, would be
held responsible if Joanna were deemed unready. Or – frightening
thought – unsuitable.

   I am not unsuitable, she told herself calmly, her hand unconsciously going to her bear's claw and clutching it. And I do not
believe that I am unready.

They came for her in the third week of January. In the realm of the
Outworlders, Queen Eleanor was tearing her hair in anxiety over
her captured son. And a small group of people – foreigners, far
from home – wandered lost and abused, trembling at the thought
of what was to happen to them.

   Deep in the forest, Joanna was ready. She had prepared a

small pack and made a sling out of soft, supple leather in which Meggie was to be carried. The straps of the sling were padded with sheepskin and fitted over Joanna's shoulders. Its pouch, gently cradling and supporting the baby's sturdy little body, hung over Joanna's breasts. The pouch had to be comfortable because Joanna was going to bear her burden a very long way.

Lora led the procession that came out of the trees and into the clearing. Behind her were some twenty others, men, women and children. Some of them Joanna knew; with them she exchanged grave bows and courteous greetings. The ones she did not recognise smiled at her. 'I'll not waste time with names right now,' Lora said, 'you'll soon pick up who's who as we go along.'

Then they set out.

The journey took the best part of a week. They walked for most of the daylight hours, stopping three or four times to rest briefly, eat a little of their dried, easily portable supplies and drink some water. They kept to the forest: in that age of the world, it was possible to walk more than a hundred miles north westwards from the heart of the Wealden Forest in virtually a straight line, always with a canopy of trees overhead.

The weather helped them to make good, steady progress. It was cold, still and dry, which made walking easy; no mud, no flooded rivers and streams to negotiate or around which to make long detours. No driving rain in the face, hour after hour, no wind to find its way inside damp clothing and chill the flesh. No danger of sweating profusely from the exertion. Once she had overcome her initial fears over whether, new to long distance walking, she would be able to keep up with the others, Joanna began to enjoy the journey very much.

At nightfall they would find a way into some deep forest glade where it was safe to light a small fire without being observed. After eating, all twenty-three of them would huddle close together, preserving their body warmth and each sharing it with one another, lying on a bed of dried leaves and wrapping themselves in what blankets and cloaks they had brought with them. The children and the babies would be carefully watched to make sure they did not become chilled; not that there was much fear of that, with every adult keenly aware of the young, their senses open to the first intimations of distress.

Sometimes as they lay around the fire one of the elders would start to speak, telling one of the old stories. Joanna, who knew only a few of the people's traditional legends, welcomed these nights above all.

When, one sunlit morning, their destination at last came into view, one of the older men let out a cheer, taken up by the others. Joanna, unable to see anything that might look like the place to which they were heading, was therefore amazed when, from the middle of a thick stand of pine trees, an answering call went up. And, moments later, she saw a flood of people come running towards them out of the trees, laughing, smiling, crying out greetings.

A young woman of about Joanna's age, her thick plait of hair reddish-fair where Joanna's was dark brown, came up to her, put her arms round both Joanna and Meggie in a warm embrace and said, 'Welcome! Welcome to the festival!' She kissed Joanna on both cheeks, chucked the fascinated Meggie under her round little chin and added, 'Beautiful child! May I hold her?'

'Yes!' Joanna loosened the straps of the sling and extracted her daughter. 'She's not very used to strangers – until a few days ago, she's mostly only had me for company – so she may yell.'

But Meggie was relaxing in the fair woman's arms, her small face creased up as she tried to smile, gurgling her pleasure. The young woman gave Joanna an affectionate grin. 'We're not strangers,' she said gently. 'Not to one like her. Come, I'll take you to your place.'

Following her, Joanna thought back to the night of Meggie's birth. Then, too, someone had hinted at the same thing: Lora, gazing into the newborn child's wandering eyes, had predicted that she would have the Sight. That she would be, in Lora's own words, one of the great ones. It was an awesome thing to be told about one's new baby; even now, three months later, Joanna was not entirely sure what she felt. And now this kindly young woman had said, *not to one like her*. As if she, too, recognised some quality in Meggie that set her apart. Something that her own mother could not see.

I must not let it disturb me, Joanna ordered herself. I must keep an open mind and hope that, if I am patient and keep my eyes and my ears open, soon I shall understand what they mean.

Slinging her pack across her shoulder, she set off up the slope to the trees.

She would never have found the stone circle had they not led her to it. That, she supposed as she found the place in the temporary camp that had been set aside for her, was the whole point. Nobody except the forest people was allowed. The thought gave her a thrill of anticipation.

The camp had been made of simple, natural materials. A large number of dead branches had been dragged out of the surrounding woodland, trimmed and erected to form a rough framework, over which great bundles of last year's bracken had been tied to act like thatching. Joanna was impressed to observe how her people used only dead wood and plants; even for a great festival, they did not cut down living things. Joanna's place was at the end of one of the long structures. Her companions were all other young women with babies or small children; happily anticipating a few days in their company, Joanna realised that she had missed talking to other mothers, comparing her baby's progress and habits with those of their children. Reassuring herself when, as sometimes happened, some small anxiety about Meggie escalated into a real concern. Not that she ever felt entirely alone – there was something about her area of the great forest, some benign spirit, perhaps, who looked out for her – but it was not quite the same as a good long talk.

Their camp, Joanna was informed, was one of many. The mothers and children had been given one of the choicest sites close to the centre of the festivities. When she asked why, her

132

informant – a raven-haired, blue-eyed girl who spoke with a soft accent unfamiliar to Joanna, answered, 'So that we can slip away from the feast now and again to make sure the babies are all right.'

Joanna, who had half been expecting an explanation involving some strange arcane rite, almost laughed aloud at the sheer common sense of it.

In all, there were almost five hundred people in attendance. Joanna did not think she had ever been a part of such a huge gathering. The black-haired girl – whose name was Cailleach – said that this number was relatively small; Joanna should come to Samhain or the Midsummer Fires, then she would see a *real* crowd.

I will, she promised silently. Oh, I will.

Early in the evening when the babies were settled, a group of the mothers who, judging from the amount they were finding to say to one another, appeared to be old friends, said they would stay in the camp so that the others could slip out and have a look around. Joanna took the opportunity eagerly and Cailleach went with her.

They followed a well-defined track from the camp clearing through the pine trees and very soon emerged into an open space. They were on the summit of a low hill, part of a long ridge that rose up over the flatter lands below. The wide area in the middle of the surrounding trees was marked out by a circle of stones.

'What are they?' Joanna asked in a hushed voice.

'Outworlders call them the Rollright Stones,' Cailleach replied. 'They're frightened of them – they won't come here.'

'Why should they be frightened?'

'Because they sense what we sense but they don't understand it. They make up tales to explain the stones – they say they're soldiers of some old king's army turned to stone by a witch, and they say that nobody can count them and get the same result twice. They even say the stones go down to the stream by night to drink.'

'And how do you – how do we view the stones?'

Cailleach turned to look at her. 'This your first Great Festival?' Joanna nodded. 'Then I won't spoil the surprise,' she said kindly. 'Wait and see!'

The feast of Imbolc, the celebration that honoured the first stirrings of new life, was held a few days later, as January gave way to February. Joanna sat feeding Meggie early in the morning of the festival, calling to mind all that she knew about it. 'The ground may still seem as hard as rock and all of the Great Mother's creation still fast asleep beneath it,' Lora had told her, 'but the first signs are there, for those with the eyes to see. The ewes are in lamb, see, and their milk's coming in. That's the signal. That tells us that all's well, that the Light's coming back and bringing renewed life with it. The Goddess has borne the Star Child and he's growing strongly. She doesn't have to worry over him, so she's got a little time on her hands away from child rearing to look around her and enjoy herself. It's especially for mothers, Imbolc,' she stressed, 'that's why it's important that you're there. It's a time of initiation.'

'Initiation,' Joanna said softly to herself now as Meggie, alert dark eyes looking all around at the unfamiliar crowds of people, let her mother's nipple slip from her mouth. 'This night will be my initiation.'

Then Meggie burped loudly and Joanna, smiling, found herself abruptly brought back to Earth.

Nothing could have prepared her for what happened that night.

The babies and children were settled and two of the older women were left to watch over them; they would be relieved after a time and others would take their place. 'Not you,' Joanna had been told when she had offered to share in the duty. She had felt a faint shiver of apprehension.

She was taken out of the encampment and led away, apart from the other young mothers, to a place deep in the pine trees where someone – a man, she had no idea who he was – gave her a white robe. She was ordered to strip off her own robe, wash herself and then put on the white garment. A bowl of very cold water had been put out for her and, forcing herself to ignore the shivering protest of her naked flesh, she washed herself thoroughly. Then she dried herself on a linen towel and put on the white robe. It was simply made and hung down straight from the shoulders, flaring out generously towards the ground-brushing hem. The sleeves were long and deep. When she was dressed, the man wrapped a green sash over her right shoulder and tied it in an intricate knot on her left hip. He put a garland of ivy and evergreen leaves on her head and wrapped her in a cloak of some dark material.

Then he said, 'Behind you is a bunch of the first flowers. Pick them up.'

She did so; they were snowdrops. She felt something hidden among the slim, delicate stalks of the flowers and, looking down, saw that it was a small beeswax candle, set inside an open-topped cone of some hard, transparent substance. It was a long time since she had held in her hands so costly an object as the candle. She bent to smell its sweet scent.

Then the man put a blindfold over her eyes. 'You will be left alone here,' he intoned. 'You must find your way into the circle, where we shall be waiting for you. Do not set out from this place until you hear the hoot of the owl.'

Trembling, the sense of unreality growing rapidly, Joanna stood, blind, and waited. After what seemed a very long time, she heard the owl.

Holding the snowdrops in her left hand, she put her right hand up to hold the bear's claw. As her fingers closed around it, she seemed to see his eyes. They were warm with love and she felt her fear begin to diminish. When she felt brave enough to put one foot in front of the other, she set out.

She had no idea in which direction the stone circle lay. There was a path by which she had arrived – should she get on to it, follow it back to the camp and make her way from there to the summit of the hill? But where was the path? And how, blindfolded as she was, would she find it?

Something that had just flashed through her mind seemed to call her attention back to it. She waited, stilling her thoughts. It returned: *the summit of the hill.*

Of course! The stone circle was at the top of the slope, so all she had to do was to walk uphill.

Still clutching the snowdrops, she put her right hand out in front of her face and tried a few steps, first one way, then another. One way led her straight into a bramble bush; the next went, she was almost sure, downhill. She tried again, and then again. She was just beginning to feel the unpleasant, unwelcome sense of her fear returning when she half-tripped on something, lurched forward and took three or four short, involuntary steps. They were enough for her to discover that she was climbing. Eagerly she started to go on up the hill, stepping tentatively at first – she met another bramble and felt the low branch of a pine tree whip her left cheek – but then, as the path appeared to open out, she began to go faster.

Because her eyes could not see, her other senses had sharpened. And, although she did not then appreciate it, Mag's teachings and almost a year of learning the old ways had changed her subtly. The combined effect was that she knew, suddenly, that the stones were close; she could feel their power. Putting out her right hand, she extended the fingers . . . and touched cold stone.

Which way now? They would all be out there watching, even if she could not yet sense them; she did not want to stumble about, perhaps in quite the wrong direction, and trip over her own feet. Although the impulse to hasten on was strong, she made herself stop. Standing quite still, she quietened her breathing and waited until her racing heartbeat had slowed down.

Then she listened. And, with her newly sensitive skin, felt. She thought: power from the stones *there* . . . and *there*. So the line of the circle must run around just in front of me. The open space has to be right before me, and so the people must be standing over there . . .

She strained to hear. Nothing. But then, as she tried harder, she seemed to sense a tension in the air as if a great crowd waited expectantly.

Yes. They're there.

She stepped forward confidently into the stone circle.

Instantly, where there had been silence came noise. And, even through the cloth covering her eyes, she could vaguely see them, running and dancing, jumping for joy. Somebody behind her whipped off the blindfold and in the light of the waxing moon she saw the stones circling the summit of the hill, the protecting trees crowding around as if they, too, were eager to be a part of the celebration.

The circle itself was empty. But, as she had suspected, the people were gathered all around it, the majority of them on the far side. Seeing her standing there they began to cheer, smiling at her and calling out her name.

With tears streaming down her face, she smiled back at them. She could not think of any moment in her entire life when she had been quite so happy.

# 12

Then one of the oldest of the women stepped out of the shadows and walked towards her. She was holding a flaming torch in her hand. By its light, Joanna could see her face. The deep-set dark eyes held the wisdom of years, although the skin was smooth, like a young woman's. The long hair was silver. The woman wore a dark robe over a gown that sometimes appeared white, sometimes silver. It looked almost as if it had been made out of moonlight.

Around her neck she wore a heavy silver lunula.

Joanna knew who she was. Although she had not met her before, they all spoke of her. In whispers, with awe and wonder in their voices.

She was oldest of the old, wisest of the wise. She was the Domina.

She removed Joanna's cloak, revealing the white robe and the green sash. Joanna heard a sigh like a soft breeze flow through the assembled crowd. The woman indicated the snowdrops and the candle that Joanna carried. She put up her hand and the woman lit the candle from her torch. Then she said, 'Give the people light.'

Joanna walked slowly around the circle, holding up the candle in its sheltering cone, protecting the flame with her other hand. The others put their candles to hers, lighting them and carefully shielding them, taking them to light a series of small fires all around the circle.

Then the Domina led Joanna back to the centre of the circle. She said, 'Joanna, you have passed the test and found your way to your people. By so doing you have proved that you belong with us. You have spread the Light. Now the moment has come for your initiation.'

Smoke from the fires filled the stone circle. Joanna caught the sweet-sharp scent of some herbal mix, and knew that the people were using their skill and their wisdom to cleanse the sacred space and enhance the mood. She watched as, slowly at first and then with accelerated speed, the great crowd outside the circle began to move. Round and round they went, always outside the standing stones. Then, at some signal that Joanna did not perceive, they all advanced inside the stones' encircling ring. As they went – closer to her now and faster, and with a repeated pattern of steps as if they were dancing – she heard the chanting.

Beside her the Domina stood utterly still. There was such power in her that some element of her reached out and compelled Joanna to be equally still. Staring out at the standing stones, it seemed to Joanna that she was the hub of the great wheel that they formed on the hilltop. Then, as if the image developed by itself, without prompting from her, it seemed that the wheel of stones was moving, turning on itself. On she who, with the Domina, stood as its axis.

The purifying smoke, the movement and the endless chanting combined into a great force. Before Joanna's entranced eyes there appeared to grow out of the circle a faint cone of bright, pure white light, its point shooting straight upwards into the night sky. Aiming for the Moon.

And then at last the Domina broke her stillness and her silence. Moving a pace or two away from Joanna, she stood right in the centre of the circle. Raising her arms, she cried out in a surprisingly powerful voice, the words soaring up into the sky. Joanna did not understand all that she said, but it did not matter; she knew that the Domina was making her invocation to the Goddess. On behalf of the people, she was making the ritual observance of Imbolc.

When she had finished – Joanna had lost track of time and could not have said how long the chanting went on – she lowered her arms and slowly turned to face Joanna. In the firelight, Joanna could see exhaustion in the old face; the Domina at last looked her years. Putting out her hand, the Domina said, 'Come, Joanna. Come and stand in the centre of the power.'

Joanna did as she was commanded. As she joined the Domina on that central piece of the springy green turf, she felt a forceful jolt enter her body and she was shaken from the soles of her feet to the crown of her head. Her face must have expressed her shock, for the Domina, studying her intently, gave a sudden brief smile.

'Good,' she murmured, 'very good.'

Then, opening her arms, she took Joanna in a close embrace and hugged her to her breast. She whispered, for Joanna alone to hear, 'Welcome, child. Welcome to your heart's home.'

As they stood there so close together, Joanna felt the bear's claw on its leather thong pressing into her breast. The Domina must have felt it too, for, breaking the close contact, she reached out for the thong and pulled it and the claw out from where they had lain concealed beneath Joanna's white robe.

The Domina held the claw out so that the firelight fell on it. She ran her fingers up and down its length and felt the sharp tip. Then her deep, dark eyes met Joanna's. She said nothing, but Joanna had the strong impression that she was surprised.

Joanna wanted to explain, to say how the man of the forest people had slipped away from the Yule festivities to visit her and remind her that they had not forgotten her in all the revelry. She opened her mouth to speak but the Domina gave a faint shake of her head.

Then she replaced the claw inside Joanna's gown.

The power was still singing and crackling through the air all around the circle. Now the Domina stepped forward and, once more raising her arms, began to chant again. Joanna, so close to her, felt the strength flow from her as she earthed the power. Then, her voice taking on a different timbre, the Domina, at long last beginning to droop, gave thanks.

And, finally, broke the circle.

Some time during the long night of celebration that followed, a woman whom Joanna did not know sought her out and said that the Domina wished to see her.

Feeling very nervous, Joanna followed where the messenger led. In a clearing in the pine trees, a short distance away from the stone circle and the lively gathering of happy people, a small shelter had been made. Like the dwellings of the camp, it too was constructed of dead wood and bracken. This one, however, was only big enough for one person. Inside, wrapped in luxurious furs before a fire burning in a small stone hearth, sat the Domina.

She seemed to have recovered some of her strength. She had eaten – there was an empty platter at her feet – and she was sipping at some drink in a pewter cup that gave off curls of steam and a wonderful aroma. The Domina's dark eyes were very bright.

'Sit, Joanna,' she ordered, with a wave of her hand. Joanna obeyed. 'You have done well this night, child,' the Domina went on. 'The faith that your teachers have in you is justified.'

'My teachers?' She must mean Lora and the others, Joanna thought, since she speaks of them in the present tense. But then that means that she's forgotten about Mag Hobson, who was my first teacher and, really, the one who—

'Of course I have not forgotten her.' The Domina's voice held faint amusement. 'She would not let me, even if I would have it so,' she added in a murmur. Eyes boring into Joanna's, she said, 'Mag was one of our great ones, child. Did you not know?'

'I – she died for me.' Joanna found that she was fighting back tears.

The Domina regarded her intently. 'She gave up her earthly body, yes,' she said. 'For which act she had a very good reason.'

'She died because she would not reveal my whereabouts!' Now the tears were streaming down Joanna's face. 'And I *miss* her, I still miss her so much!'

The Domina waited until the storm of grief eased. Then she said, 'But, child, she is still with you. Have you not felt her presence?'

Joanna had no idea how to reply. What was she expected to say? Mag still with her? No, that could not be so; Mag was dead.

And yet there were those strange moments in the peace of late evening, after the sun had set, or in the bright early mornings when, alone and thinking of nothing in particular, suddenly Joanna would feel a lift of the heart and begin to sing. One of the old songs that Mag had taught her. And there were the times when, with the other forest people far away, some minor crisis would occur, usually to do with Meggie; it was not easy, Joanna had discovered, to bear sole responsibility for the health and well being of a beloved child. Sometimes, feeling close to despair, she had heard Mag's wise voice speaking inside her head. *Do this, comfort her in this way, make her a drink out of this.*

The remedies had always worked.

If she had stopped to think about it, Joanna would have said that Mag was still there in her memory, vivid, full of life, and that she was recalling instructions that Mag had given her in the past. But, now that the Domina seemed to be suggesting an alternative explanation, it occurred to Joanna that Mag hadn't given her any instruction in the care of young babies. Meggie had been born – had been conceived – after Mag had died.

Joanna raised her eyes and stared into the Domina's.

The Domina nodded, smiling her satisfaction. 'Good,' she murmured. Then: 'You named your child after her.'

'I did. She is called Margaret, but I usually shorten it to Meggie.'

The Domina's smile had widened and now there was an uncharacteristically soft expression on her face. 'We used to call Mag by the same pet name,' she said softly.

Joanna was still trying to absorb the implications of that when the Domina said, in quite a different voice, 'You wear the claw.'

'Oh! Yes. I was given it at Yule. I was alone – too busy and preoccupied with Meggie to attend the festival – and one of the men came to see me. He was wearing his animal mask and cloak and he left me this.' She pulled the claw out from inside her gown. 'It was such a kindness,' she said quietly, 'to leave the celebration and pay me a visit. It made me feel that I was not forgotten. I suppose the festival must have been held quite close by but, all the same, he missed quite a lot of it for my sake.'

The Domina made no reply. Surprised, Joanna looked up from

142

her contemplation of the claw. The older woman was staring at her. When she had assured herself that she had Joanna's full attention, she said tonelessly, 'The festival of Yule was held three days' walk from where you have your forest house.'

'But then—' Joanna could not take it in. 'But did he not attend the festival, then? Did he stay away too?'

'Who do you mean by *he*?' the Domina asked.

'I – well, one of the forest people who live close to me, I suppose.' She had not really thought about it before. 'I have encountered a few of them. They have helped me out sometimes, and some of them have called by to show me something or teach me a new skill. I imagine it was one of them.'

'Did you recognise him?'

'No. As I said, he wore his bear mask. But—'

But what? She did not know.

After quite a long pause, the Domina said, 'Do not assume, child. Keep an open mind.'

And, a few moments later, she waved her hand again and Joanna was dismissed. As she turned to leave the little shelter, the Domina spoke again. 'You have been initiated as one of our people, Joanna,' she said. 'You have done what was required for this first step.'

A first step? Oh, did that mean there would be more? Joanna felt her heartbeat quicken in faint alarm.

'Have no fear,' the Domina went on calmly. 'You will not be asked to do anything that is beyond you. When the time comes, remember that what you have done before, you can do again.'

Joanna waited to see if she would enlarge on this enigmatic piece of advice. But there was nothing; watching the Domina, she saw her close her eyes and sink back into her furs.

Back within the circle, somebody gave Joanna a drink. She gulped it down thirstily, and they gave her some more. Cailleach came by, dancing in the midst of a long chain of young men and women. Two of the men took Joanna's hands and swept her up with them. Laughing, singing, she danced with her people.

The celebrations went on for a long time. Only as the faintest break in the darkness beyond the stone circle began to appear did men and women begin to slip away. They went in pairs, happily, joyfully together. They would, Joanna was well aware, find a quiet corner in which to lie together, honouring the Great Mother in an act of love.

Her body yearned to do the same. But she knew nobody, had met no man who was likely to seek her out and entice her to lie with him amongst his warm furs.

As the chain of dancers dwindled to the last few, she turned away. Heading out of the circle and towards her camp, her feet dragged. It was very dark under the pine trees and, as soon as she was away from the fires, also very cold. She shivered, wrapping her cloak more tightly around her.

The path back to the camp was longer than she remembered. Feeling the beginnings of alarm, she wondered if she had managed to get lost. Oh, surely not, she thought, how could I be so foolish? After all, it's not far.

Concentrating, trying to peer into the darkness of the trees for a familiar sign, she thought she recognised the track. Relieved, she set off confidently down it.

Only to realise, a little later, that it could not be right after all. If it were, she should be at her camp by now.

What to do? Go on? Turn back?

Go on.

She did not know where the command came from. Nevertheless, she obeyed it. Moving now as if in a trance, she followed the path. Her feet fell with a soft thud on the aeons of fallen pine needles that made up the ground; she seemed to feel a warmth emanating from them, as if the very ground was magical.

Then she came to a tiny clearing. A space had been made right in the midst of a thicket of bramble and bracken, and within it burned a little fire. Beside the fire was a dark shape lying in a den of fur.

She knew who he was.

The great head was raised in greeting, and she saw the smile

144

of the man within the mask of the bear. Without a word being spoken, she knew that he had heard her silent yearning and called her to him.

Quite unafraid, she went through the bracken and knelt down beside him. He welcomed her into the circle of his warmth and she felt the soft bear fur brush against her skin. His breath smelt of the forest. Pulling her close to him so that she could feel the slow, steady, powerful throb of the great heart that beat within his breast, he bent his head and kissed her.

She would have expected to feel very cold without her cloak and her gown but he had heat enough for them both. Wrapped in his arms that were at the same time human and animal, she gave herself to him and he surrounded her with the essence of himself. His strong aura embraced her and, in total trust, she surrendered into his care. He was a bear, he was a man; he was both. Yet, when at last the moment came and he entered into her, it was, as she had all along known it would be, as a man.

They lay there in the light of his fire and she relaxed, utterly spent, into him. She felt his large hand gently stroke her sweat-damp hair from her face and turned her head a little to look at him. She saw both images, the bear mask and the human smile. Returning the smile, she pressed her breasts into his pelt. She felt the claw that she wore around her neck digging into her skin.

'Thank you for the gift,' she murmured. 'I treasure it.'

Inside her head she heard him reply. *You will never be alone now.*

'I know.' She caressed the strong, heavily muscled shoulder. 'I feel . . .' She wanted to tell him that what he had done for her made the difference, so that now she felt at home in the forest where before she had been merely visiting.

While she was still fumbling for the right words he answered. *It is understood.* A pause, then: *It is right.*

Relaxing, feeling sleep overcome her, she knew there was no more to be said.

★　　★　　★

She awoke to thin daylight. The fire had all but gone out but, snugly wrapped in furs, she was warm.

She was alone.

Stretching luxuriously, she felt the kiss of the pelts against her naked flesh. Memory came flooding back, and she felt again the violence of her climax. Oh, but she had needed that! And she had not even suspected her need; it was only when the dancers had begun to creep away that she had felt the stirrings of that primal hunger.

He had known. And he had called to her.

Smiling, she turned over, curled up and went back to sleep.

When she stirred again, it was a different sort of hunger that woke her. Blinking in the sunshine filtering down through the pine trees, she tried to think when she had last eaten. Unable to remember – and quite sure that it was far too long ago to be good for her – she got up, dressed and made her way back up the track towards the stone circle.

It occurred to her when she was only a short way up the path that perhaps she should roll up those beautiful furs and make some attempt to return them to their owner. He had quietly left her to sleep, and it seemed a little ungrateful just to abandon their bed. She turned and went back along the track.

She could find neither the furs, the dead fire, nor the thicket of bramble and bracken.

Shaken, for the first time afraid and suddenly desperate to get back to Meggie, she ran away up the path.

Back in the cheerful company of the young women's camp, she soon forgot her fright. Many of them, it seemed, had had strange experiences during the night just past, yet none was perturbed. On the contrary; they appeared to regard the occasion as one for which to be deeply thankful.

Suckling Meggie – who, according to the women who had been watching the babies, had taken a small feed from her and then slept soundly for the rest of the night – Joanna felt her feet slowly return to Earth. When, a little later, Cailleach returned to the camp with a deep purple love bite on her neck, Joanna had to suppress a giggle.

The two of them talked for a while, teasing one another, and some of the other young women joined in. To begin with, Joanna was quite surprised at their ribaldry, but then she thought, why should I be shocked? What possible evil can there be in men and women lying together in the Great Mother's name, giving and receiving pleasure and, for a time, love?

But as she thought on this, something occurred to her. She had borne two children and knew herself to be fertile. Meggie was her delight, and she would not be without her for the world. But to bear another child, that was another matter. What if it should be a boy? Life in the forest was not the life for a young man.

Or was it?

This morning, after all that had happened, she found that convictions which she had formerly held so rigidly were taking on an air of uncertainty.

Nevertheless, she beckoned Cailleach over to her and asked in a low voice, 'Do we – I mean, do any of the girls become pregnant after the festivals?'

Cailleach laughed. 'Of course! It is the same act of love, Joanna, even if it comes at the Goddess's bidding. Children born of the festival nights are especially blessed because we believe they have Her kiss on their brow.'

It was a lovely concept. But still Joanna was not entirely happy. 'Do we – that is, what if we think that it's not actually the right time for a baby?'

Cailleach regarded her kindly. 'We put our trust in the Great Mother,' she said. Then, a smile breaking out on her face, 'Although there are steps that we can take if we are not ready for a pregnancy.'

'Are there?' Joanna was amazed.

Cailleach laughed delightedly. 'You have lived in the old ways for a year and you do not know?'

It hasn't been relevant until now, Joanna thought. But she merely said, 'No. Please tell me, Cailleach.'

Cailleach sat down on the ground beside her and told her of the workings of her body. Then she explained how to make conception more likely, and how to make sure it did not happen at all. She told Joanna of the mysterious cycle that kept pace with the Moon, how to calculate which were the most and the least fertile days.

'You wish to know whether you conceived last night, I would guess,' Cailleach said when she had finished the lesson.

'Yes.'

Cailleach studied her for a moment. 'No. You did not.'

'How do you know?' Joanna burst out.

Cailleach grinned. 'You are about to have your courses. Tomorrow, perhaps even later today, the blood will flow.'

'But—'

From close at hand, another of the women laughed. 'Is that Cailleach working her magic again?' she said, eyes on her child feeding at the breast. 'You believe her, young Joanna, she is never wrong.'

Joanna gazed at Cailleach. 'How do you *know*?' she asked again, whispering now.

'Experience,' Cailleach said modestly. 'Anyone can do it with practice.'

Watching her as she gracefully got up and wandered away, Joanna thought, there has to be more to it than that. She's only my age, if that, so just where has all this experience come from? She hasn't had the time!

And, as if in confirmation, the woman who had laughed said, 'She's a midwife in a hundred, is Cailleach. They nickname her Mab because they say the fairies taught her.'

Then, as if her remark had been nothing more than some mundane utterance about the weather, or the plans for the next meal, she calmly returned to feeding her baby.

There was one more day of celebrations – far less exuberant than the one before – and then the gathering began to break up. One by one groups set off from the hilltop, seen on their way by the singing of the others. Joanna, busy with tying up her pack, felt a tap on her shoulder.

A young man stood there. He had thick auburn hair, smoky grey eyes and a shy smile. He said, 'I'm a silversmith. I heard tell you were looking for one.'

Too much had happened in the last two days for Joanna to ask who had told him or how he had found her. She simply said, 'Yes, I am. Thank you for seeking me out.' Then, pulling out the claw on its thong, she held it out to him. 'Could you set this in silver, with a ring on the top from which to hang it?'

He was staring at the claw, his eyes wide. 'Yes, I can,' he said slowly. 'It'll be a rare test.'

'Is it a difficult task, then?'

He looked up at her, smiling briefly. 'Not difficult, no. It's the honour, see.'

She thought she did see. 'I do not know how I can pay you,' she said. 'I have some skills, so perhaps if you name your price?'

But he shook his head. 'I don't want payment,' he said gently, 'thank you all the same.' Before she could protest, he added, 'That piece of thong's all very well, but a thing such as this should have something better.'

'It's all I have.'

Again he gave her his gentle smile. 'You just leave it with me,' he said. 'When I'm done I'll come and find you.'

She passed the thong over her head. Without the claw resting over her heart, she felt suddenly vulnerable. Reluctantly she held it out.

The young man took it. Studying her, he said, 'Don't worry, lass. I'll be swift. You will have your treasure back before you sleep this night.'

He was as good as his word.

Joanna and her group left the hillside after the midday meal. They marched for a few hours then, as night fell, found a place to

149

camp for the night. As she was settling herself after the evening meal – she had just begun to bleed and was uncomfortable, feeling bloated and in some pain – the silversmith came to find her.

He held out the bear's claw for her to see. Now it was set in solid silver and it hung on a fine silver chain, of some intricate design that she had never seen before. Putting out her hand to take it, she said, 'It is beautiful, even more so now that your work has enhanced it.'

He bowed his head at her words. 'Thank you. I am glad that you are pleased.'

'More than pleased!' she exclaimed. 'I don't know how I can repay you.'

He backed away as she spoke, making a gesture with his hands. 'There is no need for that, as I said. It has – I mean, the task is its own reward.'

Then, bowing to her, he backed away and disappeared into the darkness.

She never saw him again.

# 13

Home once again in her own dwelling, Joanna looked back on Imbolc as if on a dream. All that had happened at the festival was so far removed from everything that had hitherto made up her normal experience that there seemed little else she could do.

One thing, however, remained at the forefront of her mind: she had to face – and pass – another test.

As the February days went by, she was unconsciously preparing herself.

She had been on a hunting trip. Her prey was not, however, any living creature; she had been taught only to kill when she was in dire need, and she preferred to live on what she could grow in her little garden. She had been hunting for sheep's wool to spin and weave into cloth for Meggie's clothes, and the best places to go were the gently sloping hills and vales of the Weald where flocks of sheep caught their woolly coats against brambles and twigs.

It took a long time to find enough wool to make even a baby's garment, but then Joanna had plenty of time. Although the February daylight was short, there were few tasks that had to be done in the course of a winter's day. Nothing yet grew above ground, so there were no tender young plants to protect and nurture. She had to collect wood for the fire and prepare food and drink for herself – Meggie was beginning to try other mashed and blended foods although she still fed primarily off her mother – but those jobs were easily and swiftly done because she did them every day.

Today she had collected a fat bag of wool. Heading home, Meggie almost asleep in her sling, Joanna was already happily anticipating getting out her spindle after supper and meditating quietly in the light of the fire while she spun her wool. Hurrying away from the sheep pasture, she was eager to get back under the shelter of the forest's guardian trees.

She always took steps to ensure that none of the Outworlders should see her. Not that there were many people abroad today; she could have believed that she had England to herself. But then, as she reached the outer limits of the forest, she heard something.

Some*one*. The sound was a low moan, as if whoever had made it could no longer suppress his – or her – distress.

Joanna felt two conflicting impulses. One was to run, to hurry away on silent feet and hide in the depths of the forest so that she did not become involved. This person must surely be an Outworlder, and Joanna had detached herself from them.

But a part of her was urging her to go and help. There was somebody in trouble close at hand, and human compassion dictated that she must do what she could to alleviate his pain.

She cuddled Meggie closer to her – the child let out a small cry of protest as Joanna squeezed her – and then turned to walk in the direction from which the sound had come.

Lying under an oak tree, huddled under a thin cloak stained with blood, was a woman. She had a veil over her head and face, held against her mouth with hands that were blue with cold, and she was sobbing quietly.

Joanna said, 'I will help you, if you wish it.'

The woman shot up, dropped the veil and stared at Joanna from terrified eyes. She was older than Joanna by perhaps a decade, round-faced, short and quite plump. Or she had been; it looked as if she had lost weight rapidly quite recently so that now the yellowish flesh had settled into pouches around the jaw, neck and shoulders.

There was a flaming, infected sore in the middle of her forehead.

Making as if to get to her feet, she stumbled, fell, and screamed in pain.

Joanna went to help her. Putting one arm around the woman's

152

waist, she got her to her feet. 'You can't stay here,' she said gently, trying to make her tone warm and reassuring, 'you're chilled enough already and if you lie here overnight you'll surely freeze to death. I will take you to my hut and look after you.'

The woman ceased her feeble struggling. Staring into Joanna's face, she mouthed something, but Joanna did not understand.

'I mean you no harm,' she said earnestly. 'I am your friend, I promise you.'

One word seemed to have penetrated; slowly the woman repeated, '*Fren. Fren.*' Then, leaning against Joanna, she allowed herself to be led away.

The journey back to the hut took some time. The woman tried to be brave but could not always contain herself; even had she not cried out loud, all Joanna's healer instincts told her that the woman was suffering severely. It was all in the way she held herself, in the way she moved so carefully to save herself further pain.

And Joanna had to think about Meggie, too. It was awkward carrying a baby in a sling and trying to half-support a grown woman at the same time.

When they finally got to the hut, Joanna was sweating and her back was aching. Swiftly she put Meggie into her cradle and, ignoring the child's hungry cries – 'You will have to wait for a while, sweeting, there is another here whose need is greater' – she gently sat the woman down on the floor beside the little room's central hearth. The embers of this morning's fire were still glowing faintly and it was the job of moments to get a good blaze going.

By its light, she turned to look at her patient.

Having given herself into Joanna's care, all the woman's resistance had leached out of her. She sat slumped, hands cradling the opposite shoulders, exposing the damage that somebody had wrought on her back.

Somebody had beaten her.

Joanna warmed water and added some of her precious supply of salt; Mag had demonstrated to her years ago that lightly salted water was less painful on raw wounds than pure water because it was closer to the body's own fluid. Then she soaked a clean piece of linen and, with as light a touch as she could manage, began to moisten the remains of the woman's gown until it was washed from her torn skin. The woman was quietly sobbing. Realising that even such gentle treatment was causing her great pain, Joanna fetched a selection of the little wooden boxes that she kept safely stored away on a high shelf.

She gave the woman a dose of the strongest painkiller that she had. It would make her sleep – maybe for a day, a day and a night – but then that would do her no harm. Joanna would look after her.

As the draught took effect, Joanna laid her patient down on the floor, cushioned on Joanna's own furs. With the woman slipping into unconsciousness, Joanna was able to work faster. Soon she had the wounds of the lash anointed and dressed, and she turned her attention to the woman's brow.

When she had cleaned the wound, she saw what it was. Somebody had branded the woman with the letter H.

Joanna, who knew full well what it stood for, felt a tremor of fear run through her. If there were people hunting heretics, then she was in danger herself. Oh, no, and she had brought this woman right *here*, into her home, her own private place! Supposing whoever was after her had seen? Was even now making his way stealthily through the forest, about to order his men to surround the hut, pounce, kill the woman and Joanna?

Oh, dear Goddess, and Meggie!

Danger to herself and her patient had been enough to freeze her temporarily in terror. Danger to her child brought her swiftly out of her paralysis.

She knew what she must do. She had prepared for this and she need not sit there helpless while they – whoever they were – came searching for the woman. For her. She picked up Meggie, fed her and cleaned her, then put her back in the sling. It was dusk now, and there was no time to waste. There was not a great deal that she could do before night fell, but what she could, she must.

She checked on the woman – sleeping deeply, well wrapped and warm – and then, collecting her ash staff from a far corner, slipped out of the hut. The first task was to conceal any tracks that she had made in bringing the woman here to the glade. She found her broom and spent a while sweeping vigorously until there were no traces of stirred-up leaves or footprints to mark their passage. Then she collected brushwood and bracken and fabricated a sort of screen in front of the hut. It was not perfect – she stood considering it – but it would have to do. Now the falling dark was on her side; soon it would be night and the hut would become as near invisible as made no difference. She had banked down the fire in the hearth before she left, so that it was now giving off hardly any smoke. What there was became absorbed in the thick reed thatch of the hut's roof.

Standing a few paces from the hut behind its screen, she remembered something that Lora had taught her. It was a way to make yourself invisible in a crowd; Joanna had laughed at the time and remarked that this was a skill for which she would not be likely to have much use. Lora had looked at her darkly and said, 'You cannot know, child. Never turn down knowledge.'

The way in which this invisibility was achieved was to make people look straight past you. You had to blend, Lora had said, you had to *become* your surroundings. Like many of the old skills, it was a question of believing; in this case, believing yourself to have melted into the background. Deed followed thought, and there you were, unobserved.

Joanna wondered if it also worked for large objects such as huts. Taking a few moments to slow down her breathing and concentrate her mind, she began to make a picture in her head. She imagined that the hut's outline was softening, that long strands of creeper and kindly, helpful leaves and branches were slowly covering it, hiding it, making it safe from eyes that had no business seeing it.

When she brought herself back to normal consciousness, she had quite a hard job seeing the hut at all.

155

Smiling, she picked up her staff, turned and strode out of the clearing.

Her destination was no great distance away. She knew she must hurry – the light was fading – but nonetheless she trod lightly, careful not to leave any record of her passage. After a short while she arrived at the foot of a huge, ancient yew tree. Looking up into the dense, dark green of its foliage, she studied the convolutions of the thick trunk. It would have taken three people holding outstretched hands to encompass it; legend said that the yew was a thousand years old.

Joanna raised her staff and, standing on tiptoe, poked it into the fork where one of the lowest branches met the trunk, perhaps two or three man-heights above the ground. After a few attempts, the hidden rope that lay curled up there came tumbling down. Checking that Meggie was secure in her sling, Joanna quickly climbed the rope. Once she was safe on the branch, she pulled the rope up after her and put it back in its hiding place.

She now did the same with a second rope that was tied to a branch further up the tree. Once she had gained that higher branch, it was easier; she had made herself a rough rope ladder, which hung there permanently since it was quite impossible to see it from the ground.

The rope ladder led up to a platform in the middle of the place where the yew's great trunk divided into four. The platform was very old; it was made of oak planks, beautifully sawn and planed, smoothed to a glossy finish. The joints were pegged, as secure and solid as on the far-distant day that they were made.

Lora had told Joanna about the yew tree's secret.

'It's a refuge, see,' she said. 'There's been times when our ordinary places of concealment haven't been enough, or at least we've feared so. Our forebears in their wisdom made the secret refuges, where our people could go when there was danger and where they could remain until it was past.'

She had taken Joanna to the yew tree and told her to make new ropes, since the old ones had rotted almost to nothing. It had been

Joanna's own idea to make the rope ladder for the topmost stage. She had sat for many evenings during her pregnancy cutting pieces of oak and whittling the rungs. The lengths of rope she had fetched from the house that her mother's kin had left her.

It was not advisable, she had decided, to work on the platform whilst pregnant. However, soon after Meggie's birth she had begun. First she had cleaned off many decades of dark green, sticky residue, apparently made up of foliage, berries and bits of twig, and she inspected the planks for damage. They were sound. Then she set about making a shelter; if she ever had to use the platform in bad weather, it was possible that Meggie, so tiny and so vulnerable, might not survive unless Joanna contrived to make waterproof, weatherproof walls and a roof up there.

The work was so hard that she almost gave up. She had to take up posts to make uprights for the walls, hazel to weave between the posts and then wattle and daub to fill in the gaps. Then she had to take branches and reed thatch for the roof. And she had already climbed up with two posts when it occurred to her to use the rope as a pulley.

After that, progress was a lot quicker. Even Lora, sternest of judges over any matter involving security, had to praise her for her speed. And for her thoroughness; kneeling up on the platform – the roof was too low to allow anyone taller than a child to stand upright – she bounced a few times, leant against one of the outer walls and nodded.

'Good,' she had said. 'It'll do.'

Now Joanna inspected her shelter. Opening the plank door, she peered inside. It was too dark to see much, but the place smelt wholesome. She put her hand down and felt the platform: very slightly damp, but not soaked. It looked as if the roof had not leaked.

Tomorrow, Joanna thought, I shall bring bedding, furs, blankets – everything that I have. Somehow I must make this shelter warm, for there is little use in saving us from those who would hunt us down if we all die of the cold.

She was very tempted to lie down inside the shelter and spend the night there. It was safe, and at that moment that was the main consideration. But already she was feeling chilled; her under-robe had been damp with sweat earlier, when she helped the woman back to the hut, and the exertion of climbing up to the platform carrying Meggie in her sling had made her sweat again. Now that she was still, the sweat was rapidly cooling and she knew she would soon begin to shiver. Besides, although Meggie was with her, dozing snug and peaceful in her sling, the woman was not.

No. She could not contemplate a move to the refuge until tomorrow.

Resolutely she fastened the door behind her and began the climb down.

She spent the night watching over Meggie and the woman. She dozed off sometimes, but each time it was to wake with a start of fright from some dire dream where black hands with long, claw-like fingers were stretching out to open the door of the hut. She was very relieved when dawn broke and the new day began.

She spent the first part of it waiting impatiently for the woman to show some sign that she was returning to consciousness. It's my own fault, Joanna told herself, and it's quite unjust to blame her, poor soul – I should not have made the draught so strong.

As the Sun reached the zenith, the woman stirred, but then slept again. Heartened by this, Joanna began on the plan that she had worked out during the night for heating the refuge in the yew tree. She had already taken up what blankets and coverings she could spare; now she fetched a heavy bucket made of stout hide and lined it thickly with straw. Then she took out the first of a series of large stones that she had put in the fire to heat. It was awkward to handle – she had to be so careful not to burn her hands and render herself helpless – and she tried several methods before hitting on the best, which utilised two short, stout sticks with which to raise the stone on to the surrounding hearthstones. From there it was relatively easy to flip the hot stone into the straw-lined bucket.

Then she covered the stone with more straw and took it out to the yew tree, climbing up with it and wrapping it, still in

158

the insulating straw, inside the thickest of the blankets. She repeated this procedure seven times. Because she was carrying such a potentially dangerous load, she did not dare take Meggie up the tree each time; instead she laid her carefully in its roots, warm in her furs. It was a relief, in every respect, when the job was done.

The woman woke up in the mid-afternoon. Her eyes looked dazed and vague and, when Joanna asked if she were in pain, slowly she shook her head. Joanna gave her water and offered food, but the woman refused it. Joanna was not surprised; the painkilling draught was reputed to take away appetite.

Joanna had a quick look at the woman's wounds. On neither her back nor her brow was there any sign of that dread smell that indicated corruption of the flesh and, indeed, it seemed to her that the bright red inflammation had receded a little. Joanna said encouragingly, 'It's good! You are beginning to heal,' and, for the first time, the woman gave her a very small smile in response.

'I am called Joanna.' She pointed to herself. 'My baby is called Meggie.'

The woman was nodding as Joanna spoke. 'I, Utta.' She put a hand on her chest. 'Not – not speak good. Just a little.'

'Where do you come from?' Joanna spoke slowly and clearly.

'Home – is Liège.'

Liège? Where was that? Joanna tried to think. In the Low Countries? She thought so. 'Why did you come to England?' she asked.

'*Frens* bring. Man said to come, to tell the word.'

'Your friends brought you? What happened to them?'

The woman's eyes filled with tears. '*Frens* – friends – taken. Whip, brand. In prison. Dead.'

Joanna was beginning to understand. If she was right and H did indeed stand for heretic, it sounded as if Utta had been part of some sect that had come to England from the Low Countries to seek converts. Perhaps to seek refuge, although if they had hoped

159

for that then it seemed they had been sadly disappointed. They had clearly been caught and punished.

Joanna knew what happened to heretics in England. They were few in number, or so she had been told, and the law was relatively silent on the matter of their treatment. Having been convicted, they were to be punished and then exiled; anybody found harbouring them or otherwise helping them was to have his house burned down.

It was one thing, she now thought, to be aware of a fact. Quite another matter to see evidence of it before her own eyes. 'They beat you and then turned you out into the bitter weather?' she asked, sympathy strong in her voice.

Utta nodded. 'They say, go away and not come back. I go, but nowhere to shelter from cold.'

'You did not go with your friends?'

The tears flowed more freely now. Utta said, 'My friends in prison. Frieda, Arnulf, Alexius. Guiscard also, I do not know. Frieda have – man. But he not love her, he tell men about her, about us all. Aurelia and Benedetto . . .' With a weak shrug, she gave up.

'Seven of you,' Joanna murmured. 'And one of you met some man – an outsider – who, in betraying her, also betrayed the rest of you. You were punished and then either turned out in the cold or put in prison.' There was one thing she had to ask. Staring intently into Utta's soft blue eyes, she said, 'Are they still looking for you?'

Utta gave another shrug. 'I not know. I think, men say to let me go. But not the Black Man, he say no, that we must all suffer death.' She dropped her face into her hands and her shoulders shook with her sobbing.

Joanna put her hand on Utta's shoulder, murmuring gentle, soothing words. Her mind racing, she tried to think. The Black Man. What did Utta mean by that?

Then she thought, but it doesn't matter who he is. Utta says he may still be searching for her. If so, and if he tracked her to the place on the forest fringe where I found her, then he may soon start hunting for her within the forest. He may bring others with him.

There was no time to lose.

Speaking slowly and calmly, she said, 'Utta, I have a place of safety. We can go there, you, me and Meggie. It will be hard for you because of your injuries, but I'll give you more pain-killing herbs, which will help. But we must go *now*.'

Utta stared back at her. For a moment it looked as if she would refuse, and Joanna could hardly blame her; when you were in pain, the last thing you wanted to do was to stagger to your feet and set out on a journey. And she hadn't yet told Utta about the yew tree. But then Utta nodded. 'Yes,' she said. 'I safe, you safe.'

Good woman! Joanna thought. You understand that if you're safe then I am too. Me and Meggie. She said bracingly, 'Come on.' Utta was already trying to get up, and Joanna put out her arms to help her.

Today's walk was slightly better than yesterday's. Utta even offered to help carry some of the covers, so Joanna folded a couple of light woollen blankets and laid them across her arms. Joanna carried both the furs and Meggie in her sling.

When they reached the yew tree, Utta looked up at it in amazement. Joanna, who was just realising what a task she had set them both, made up her mind that this was no time to be half-hearted. Jerking down the rope, she said, 'Up you go, Utta. I will put Meggie down – look, she's quite safe here among the roots – and I will help you.'

Utta put her hands to the rope. But Joanna could see straight away that there was no strength in her arms; quickly she made a loop at the end of the rope and showed Utta how to put her foot in it. Then she threw the slack middle section of the rope over the branch and, before Utta could protest, began to haul on the end. Utta was jerked off the ground; she clutched on to the rope with one hand and fended herself off from the yew's trunk with the other. In moments, she was up on the first branch.

Joanna, sweating profusely and panting from the effort, pulled the rope back down and quickly climbed up it. She got Utta up the second stage using the same method then, showing her the rope ladder, let her climb it on her own, following close behind in case she slipped. Eventually they reached the platform, and Joanna got Utta inside the shelter.

Turning to Joanna, she gave her small, gentle smile again. She said simply, 'Safe.'

Joanna, grinning, muttered, 'I hope so.'

She went back down to the ground and brought Meggie up, making her a secure little nest in a corner where a fold in the yew's trunk made a triangular space the right size for a small baby and her wrappings. Two more trips for food, water and medicinal supplies for Utta, and Joanna was finished. Utta, welcoming her into the shelter with a grateful look, helped her to secure the door.

Then Joanna uncovered the hot stones she had brought up earlier. The insulation seemed to have worked; the stones still gave off quite a lot of warmth. The mere presence of people inside the shelter had raised the temperature by a few degrees, and Joanna began to hope that they would survive the night.

Knowing that there would not be light once night fell – it would be folly to have a flame of any sort – Joanna got on with the many tasks she still had to do before sunset. She made a bed of sorts for Utta, putting one of the hot stones at her feet beneath a covering of blankets and furs, then she laid out a similar bed for herself. She went back to the hut in the clearing and fetched the food she had prepared earlier – hot food, a sort of porridge with root vegetables, which she carried up to the yew tree platform in another leather container – and she made sure they had adequate drinking water. Before she left the hut, she banked down the fire and put some more stones in it to heat. She was very afraid that they would soon be needing them, and she was already wondering how she would manage to climb down and up the yew tree in the dark.

Just before they settled down to sleep, Joanna gave Utta another draught of the herbal mixture. Again, it would both help with the pain and make her sleep. Joanna was tempted to take some herself; not that she was in pain, other than aching muscles as a result of all her activities over the past two days, but the idea of a long, sound night's sleep was seductive.

No, she told herself. I do not dare. Someone has to watch out for us all, and I cannot do so if I am in a drugged sleep. She would wake from a normal sleep, she well knew, if anything out of the ordinary happened; she was so attuned to the regular night sounds of the forest that she would instantly recognise anything that ought not to be there.

Finally, there was nothing left but to try to sleep. Closing her eyes, putting out a light hand to touch Meggie, deep in her infant dreams close by, Joanna said a swift but heartfelt prayer to the protecting powers and drifted off.

# 14

In the world beyond the great forest, one of Utta's companions was already dead. Frieda, who had fallen in love with a man who was not of her faith and who had betrayed both her and her friends, lay violated on the foul floor of a prison cell, her skull crushed.

Two more of them had been rescued from their cell. Driven to this desperate act, their saviour had carried out an act of violence against the man who guarded them, believing their lives to be in grave danger. He was right. The secular authorities would have been content to have the punishment administered and then turn the men loose; did not the relevant statute forbid any man to receive them in his house? The view was that the troublemakers would either return to wherever it was they came from or else perish. Whichever happened, they would no longer be a problem.

But the secular authorities had not reckoned on the Church. Or rather, to be exact, one member of the Church, who, believing in his fanaticism that a heretic ceased to be a danger only when he – or she – was dead, had a more permanent and more certain solution in mind. He wanted them dead, every one of them that could be rounded up.

Even as Joanna and Utta were waking up on the morning following their first night in the yew tree refuge, the hunt was beginning.

Daylight brought to Joanna another long spell of hard physical work. She went back to the hut for supplies and brought back to the yew tree all the dried food she had. For as long as they remained up there in the refuge, they were going to have to put

164

up with a very monotonous diet; she could not risk lighting a cooking fire and so there would be no fresh food. She also filled all the containers that she could find with stream water and lugged them to the refuge. When she had made her last trip to the hut – for her medicinal herbs, since she still had Utta's wounds to care for – she fastened the door with a special piece of string that Mag had given her, using Mag's most powerful knot.

She replaced the foliage screen and stood for a moment, breathing quietly and evenly, until she felt the strength rise up into her body from the ground beneath her feet. She closed her eyes the better to visualise the deity, then said a deeply heartfelt prayer that her hut – her precious home – should remain safely hidden away.

Then, without a backward glance, she walked away.

Utta perceived what she was trying to do and came to help. Weak though she was from loss of blood and infection, still she worked with all the little strength she had, lowering ropes, helping to pull up loads and always, even when not actually engaged in a task, nodding, smiling, encouraging Joanna in her efforts. She was, Joanna was quickly realising, a good woman.

She was also excellent with Meggie. One of Joanna's main problems in her solitary life was only having one pair of hands; whenever Meggie needed something, Joanna either had to drop what she was doing and attend to her or else endure the child's protests until she did so. Now, when a loudly crying baby was the last thing they wanted in their secret refuge, the problem was poised to escalate into a major difficulty.

Until, the first time it happened, Utta stepped in. With a swift look at Joanna as if to ask for permission, she picked the child up from her furry nest. Cradling her against her breast, she began softly crooning to her, stroking the small back with a smooth, gentle rhythm that Meggie instantly seemed to appreciate. She has the touch! Joanna thought, watching from two branches down the tree as her daughter relaxed into Utta's arms. Her heart full of relief, she sent up a swift thank you to the Goddess for sending her someone so very useful.

When the two women sat down to eat at noon, Joanna was exhausted. She had stripped to her undergown and, as she downed a very welcome draught of water, she realised something.

The weather had improved.

It was nowhere near so cold, and the Sun now really had some heat in it. The hardest task – of keeping the three of them warm enough – had just been made a great deal easier.

Again, Joanna sent up her thanks. Whoever was up there in the Heavens keeping an eye on them, they certainly seemed to be on Joanna and Utta's side.

They heard the hunt early in the morning of the next day.

At first they thought that it could have been horsemen after deer or boar; such parties came into the forest from time to time, as Joanna well knew since she had sometimes had to hide from them. Usually they were rich, well-mounted men who had the King's permission to hunt in his forests.

Joanna, hurriedly pulling up the rope ladder and securing it, found herself a vantage point; there was a small hole in one of the planks, in a place where the platform sat above thinner branches and empty air instead of right over the thick trunk. Quickly she checked on Utta and Meggie; Utta was crouched down against the trunk, wide-eyed with fear, and Meggie was asleep in her nest. Then, lying flat on the floor, Joanna put her eye to the hole and stared down.

The yew tree stood in the midst of undergrowth, but some faint animal tracks led here and there around it. A little further off, one of those small tracks met a larger one, which in turn led to a wider ride that gave on to a clearing. By angling her head, Joanna could make out the end of the ride and the very edge of the clearing.

She could see the men now. There were five of them, well dressed and well mounted. As she watched, three of them dismounted and gave the reins of their horses to the other two. She heard the faint murmur of conversation, then the three men on foot walked towards where the ride branched off from the clearing.

It became clear then that the men were no hunting party. There was a rustling in the undergrowth and then a large boar, presumably disturbed by the men and the horses, suddenly broke cover almost under their feet and raced away across the clearing and into the bracken on the far side.

The men just stood there. Someone made a comment, and somebody else laughed briefly.

Then the men on foot set off along the track.

Joanna did not move. She lay frozen in position, her eye fixed to the men walking so stealthily towards her. She did not dare lift her head to see how Utta was doing; she took the total silence from behind her as a good sign. If only Meggie did not choose this moment to decide she was hungry . . .

As the men came steadily closer she could occasionally make out what they were saying. They seemed to be talking about some escaped prisoners; one of them said something about a dead gaoler. Then – and she started with terror – one of them looked straight up into the branches of the yew tree.

She stared down at him. He was a good-looking man; she could not help but notice it, although she berated herself for the irreverence when this very man might be on the point of making a move that would lead to her death. If he spotted the refuge, if he managed to scale the yew's trunk and came up to investigate . . .

He said, in a blessedly ordinary voice, 'Great old tree, that one, eh, Robert? It's stood there a thousand years, they say. It must have seen the Romans as they marched along these tracks.'

One of the others answered him, making some laughing comment about a legion needing a wider road than this insubstantial path. The third man had come to stand right under the tree.

Suddenly the first man cried out, making Joanna jump out of her skin. 'Stop that!' he roared. 'Have some respect, damn you, and shed your water somewhere else!'

The man under the tree, grumbling, turned away, walked a few paces into the dead bracken and then, raising his tunic, splashed a loud stream of urine into the thick, rusty foliage.

Even if the man in the lead were her enemy, Joanna thought, he had one redeeming feature.

He was still looking up into the branches, but she no longer feared that he had discovered her secret refuge; his interest appeared to be in the old tree itself. Now, coming to stand beside the trunk, he gave it an affectionate pat. He said something in a low voice – Joanna could not make out the words – and then, turning away, led his men off along the track and back to the wider path.

They waited in silence for what seemed like hours. From time to time they heard the two men who had stayed with the horses making remarks to one another. They had both dismounted now, and one of them kept swinging his arms around himself, slapping his hands against his jerkin as if in an attempt to keep himself warm. They were in deep shade down there in the clearing, Joanna thought, and had not the benefit of the Sun whose beams she could see on the open section of the platform. The other man led the horses across to where there was a small rill leading from the stream that ran through her own glade, waiting with them while they drank.

Eventually she heard the sounds of the other three making their way back. They were returning via a different path, one that passed further away from the yew tree.

One of the men in the clearing called out, 'Did you find anything?'

The man who had led the searchers called back, 'Deer tracks, boar tracks, plenty of signs of animal life. But I don't think there's a human being within five miles.' One of his companions laughed and said something about Hawkenlye Abbey and the man, laughing too, replied, 'Ah, yes, Robert, but we are not hunting pious Christian women, especially not nuns.'

Joanna turned over on to her back, closing her eyes.

So it was true. They *were* hunting for Utta and her party.

After a moment, opening her eyes again, she stared across at Utta, who met her gaze steadily. She tried a smile, a gesture of such gallantry that Joanna's heart went out to her all over again.

I cannot protect her friends, she thought to herself. But I vow that, if it is in my power, I shall keep Utta safe.

They spent the remainder of the day trying to recover from the fear engendered by the presence of the huntsmen. Joanna attempted to take Utta's mind off her terror by keeping her occupied. It was not easy, in their restricted circumstances – and nothing on Earth would have persuaded Utta to descend from the safety of the yew tree – but she did what she could. First, there were Utta's wounds to look at. She was healing well and Joanna realised that the enforced idleness up in their refuge was a blessing in disguise. The brand mark on Utta's forehead was still angry and inflamed, but Joanna was sure that the area of heat around it was growing smaller. She encouraged Utta with nods and smiles, to which Utta responded with pathetic gratitude.

'I have – mark?' she asked shyly, pointing to her brow.

'Yes, Utta. You bear a mark.'

'It will—' Utta paused, clearly thinking how to ask what she wanted to know. 'Mark will stay?'

Ah, of course, Joanna thought. She's asking if she will be left with a scar. What woman would not want to know that?

Weighing her words carefully so as to sound neither over-optimistic nor over-pessimistic, she said slowly and clearly, 'Usually a branding iron will leave a scar. But your wound is healing very well and I believe that the herbs that I have used will mean that eventually you will only have a faint mark.' Leaning forward, she reached for the edge of Utta's veil and said, 'May I?'

Utta nodded, her blue eyes puzzled. Joanna draped the veil low over Utta's eyebrows, covering the brand mark. 'If you wear your veil a little lower,' she said, 'like this, I think that nobody will see the mark.'

Relief flooded Utta's face. Taking Joanna's hands in both of hers, she squeezed them warmly. 'You – good woman,' she pronounced. 'You save Utta's life, also save her face.'

Something about the way she phrased her gratitude made Joanna giggle. Utta joined in and, as their fear gave way to laughter, they looked at each other, both aware that some new factor had entered their relationship.

I wish, Joanna thought, that I could ask her why she has been branded a heretic. What is her faith? What do her people believe in? But, given Utta's limited command of Joanna's language, she realised that her wish was to remain unfulfilled.

They both slept more soundly that night. Joanna gave Utta some more of the painkilling draught, ensuring that she would have a peaceful rest, and Joanna felt able to relax to a greater degree. But she knew that having had one visit from those who hunted for Utta did not necessarily mean that there would not be others.

Sound sleep might have come to her, but it was full of dreams, the content of most of which Joanna did her best, on waking, to forget.

He came late in the afternoon of the next day.

Joanna never knew why he should have found his way to that particular area of the great forest. Since nobody told her otherwise, she concluded that it was nothing more than mischance.

She had just fed Meggie and settled the child in her furry nest. Meggie went quickly to sleep, one small fist clenched under her chin slowly uncurling as she relaxed; Joanna tucked the hand beneath the fur covers.

Utta was wrapped up in her own rugs, leaning a shoulder into the spongy trunk of the yew. Patting the tree, she was haltingly saying something about its wood being comfortable to rest against when Joanna heard a sound.

She held up her hand for silence and instantly Utta obeyed. It sickened Joanna to see the terror in Utta's eyes; in that one brief moment, she had gone from being a happy, relaxed woman anticipating an evening with a congenial companion to one who looked as if she expected to die in the very near future.

Trying to reassure her, Joanna put her mouth close to Utta's ear and whispered, 'They did not find us before so they will not now. Anyway, it may be nothing but a forest animal.'

But Utta did not appear to be reassured. Moving so stealthily that a moth would have made more noise, slowly she crawled right to the back of the shelter, covering herself in both her and Joanna's furs and rugs and crouching down until she was no more than a vague heap in the gloomy light. Joanna could see nothing of her but her eyes, wide with fear.

There was, Joanna knew, no need to tell her to be absolutely silent.

Turning her back on Utta, Joanna lay down on the platform and once more put her eye to the spyhole. At first she could see nothing. She was not entirely sure from which direction the sound had come so she waited, holding her breath, to see if it would come again. After a few moments, it did.

It sounded as if someone – or something – were moving cautiously along the track. Not the main track, up towards the clearing where the horsemen had waited for the hunters, but the smaller path that led off towards the yew tree. Watching, every sense straining, Joanna looked out for movement. It was almost sunset and the light was fast fading down there beneath the trees. If we have been scared rigid by nothing more threatening than a boar, she thought, peering along the line of the path, then I may never even *see* the creature . . .

But then there was another, louder sound, swiftly followed by an exclamation. Whoever was down there had just tripped over something. And he was not a boar but a man.

Joanna moved slightly so as to get a better view. The sound had come from the path, at a point where the smaller animal track led off towards the yew tree. Straining to see, she stared down into the gloom.

As she watched, he came down out of the undergrowth and stood on the path. It seemed likely that he had been making his way under cover of the low growth beneath the trees, almost as if he knew somebody would be looking out for him and wanted to ensure that he stayed hidden. But, having damaged himself when he tripped – he was reaching down to inspect an ankle – he had decided to come out on to the easier way offered by the path.

Joanna could see little of him but the top of his head – he appeared to be bald – and his slight shoulders. He was dressed in some dark garment that might have been deliberately chosen to make him hard to spot in the dim light. As she stared intently down at him, he straightened up and began to creep on down the path.

Stay on that track, Joanna willed him, follow it wherever it leads you, and do not turn aside.

It seemed as if he would obey. Turning his head to look from side to side, he paused for a moment to stare at the animal track leading off towards the yew tree – Joanna felt her heart stop – but then, apparently losing interest, he made as if to go on.

Just at that moment, Meggie stirred, gave a little hiccup that brought up a mouthful of semi-digested milk, and let out a small, soft sigh.

He can't have heard, Joanna told herself, he is too far away!

But the man had stopped. Turning with infinite slowness towards the yew tree, he raised his head and stared right up at the place where the platform sat hidden in the tree's thick branches, still clad in their dark-green foliage. Only then, when danger really threatened, did Joanna fully appreciate the wisdom of her people in constructing the refuge in an evergreen tree.

Keep still! Joanna ordered herself. And, instantly disobeying her own command, she stretched out a hand to Meggie.

Who, not aware of the terrible drama being enacted around her, merely perceived her mother's particular scent. And, as she always did when her mother came close, she gave a happy little gurgle.

Even as Joanna watched the man hurl himself along the faint track she thought, what an irony, to be betrayed by a baby's delight.

There was still hope. Twisting round to give Utta a furiously intent look – stay still! – she put her eye back to the spyhole.

He was very near now, standing just outside the protective ring formed by the outer branches of the yew tree. It seemed almost as if he were reluctant to enter under the dense green foliage. Putting all her power into her thought, Joanna commanded him: *Keep away!*

It was almost as if he heard her. With a low laugh – a truly horrible sound – he bent down and, coming forward in a crouch, straightened up again right beside the trunk.

But he could not get up to them, Joanna thought frantically, not without a rope! And if he went away to fetch one – to fetch more men too, probably – then she and Utta could escape while he was gone.

There was silence for so long that she thought he had already gone. But then, sounding frighteningly close, came his voice.

'I know you are there, my pretty maid,' he said. 'And, by the sound of it, you have one of your accursed offspring with you, although they did not tell me that you had whelped. Still, the fires that consume you will accept your young, have no fear.'

Then there was a whisper of sound, quickly repeated once, then once again; he must have brought a rope with him, for he was trying to cast it over the lowest branch so as to haul himself up.

Joanna heard a muffled sound behind her: Utta, stifling her agony with a corner of a blanket. For an instant, Joanna met her eyes. Then she looked at Meggie, grinning gummily up at her from her little nest.

This was Joanna's test. Suddenly she knew it, without any doubt. She heard the Domina's words in her head: *When the time comes, remember that what you have done before, you can do again.*

Feeling her fear run out of her as resolve took its place, Joanna climbed off the platform and silently descended the rope ladder. She was thinking, as her bare feet effortlessly found the rough rungs, of that earlier time, that occasion – which the Domina must have known about – when once previously Joanna had acted out of love for another. What you have done before, you can do again.

Yes. The Domina was quite correct. And if this was the task, and the Domina had known about it and prepared Joanna for it, then it must be the right thing to do.

The last of her doubts left her. Standing now on the branch from which the upper of her two ropes habitually hung, she uncurled its length and let herself down to the lower branch. She slid down the rope too quickly, burning her palms, but speed was now essential: he had managed to get his own rope over the lower branch and even now he was securing it.

Then he began to climb.

# Part Three
## Hawkenlye Abbey
### February 1193

# 15

Three days after Father Micah's death, neither Josse nor anybody else within the Hawkenlye community yet had any idea how he died.

Soon after noon of that day, Josse stood in the road outside the Abbey gates staring after the retreating figure of Gervase de Gifford. He was going over in his mind all that de Gifford had told him concerning the group of strangers. The heretics, as he now knew them to be.

He was trying to decide exactly how – indeed, what – he was going to tell the Abbess. Briefly it crossed his mind that he might not reveal the group's identity; would it really do any harm if she did not know? He had given his word to de Gifford to respect the man's confidences, although with the proviso that only if by so doing he did not compromise anyone else. Not telling the Abbess would certainly save the almost certain introduction of friction in his relationship with her for, no matter that he knew her to be a compassionate and fair-minded woman, she was also Abbess of Hawkenlye. And, as such, she was answerable to those above her in the religious hierarchy who decreed what the attitude to heresy and heretics must be.

Aye. He gave a deep sigh. No matter what her own heart told her, she would obey the rules, as she had vowed to do. And he realised that he had to tell her; tempting though it was to leave her in ignorance, it might prove dangerous for her. It was quite possible that there were other priests as well as the late Father Micah out there on the heretics' trail. If one of them came to Hawkenlye and found out that the Abbess and her nuns had tended a heretic woman in the Abbey infirmary, then she – and probably Sister Euphemia and Sister Caliste – would be severely punished.

To refrain from telling the Abbess that Aurelia was a heretic would certainly compromise her.

He sighed again, turned back inside the gates and went to find her.

Launching straight into his story, he told her what de Gifford had just told him. 'They're a band of heretics,' he said baldly. 'Some from the Low Countries, some from the south; some place in the Midi called Toulouse, or perhaps Albi. That's why Father Micah treated them so savagely. And the letter on Aurelia's forehead isn't an A but an H.'

For some moments she just sat and stared at him. Then she said, very quietly, 'She's a heretic.'

'Aye.'

He had expected her to be surprised – shocked, even – but nevertheless the pallor that spread over her face alarmed him. 'My lady?' he said anxiously. 'May I fetch you water?'

'Water will do me no good whatsoever,' she snapped back. Then, eyes blazing, she cried out, 'Heretics say terrible things, Sir Josse! They claim that Christ is not divine! They say that there is not the one true God but two deities, one good and the other evil, and that this world and everything in it is the creation of the Dark One! Dear Lord, but they claim our very existence here on earth is but an exile until our material bodies die and we are reunited with our souls!'

'But—' He tried to interrupt but she was in full flow, stung to fury by heresy's terrible, hurtful slur on the loving Son of God she worshipped.

'They reject marriage and baptism, they scorn the clergy and they say that each and every man and woman may address the deity personally!' she stormed. 'Just how, pray, is a man of the Church supposed to respond to *that?*'

'Perhaps we should—'

Again she rode him down. 'Think of the people, Sir Josse! What is to become of them if they do not have the strong, steady hold of the priesthood keeping their souls safe from temptation? If they fall into sinful ways and are not brought to confession and given God's forgiveness, then when they die they will go to eternal damnation!' She paused, panting from the effort, then, after a moment, said in a quieter tone, 'That is why heresy must not be allowed to spread. Because it will lead directly to men and women dying in a state of sin, and I cannot believe that you would wish it on a fellow human being to appear before the terrible judge without having been reconciled by penance and fortified by Holy Communion.' She sniffed, eyeing him suspiciously. 'Even if you can accept that threat, I certainly cannot.'

'What will you do, my lady?' he asked frostily. 'You now know that a heretic woman lies in your infirmary, where you yourself have looked down with pity on her wounds. Will you now go out and find whichever priest holds sway here in place of Father Micah and tell him? Watch as Aurelia is taken away, imprisoned, even burned, perhaps, simply because she views these vexed matters of faith differently from the way in which you and the Christian Church do?'

'She will not be burned!' the Abbess cried furiously. 'She will be – they will . . .' Her words petered out. 'Well, they'll probably just let her go.'

'Aye, and just how long will she last, do you think?' he demanded. 'She's badly hurt, her wounds are infected and she is weak with fever. The month is February, my lady, in case you have forgotten, and she will find no food and precious little to drink all the time the ponds and streams are frozen. If she approaches some far-flung hamlet and creeps into an outhouse for shelter, the inhabitants will denounce her for fear of having their dwellings burned down over their heads in punishment for harbouring a heretic!'

The Abbess had dropped her flushed face into her hands. Feeling a surge of pity for her, he stepped forward, about to offer to help her think up a solution to the dilemma in which she found herself.

But even as he did so she removed her hands and shouted up at him, 'I cannot risk the safety and integrity of Hawkenlye! If I had a hundred heretics hiding here, I should have to report it, even if it meant they were all taken straight to the stake for their treason!'

'I do not believe that,' he said flatly. 'I have known you too long and too well to think you capable of such cruelty.'

'They deny Christ!' she cried. 'They spit on the Cross and profane his holy name, he who suffered so for us!'

'Who says they do?' he shouted back. He saw that she had tears in her eyes, but was too angry to let it affect him.

'The priesthood tells us,' she said earnestly. 'They know about these things – they find out, and it is their job to inform us.'

He knew there was a flaw in her argument – something to do with priests only passing on their own version of what they had learned – but just then he heard a faint sound from the cloister outside. He was about to go and investigate when she said, 'Sir Josse, I have no choice. Do you not understand?'

He spun round to face her again. 'Give Aurelia a few more days,' he urged. 'Let her receive the benefit of Sister Euphemia's and Sister Caliste's loving care a little longer, until she is strong enough to get away from here and out of immediate danger. Nobody is aware that you know her to be a heretic – I won't tell anybody that I told you.'

'But I do know,' she said dully. 'And it is not right that I should allow you to lie.'

'Leave it to me to take care of my own soul,' he said gruffly. 'And if your conscience pricks you, you can do the hardest penance ever devised after she's gone.'

She was staring at him and for once he could not read her expression. Sensing – hoping – that she might be weakening, he said softly, 'What do you think the Lord Jesus would have done? Would he have turned a sick woman out to fend for herself and be hunted down by her enemies? Or would he have given her love and tended her hurts?'

'She is a heretic woman who denies His divinity,' the Abbess muttered.

'She is still a human being,' he insisted. Hoping that he had the words exactly right, he said, '"A new commandment I give unto you, that ye love one another as I have loved you."'

'But—' She stopped. It seemed to Josse, watching her so intently, that it had perhaps occurred to her that there *was* no 'but'.

Deciding that it would be wise to slip away and leave her to think, he murmured, 'I will leave you to your contemplation, my lady,' and eased himself out of the room, closing the door gently behind him.

As he walked along the cloister, he sensed someone move in the shadows. He called out, 'Who's there?'

A black-clad nun stepped out from the dimly lit corner where two arms of the cloister met at a right angle. She gave him a graceful bow and, as she straightened up, he found himself looking into the bright blue eyes of Sister Phillipa.

'Sister! How goes the Hawkenlye Herbal?'

'Well, thank you, Sir Josse. Although I have had another task to do these last few days that has kept me from my work.'

'Indeed?'

'Yes.' She looked doubtful suddenly. 'I had thought that you might know of it.'

'No. What have you been up to?' He gave her an indulgent smile.

But then she said, 'Sister Bernadine believed that someone had been going through the Abbey's precious texts. I was ordered to help her to make an inventory and see if anything had been stolen.'

'I had no idea!' He wondered why the Abbess had not told him; theft of one of the manuscripts would be a dire blow for the Abbey. 'And is any document missing?'

'No, that's the strange thing.' Her straight brows knotted into a frown. 'Everything that is meant to be there – everything on the inventory – is there, and undamaged, as far as I can tell. Nothing's been stolen but, Sir Josse, something's been put *in*.'

'What sort of a something?'

From beneath her scapular she pulled a small parcel, wrapped in linen. It was rectangular in shape, about as long as a large man's hand and perhaps two-thirds as broad. After looking in each direction to make sure that nobody was watching, Sister Phillipa unwrapped the linen and held out what it had concealed for Josse to see.

It was a book made from some eight or ten sheets of fine vellum, bound down the left-hand side with a narrow leather cord woven in an intricate pattern. The first page was densely covered in letters, but what they said, or even what language they were in, Josse had no idea.

'There are some wonderful illustrations,' Sister Phillipa whispered, right in his ear; she was so close that he felt the brusque touch of her starched headdress brush his cheek. 'Look.'

Carefully she took the manuscript from him and turned a page or two. A lively picture leaped out at him, its style so vivid and its colours so vibrant that the tiny figures almost appeared to move. He studied them; they were dressed in long black robes and seemed to be standing in a circle and holding their arms up in an attitude of reverence.

'What are they doing?' he asked softly.

'I have no idea,' Sister Phillipa murmured back. 'I have never seen anything like these pictures before. There's a strange cross' – she turned another page – 'and there's a really frightening picture of two worlds side by side, one all light and brilliant, one dark and seething with weird distorted beings . . . There!'

He saw instantly what she meant. The dark world was a nightmare landscape of chaos and misery, with people in torment, wailing and tearing at their hair. Nature was distorted and corrupt, twisted and cruel. The light world, by contrast, was filled with fluffy cloud and bright sunshine, and yellow, gold and pink were the predominate colours. All was ethereal and with an almost unreal quality, and the groups of human-like figures were slightly vague and dream-like.

Josse said wonderingly, 'These are like – like illustrations of a tale only half-remembered. I've never seen anything similar, either, Sister.' He raised his eyes and looked at her. 'Any ideas?'

She said tentatively, 'At first, no. I thought that both the writing hand and the paintings were very beautiful, perhaps the most perfect work I have ever seen, even though I was bothered by the strangeness. But then I remembered something that my father once told me about a religion that believed in two different forms of existence, one all good and the other all bad, and I wondered if this painting' – she pointed at the page that Josse was still looking at – 'could have something to do with it.'

Aye, Josse thought. We have a heretic woman in the infirmary, brought here by the man we believe to be the bodyguard for the whole group. Having carried out his task and brought her to safety, he disappears. But to imagine that this heretical text appeared coincidentally just at the same time is just too incredible.

Benedetto must have hidden it.

Josse said, not meeting Sister Phillipa's eyes, 'What were you going to do with it, Sister?'

She said instantly, 'I was bringing it to the Abbess. But when I stood outside her door I heard you both arguing. I'm sorry to confess that I listened, and I understood what it was that made you both so heated.' She stared at him, her blue eyes troubled. 'Sir Josse, I am very afraid that if I do as I should and give this manuscript to the Abbess, she will destroy it.'

'And the artist in you, Sister Phillipa, cries out in protest against flinging this beautiful work, which must have taken its creator so many painstaking hours to complete, into the flames. Yes?'

She nodded. 'Yes. But what should I do? I cannot put it back, can I? I promised to tell Sister Bernadine if I discovered that anything was missing or damaged, but even if that is not so, surely it is not right to put this manuscript back and say that nothing at all is amiss?'

'I don't know, lass,' he admitted. 'I agree with you that it would not be a strictly honest thing to do. But I also agree that this should not be destroyed.'

They stood in silence for a few moments. He could almost

hear her unspoken appeal and after a while he said, 'I will take care of it.'

She said fervently, 'Thank you. They said you are a man to depend on and they're right.'

Flattered, too modest to ask who *they* were, Josse rewrapped the script in its linen cloth. 'Perhaps you might merely report to Sister Bernadine that you found nothing damaged and nothing missing and that you have put all the Hawkenlye documents neatly back where you found them,' he suggested. 'That would be the truth, other than a small omission. Can your conscience bear that?'

'I believe it can.' She gave him a brilliant smile. 'And any penance that I have to do will be worth it to see poor Sister Bernadine relieved of her anxiety.'

With a repeat of her graceful bow, she turned and walked away. Absently tucking the linen-wrapped package inside his tunic, Josse wondered what on earth he was going to do with it.

Josse did not notice, but while he had been engaged in his clandestine discussion with Sister Phillipa, Helewise had slipped out of her room and gone across to the Abbey church.

Now, all alone and on her knees before the altar, she asked for guidance. I do not know what to do, dear Lord, she prayed silently. I know now that the woman Aurelia is a heretic, who has been punished according to the Church's dictates and who bears the mark on her brow to warn good Christians to be on their guard against her. I am sworn to obedience and it is my clear duty to report her presence here to the Church authorities immediately.

But, oh, dear sweet Jesus, she is so hurt! She is sick and in pain, and if I do as I should, she will suffer more. Much more.

For a few terrible moments, images of somebody being burned at the stake filled Helewise's mind. She did not try to push them away; if I give up Aurelia, she told herself sternly, then there is a strong possibility that this is the fate that awaits her. Can I do that? Condemn a woman who has done no wrong other than to believe in a different picture of the deity?

Out of nowhere she seemed to hear a voice: *All gods are one god, and behind them all is the one great Truth.*

Helewise waited. As she knelt, silent and still, she began to feel less agitated. She waited a little longer, and a deep peace descended on her.

After a while she opened her eyes. Looking up at the altar, she asked, is that your answer, Lord? Is the calm that I feel in my head your response to my appeal? I kneel here and I begin to think that I must not give Aurelia up to those who would harm her, and from you I hear nothing but silence.

Does this mean that you approve?

The deep peace continued. Then Helewise saw herself when she had believed that de Gifford had come for Aurelia. She watched herself leap to Aurelia's defence, crying out *You shall not have her*!

That was the proper instinct, Helewise realised, and the force of her conviction told her that she was right. She remained there on her knees for some time. She had just been in communication with her God; he had listened and he had given her what she prayed for. She felt it was only fair to thank him.

Later, when the rest of the community had filed in for Nones and after they had finished the office, Helewise decided what to do next.

First she went across to the infirmary. Sister Euphemia confirmed that it was all right to visit Aurelia and Helewise went and stood by her bed, staring down at her. The woman was asleep – Sister Caliste, appearing beside Helewise and smiling a greeting, whispered that Aurelia was still in considerable pain and being given regular doses of a sedative.

Helewise put out a very careful hand and felt the hot, tight skin around the brand on Aurelia's forehead. 'Will it leave a scar?' she asked Sister Caliste softly.

Sister Caliste frowned. 'We believe so, yes, my lady. The infection must have set in swiftly and had already taken too strong a hold by the time she was brought to us. Sister Tiphaine has prepared a special salve to help healthy skin grow back, but we fear that there will always be a mark.' Suddenly her serene face fell into lines of a rare bitterness. 'It is a savage thing to do to a person, is it not, my lady? Whatever their crime, I cannot think it warrants inflicting such agony and such permanent damage.'

Helewise said quietly, 'I agree, Sister. Nothing warrants this.'

Then, giving the young nun a brief nod, she turned from Aurelia's bedside and left the infirmary.

Next she fetched the mare, Honey, from the stables and rode off once more to visit Father Gilbert. Now that Father Micah was dead, with no new priest yet despatched to the Hawkenlye community, it would have to be Father Gilbert, even though he still lay in his sickbed.

He was the only person whom Helewise could think of to whom to put the questions that burned in her.

She found the Father sitting up in bed cradling a mug of some steaming liquid that smelt deliciously savoury. Helewise, who had missed the midday meal because she had been praying, felt her belly growl. I shall suffer the discomfort of watching the Father drink his broth while I bear my hunger, she told herself, in a gesture of penance for what I am about to do. I do not intend to tell a lie, but I shall not be revealing all of the truth.

When she and Father Gilbert had exchanged pleasantries, she said, 'Father, I remember that Father Micah spoke passionately about lost souls who must be banished to the eternal fires. Can he, do you think, have been referring to heretics?'

'Heretics?' Father Gilbert looked surprised. 'I suppose so, yes, although I did not know that we had any in our area. Although, now I come to think of it, there was a rumour . . . Oh, dear, that blow to the head has left me feeling rather confused. Heretics, eh? Why do you ask, my lady Abbess?'

'Oh,' – she had prepared the explanation, but still it felt awkward and clumsy on her tongue and she felt sure he must surely be suspicious – 'oh, there is some talk of a group of heretics visiting England. Some were apprehended, I believe, to the north of Tonbridge. I know a little of heresy, that its followers believe there to be two worlds, one good and one evil, and that—'

Father Gilbert interrupted. 'You speak of only one heresy, my lady,' he said, 'that of the dualists, whereas in fact there are many, although the majority are based on dualist misconceptions. Let me see, now – the Arians challenged the divinity of Christ, the Manichaeans said that man was evil but possessed a divine spark that could be brought alight through strict religious observance, the followers of Zoroaster believed in Ahura Mazda, the Divine Light. The Romans' Mithras was a variant, you know.' He gave her a little nod, as if in confirmation of his own words. 'Then there are the Bogomils, of course. Now they are classic dualists, utterly believing in the creed of a good and an evil god.' He smiled up at her. 'Have I answered your concerns adequately?'

She returned his smile. 'Well yes, in a way, Father. But I was also wondering what a good Christian ought to do if—'

'I forgot to mention the Cathars!' he exclaimed, interrupting her. 'Which was remiss of me since they are a sect causing much distress within the Church just at present.' He shifted in his bed, rearranging his weight more comfortably. 'The Cathar heresy is spreading rather wildly,' he said in a low tone, as if crowds of fascinated Christians on the brink of apostasy were gathered outside trying to listen. 'They call themselves the Pure Ones – *kataros* is Greek for pure one – and theirs is a particularly pessimistic view of the dualist world. They are often referred to as Manichaeans; it is my own view that the two terms are used fairly indiscriminately.' He looked slightly annoyed, as if such scholarly inexactitude were inexcusable. 'The Church has been aware of them for some time – oh, more than a century, I imagine. Measures have been taken against them for almost as long. To begin with, the authorities strove hard to bring the faithless back into the fold, threatening them with excommunication if they persisted in their wrongdoing.'

'But if they were heretics, followers of a different faith, then surely they would not take such a threat very seriously?' Helewise asked.

'Indeed they did not.' Father Gilbert gave her a glance of approval. 'Sterner measures were taken and some of the heretics abjured their faith under threat of such things as trial by water. Then a strange thing happened: in Cologne, where some heretics were on trial, the common people decided that the Church authorities were being too lenient. They grabbed the heretics and burned them at the stake.'

'How did the Church react to that?'

'At first the extremity of the violence was condemned outright,' Father Gilbert said. 'After all, back then – and I speak of a time almost fifty years ago – the vast majority of the populace, throughout Europe, were faithful to the one true Church. Except, of course, down in the south, in the lands that I believe men call the Midi. Provence and the Languedoc were the breeding ground of Catharism, and in the end the Church realised it.'

'The Midi.' She tried to remember. 'Father, is there a town called Albi in the Midi? Or one called Toulouse?'

'Yes, yes,' he said, waving away her question as if impatient to return to his narrative. 'The Cathars are also referred to as the Albigensians because Albi is one of their strongholds. Where was I? Oh, yes. In 1179, the Church held a council at which measures against the Cathars were outlined. The duty of the faithful was henceforth to hunt them down, and the treatment that the heretics had received in places such as Cologne, Liège and Strasbourg began to be more widespread.'

She sat stunned. What had until then been a very personal problem – what to do about a heretic woman lying in Hawkenlye's infirmary – had just been revealed to be part of something infinitely greater.

Something that, if Father Gilbert were not exaggerating, was setting all of Europe alight . . .

He was still talking, speaking now of this Council and that pronouncement, of papal involvement and the possible interest of the King of France in a crusade to the south. But she was no longer listening.

Getting up, she said, 'Excuse me, Father, if I interrupt your most interesting instruction, but it is time for me to go.'

'Ah, yes indeed, duty calls you.' He smiled affectionately at her. 'As always.'

She spent a few moments checking that he was comfortable – she built up the fire and refilled his mug from the pot simmering beside the hearth – and then took her leave.

Mounting Honey, she rode back to Hawkenlye.

De Gifford had told Josse – who had related it to her – that two of the group of seven came from the south. From either Toulouse or Albi. It was beginning to look very much as if the members of the group were Albigensians, also known as Cathars.

One of the fastest growing and most threatening heresies that the Church had ever known.

Kicking her heels into Honey's sides and feeling the mare spring off in an eager canter, Helewise thought grimly that this fact rather altered the way in which she must treat Hawkenlye infirmary's heretic woman.

# 16

Josse was aware of the alien manuscript all the time. Although it was quite invisible to others, hidden in its wrappings inside his tunic, he felt that everyone at Hawkenlye must know what he carried.

The script had taken on the mysteriously charismatic qualities of the forbidden.

Trying to think sensibly about it, he realised that the first step was to ask the opinion of some learned, cultured person who might be able to tell him what it was. The document might not be as dangerous as he thought; simply because he did not understand the words was no reason automatically to assume that they were heretical.

Despite those strange, disturbing paintings . . .

There were some erudite women within the Hawkenlye community. Sister Emanuel, for example, whose main duty was the care of the elderly monks and nuns living out their lives in the Abbey's retirement home, had an air of scholarly competence about her. She assisted the Abbess in maintaining the Abbey's great ledgers and was reputed to be even more learned than her superior. There was also Sister Bernadine, who probably knew more about manuscripts than anyone else in the Abbey. Josse would have loved to show the manuscript to either – or, even better, both – of them.

But it would not be right. They were nuns before they were scholars and they were vowed to obedience. If Josse asked them about the script, they would, if it proved to be anything inflammatory, have to go straight to the Abbess to report it. He knew he was not ready to let her see it; he might, he realised sadly, never be ready. Not if there remained any danger of her ordering it destroyed.

Pondering the matter, Josse thought of his Lewes chess opponent, Father Edgar. The two of them had enjoyed some lively and wide-ranging discussions and the Father had demonstrated a good grasp of both the contemporary scene and the history of the land; he would be sure to shed at least a small ray of light on the provenance of the manuscript.

But, Josse thought, the same stricture applied to Father Edgar as to the Abbess Helewise; Father Edgar was a man of the Church and therefore answerable to a higher authority. It was quite inconceivable that he would say, 'Ah, yes, a heretical tract, beautifully written and illustrated; let's put it on display.' No. He, too, would cast it into the nearest fire.

*I need someone sophisticated and worldly who owes no greater allegiance to the Church authorities than the next man,* Josse mused.

His mind turned to the de Clares.

The family was certainly sophisticated; some of its members had at one time had very close connections with the royal court. William the Conqueror had given lands at Tonbridge to his close supporter, Richard Fitzgilbert, as well as the estates at Clare in Suffolk from which Richard took his title. Although he had later rebelled against William's son, William Rufus – who had attacked and burned Tonbridge Castle in response – his own son Gilbert later became a good friend to the second William.

It was said that there was a blood link between the Norman kings and the de Clares. Richard Fitzgilbert was the son of Arletta of Falaise, a tanner's daughter who later became the mistress of Robert the Devil, Duke of Normandy, by whom she had a son. That son became William the Conqueror.

The present holder of the de Clare title was Richard FitzRoger, Arletta's great-great-great-grandson. He was a powerful baron and, as Josse well knew, a man of importance at court.

Perhaps he was too important.

But what about his servant, Gervase de Gifford?

It was some time since Josse had paid a visit to his friend Goody Anne, who kept the tavern down in Tonbridge. Josse resolved to ride down there the next day, gorge himself on Anne's excellent food and ale and ask a few discreet questions about de Gifford.

He rode down Castle Hill the next morning. The day was sunny and quite warm, with an illusory promise that spring might be on its way. He made his way to the tavern and was greeted warmly by Goody Anne. After the usual flirtatious remarks, she slammed a tankard of ale in front of him and went off to fetch him a dish of mutton stew.

As always, it was a simple matter to start a conversation. This time, Josse merely turned to the man beside him – a stout fellow in early middle age who had been sharing a joke with Goody Anne and whose broad face still wore a beaming smile – and remarked on what a fine day it was.

He endured several minutes of his new acquaintance's opinion on the weather, then said, as the man took a long gulp of ale, 'I met a man from hereabouts the other day. His name's de Gifford, and I believe he is a de Clare man. I wonder if you—'

'Oh, aye, I know de Gifford,' the stout man said confidently. 'Well, that's to say, I don't know him personally, like, but I know well who he is.'

'Is he a newcomer to the area?'

'Hm? Newcomer? Well now, I wouldn't like to say. He's been a frequent visitor up at the Castle, they say, for many a day. But whether or not he's taken up residence here, that I cannot tell you, my friend.'

'Is he well liked?'

The stout man gave him an assessing glance. 'He's the law, isn't he? Liking don't much come into it, far as I can tell.'

'Is he respected?'

Again, the sly look. 'Like I say, he's the law. Makes sense for a man to respect those with power over him, wouldn't you say?'

The stout man's genial air was, Josse was realising, slightly misleading. He might enjoy a good laugh and a mug of ale, but beneath the cheery exterior there appeared to be a shrewd brain. With a nod to Josse, he said, civilly enough, 'My dinner's nearly ready. I'm away to the table over there to eat it.'

It was as clear a snub as any. Josse wished him good day and turned back to his ale.

He had just finished his mutton stew – it was excellent – when a quiet voice beside him said, 'I hear you were asking about me, Sir Josse. Can I be of assistance?'

He spun round. Gervase de Gifford, immaculately dressed in a burgundy-coloured tunic with rich gold braiding, stood behind him.

'Word travels fast,' Josse observed.

De Gifford gave a faint shrug. 'I am fortunate in that someone happened to overhear your mention of my name.'

It was more than that, Josse was quite sure. There was probably a man – maybe more than one – in de Gifford's pay who kept his eyes and ears open and reported anything likely to be of interest to the sheriff. Well, it made sense; Josse felt a moment's admiration for de Gifford's efficiency.

'I wanted to talk to you,' Josse said quietly.

'Indeed? What about?' The light green eyes studied him.

'Er – to do with the subject of the conversation we had yesterday.'

De Gifford nodded, as if in recognition of Josse's diplomacy in not mentioning what that subject had been. 'I see. There have been further developments?'

'In a way, yes, although not in the sense that something new has happened.' Josse glanced around him; the tavern was quite full and certainly no place to take out and wave about the alien manuscript. 'I have brought something to show you,' he said, lowering his voice. 'Is there somewhere private where we could go?'

De Gifford said, 'Yes. Follow me.'

Josse drained his mug and obeyed.

De Gifford led the way out of the tavern and along the road, taking a narrow alleyway between some low wooden houses. The alleyway was foul with dirty water and household waste; de Gifford, Josse noticed, stepped very carefully so as to protect his soft leather boots.

They soon left the last of the dwellings behind. The air improved quickly and Josse saw that they had come to a path that led down to the river. De Gifford headed for a spot where a fallen tree made a low seat; sitting down, he patted the gnarled trunk beside him and said, 'Make yourself comfortable. Few people come along here at this time of year and if anyone does, we shall see them approach. Now, what did you want to show me?'

Josse reached inside his tunic and withdrew the linen bundle. Unwrapping the cloth, he held out the manuscript to de Gifford, who took it from him in gloved hands.

He studied it for a long time, turning the parchment pages slowly, staring at the graceful, even writing and at the lively, colourful pictures. Josse, burning to ask what he made of it, restrained his impatience with difficulty.

Eventually de Gifford said, 'I cannot be absolutely sure, but I believe this is a Cathar tract.' Josse opened his mouth to speak but de Gifford held up a hand. 'Please, Sir Josse, do not say anything – I do not want to know how you came by this.' He glanced up at Josse. 'Yet. As I say, I am not certain. But the writing is in the *langue d'oc*, the speech of the Midi. It describes a ceremony and the illustration here' – he turned to the painting of the group of people with their arms raised in reverence – 'is a depiction of the ceremonial rites.' He stared down at the picture for a moment. Then: 'It is exquisite, is it not?'

'Aye.' Josse was thinking fast. His strong inclination was to tell de Gifford the truth; for some reason, he trusted the man. And, even if de Gifford subsequently revealed himself to be too devout a Christian to entertain the thought of preserving and treasuring a heretical document, then Josse could with all honesty say that neither he nor anybody else knew for certain how it had come to be hidden at Hawkenlye. That ought surely to absolve both him and the Abbey community from blame.

And, however hard he tried, he just could not believe in the picture of de Gifford as an obedient, devoted Christian . . .

He said, 'It was found in the book chest at Hawkenlye Abbey. One of the nuns thought she saw signs that the Abbey's manuscripts had been disturbed and a search was instigated. This was found concealed beneath the other manuscripts.'

'No doubt smuggled into the Abbey and hidden by whoever it was who arranged for the woman Aurelia to be brought for treatment in the infirmary,' de Gifford said.

'We cannot be sure of that,' Josse said quickly.

'No, of course not,' de Gifford murmured. Then, turning intent eyes to Josse, he said, 'Why did you bring it to me?'

'I needed to consult someone with learning who was not vowed to mindless obedience to the Church,' Josse replied.

De Gifford smiled. 'I am flattered on the one count, a little perplexed on the second. Why, Sir Josse, do you perceive me as potentially disobedient to our priesthood?'

'I – that was not exactly what I meant.' Josse tried to think how to explain himself. 'I suppose I just thought that, since you are neither priest, monk nor cleric of any description, you would not be bound by any vow and you would make up your own mind.'

'How perceptive,' de Gifford said softly. 'I am honoured by your judgement of me. Indeed I do make up my own mind, sometimes in matters where such independence of spirit is not altogether wise.' He was studying Josse as he spoke and, when he had finished, went on staring at him in silence, as if thinking how to go on.

'I will, I think, repay your confidence with one of my own,' he said eventually. 'You are aware of whom I serve?'

'Aye. Richard FitzRoger of the de Clares.'

'And you are also aware of the family's close connections with the Crown?'

'Aye. I know something of the Norman line. My father's lands are in France and I grew up with tales of Duke Robert of Normandy and Arletta his woman. In my country we call him *le Diable.*'

'The Devil.' De Gifford nodded.

'Arletta wed the Count of Brionne, and they founded the de Clare dynasty,' Josse went on. 'I know they have had their differences with the Crown, but, as I understand it, the blood tie always seems to manage to overcome them.'

'Yes. It does.' Now de Gifford was staring down at his booted foot, making patterns in the dirt of the path. 'Richard FitzRoger's great-grandfather once saved William Rufus from an assassination plot. And he was at the King's side in the New Forest when the Rufus fell.' Suddenly the bright, intelligent eyes were on Josse's again. 'No doubt you, who know of the reputation of the one they call *le Diable*, are also aware of what they say of his descendants who sat on the English throne?'

'In what way?' Josse asked cagily.

De Gifford gave a small sound of impatience. 'Please, Sir Josse, do not be coy. We speak in the open, with no witnesses. If I subsequently claim that you spoke of matters of which it is best not to speak, then it is but my word against yours. What they say of the Conqueror's family is that they honour the old gods.'

'I know of the rumours, aye,' Josse said. 'I've never placed very much credence in them. The Crown has been a major patron of the Church and—'

De Gifford sighed. 'You cannot deny that William Rufus was loathed and mistrusted by the clergy. Why do you think that was?'

'Because—'

But before he could get an answer out, de Gifford had forestalled him. 'Because he did not bend the knee before their altars!' he said fiercely. 'Oh yes, he went through the ceremonies for the sake of form. But they knew full well where his heart lay.'

'And you're going to tell me that his close friend Gilbert de Clare shared his beliefs?' Josse asked shrewdly. 'That, even now, the shadow of the old ways lies on the family?'

De Gifford studied him. 'No. I would not *tell* you that.' He grinned. 'I might, however, plant the seed of suspicion in your mind.'

But Josse had remembered something and was hardly listening. 'You told the Abbess Helewise that you had not come for the heretic woman!' he exclaimed. 'You said you'd have brought her to the nuns' care yourself, had you known where to find her!'

'Yes, I would have done.' De Gifford's expression was indulgent.

Josse shook his head in puzzlement. 'But she has broken the law. All of them have.'

'They have broken the Church's law,' de Gifford corrected. 'They dare to worship God in a different guise from that ordained by the men of the Church. Yet these clerics are but men, no better qualified than any other men to say that the deity is this, or that, and no other. These matters are for each man's conscience, are they not?'

'I – I don't know. No priest would agree with that, for sure.'

De Gifford shrugged. 'So? How speaks *your* conscience, Sir Josse? Do you follow without question when your priest orders you? Would you betray a fellow man to the Church for punishment because he had another faith?'

After a moment Josse said, 'No. I would not. I *have* not, indeed, for I am well aware that a heretic woman lies even now in Hawkenlye Abbey.'

'Yes. There is no need for you to prove yourself to me. I would not do so, either. Sir Josse, when I began my investigation into the death of Father Micah, I already knew about the band of heretics and I suspected that his death might in some way be linked to them. I do not believe necessarily that they killed him but, even were that so, I should keep an open mind over whether it was murder or self-defence.'

'Self-defence?'

'Father Micah threatened to kill them. If a man tries to kill you, Sir Josse, do you not hit back and try to prevent him?'

'But he is – he was a priest!'

'A vicious and over-zealous priest who belonged to a faith in which the heretics did not believe.'

Josse thought about it. 'Aye,' he said, 'I understand. Take away the religious context and it's just a man threatening to kill another and the victim hitting back.'

With a calm smile de Gifford said, 'Precisely.'

Josse sat in thought for some moments. It was, he was discovering, one thing to suspect that an urbane and worldly man of the law might be less than totally committed to the faith of his homeland. It was quite another matter to have had that suspicion confirmed.

After a while, he looked up at de Gifford and said, 'Where do you think they are?'

'The heretics?' De Gifford shrugged. 'I have no idea. There are many places out in the forest and the wild where they might be hiding, although I doubt if they would have survived the bitter weather unless they found some sort of shelter and were able to build themselves a fire. And it is unlikely that any household has taken them in for, were they to be discovered, the house would be destroyed. That particular clause of the Assize of Clarendon is, I believe, quite widely known.'

'Might they not have left England and returned to wherever it was they came from?'

'I have asked myself that question. But I do not think that they would leave Aurelia behind. Somebody obviously cares deeply for her, to have taken the risk of formulating the plan to bring her to Hawkenlye. Had the big man who carried her there stayed after delivering her to the nuns, no doubt someone within the Abbey would have insisted he be put under guard until the matter could be investigated.'

'Aye, someone did,' Josse said grimly.

De Gifford gave him a sympathetic glance. 'I see.'

There was something Josse wanted to return to, something that de Gifford had said earlier. 'When you looked at the manuscript you said it was written in the *langue d'oc* and was a – what was the word you used?'

'Cather. Yes, I said that I believed it is a Cathar tract.'

'And the Cathars are heretics?'

'Oh, yes. They are probably the biggest thorns in the Church's side that all those great spiritual lords have ever experienced.'

'I know nothing about them,' Josse confessed. 'Will you tell me?'

'Of course,' de Gifford replied. 'Catharism is a dualist faith, and its followers believe that we are here in our earthly existence under sufferance, having been torn away from our spiritual entities in the heavens against our will. The most fervent wish of a Cathar is to be reunited with his or her spirit, which is why they view their life on earth with such indifference and why they go so willingly to the stake. It is also, incidentally, why they do not recognise marriage, since to procreate means that they have separated yet another soul from its spirit and brought it down to endure life on earth.'

'If they do not marry and bear children,' Josse asked, 'how can the sect hope to continue?'

De Gifford smiled. 'I do not think that continuance on earth concerns them much. But in fact quite a lot of them have been married and had children before they become *Parfaits*.'

'*Parfaits*?'

'Perfects. Pure Ones. Men and women who refrain from sexual intercourse, who eat neither meat nor any animal products, nothing that is brought into being by progeniture or coitus. They do not kill either man or beast. They take a vow to honour all these obligations and that is called the Consolamentum. When the vow has been sworn, the man or woman becomes a Perfect.'

'So it's possible to believe in the faith without making the vow?'

'Yes. People who do that are referred to as adherents. They are accepted as such by the Perfects and they may take the Consolamentum when they are ready. It is, I understand, quite common for married couples to live as adherents until religious fervour overtakes bodily passion, at which point they forswear the pleasures of the flesh and take the vow.'

Josse, trying to absorb all that de Gifford had just told him, sat slowly shaking his head. Then he said tentatively, 'Are they – do you think that they are *good* people?'

'An interesting question,' de Gifford observed. 'Yes, I do. So, I might add, do some of the most powerful prelates of the Catholic Church. The Cathars lead pure lives devoid of violence and hypocrisy, working hard and caring for each other with tenderness and diligence, which is more than can be said for many Christians.' He shot Josse a glance. 'Even many of the clergy.'

'Hm.' There was one more thing that Josse wanted to know. He said, 'Why did they come to England? What persuaded these seven people – whether or not they are Cathars – to come to an unknown land, unsure of their welcome, in the middle of winter?'

'They came as evangelists,' de Gifford said. 'And I think that we can indeed assume that they are Cathars. The sect has been attracting many converts in the countries across the Channel and I imagine that they hoped to do the same here.'

'No wonder Father Micah dealt so harshly with them,' Josse said.

'He was afraid,' de Gifford said simply. 'He had doubtless been informed by his superiors of the situation in the Low Countries, in Germany and in France. Despite reparations – many Cathars have already died in the fires – the sect is gaining more followers by the days.'

'Will they win?' Josse found he had put his question in military terms, as if he and de Gifford were speaking of a war.

'I do not know.' De Gifford looked thoughtful. 'They are not winning, to use your word, in the north of Europe. But matters are very different in the south. The relaxed and colourful culture of the Midi is perfectly adapted for the Cathar faith, and indeed many members of the sect are flocking down to the Languedoc because it is the one place where they can be sure of a good reception.'

'You said that one of our seven was from the Midi.'

'Yes. Two, in fact. Guiscard and Aurelia. I imagine that they were sent to the countries of the north to spread the word among existing Cathars that they should head south, and to try to persuade others to convert and go too.'

'Their mission here has not been a success,' Josse remarked

soberly. 'It was their misfortune to encounter Father Micah. You said that they would not leave without Aurelia,' he reminded de Gifford. 'Do you think to put a watch over her and apprehend them when they come for her?'

De Gifford gave an exasperated sigh. 'Sir Josse, for a man of your quality you can be exceedingly slow,' he said tartly. 'Far from apprehending them, as you put it, I shall be helping them on their way.'

'You – but why?'

'Because, as you so accurately observed a little while ago, I am bound by no vow of obedience to the Church and I make up my own mind. I have much admiration for the Cathar sect and I would not see any of its men and women put to the flames for their faith. If I take them under guard, they may not suffer that fate; I do not know. But all the time that it remains a possibility, I will do nothing that might lead to it.'

He sat for some moments regarding Josse, as if deciding whether or not to speak his mind. Eventually, apparently coming to a decision, he said, 'Sir Josse, I intend to do all that I can to get them away across the Channel and on their way to what safety they can find in the south. Will you help me?'

Through Josse's mind flashed an image of another, earlier allegiance. He saw the Abbess, distressed, her face flushed from the passion of her convictions.

Addressing her silently he said, Helewise, my dear friend, in this instance I believe you to be wrong. If ever you discover what I am about to undertake, I hope that you will forgive me for the hurt it must cause you.

Then, turning to de Gifford, he said, 'Aye. I will.'

# 17

As Josse rode back up the long, sloping flank of the hillside to Hawkenlye, it began to snow. At first it was nothing much; a flurry of light flakes swirling on the air and barely settling. But the afternoon was very cold and it was likely that this initial fall presaged something worse to come before dark. Josse longed for the simple comfort of the monks' quarters in the Vale and a warm hearth to sit by. He did not envy any lost souls who were wandering out in the wild when night came.

Lost souls. His mind must subconsciously have been puzzling over the mystery of Father Micah's death, for those were the words that the priest had used. When he died, he had been preoccupied with a noble lord who had forgotten God's law – well, Josse knew now who that was; it was the Lord of the High Weald in his stronghold at Saxonbury – and with some lost souls who were to be condemned to the eternal fires.

Undoubtedly Father Micah had been referring to the Cathars. It seemed likely, in the light of all that Josse knew about him, that he had been thinking of an earthly version of hellfire to see the group on their way.

Where were they?

Pondering the question as, head down, he rode on up the track, Josse thought that de Gifford was probably right in assuming that they were still in the area. One of their number still lay sick at Hawkenlye, and all that Josse had just learned about the ways of the Cathars made him support de Gifford's view that the others would not simply slip away and abandon her.

'Arnulf, Alexius, Guiscard,' Josse said aloud, 'Benedetto who carried Aurelia to the Abbey, Frieda who died in the gaol. Who else? Oh, yes, Utta. About whose movements we know even less that we do about those of the rest of them.'

If they are waiting for Aurelia to be well enough to travel before coming to fetch her, he reasoned, then they must surely be fairly close at hand. They will have to find out how she fares, whether she's recovering her strength, how soon she will be fit to travel. How will they do that?

He was very aware of the great forest, a silent, dark and brooding presence beside him as he rode. There were places within its secret heart where men – and women – had camped. Some people lived there permanently. Mag Hobson had done so, in her neat little hut with its herb garden and its fresh stream. The Forest Folk lived there too, although from the little that Josse knew about their life and their ways, he was pretty sure that they were constantly on the move, never staying in one location for more than a week or two.

Was that where the Cathars were hiding?

God help them, Josse thought with feeling, if so.

As Horace plodded on up the rise, Josse felt his mind wander. He felt, as he so often did, that there were unseen eyes within the forest watching him. He remembered suddenly standing with the Lord of the High Weald in his courtyard, knowing with some sense beyond sight that he was being closely observed.

Aye, it had been an unsettling place, Saxonbury. Out there on top of the ridge, ancient paths and earthworks all around it; hardly any wonder, really, Josse reflected, that he had been unnerved. And that was before the Lord had begun plying him so generously and enthusiastically with ale.

His vagrant attention suddenly entered an area of his mind that he had forgotten about. It was another memory of that visit to Saxonbury and it was also, Josse realised triumphantly, the little niggling thought that he had been trying without success to locate.

Until now.

He had remembered the voices. That voice speaking in a foreign language, the one that he had presumed belonged to the Lord's

Turkish wife, suffering pain, addressing her women. He had known there was something not quite right in his memory, and now he knew what it was.

There had been a man's voice speaking that foreign language too.

Aye, Josse thought, kicking Horace and upping his pace, it might be that one of the Lord's sons speaks his mother's tongue. But it might just as well not be.

As he was contemplating the implications of his revelation, another one hit him with equal, if not greater, force. They had all been assuming that Father Micah had been referring to two different missions.

What if they had been one and the same?

He glanced up at the sky. It looked as if the snow clouds would bring darkness prematurely but, even so, surely he had time to get up to Saxonbury and back to Hawkenlye by nightfall. It was not very far. He kicked Horace again as they reached the top of the long climb, and the big horse broke into a canter. The ground was hard and the track now ran straight and level; if they hurried, they ought to be all right.

Whoever was on guard up at Saxonbury must have remembered the Lord's order that Josse was to be admitted if he came calling; even as Horace, flanks heaving and sweating profusely, came trotting up to the gate, it was drawn back. A voice said, 'Good day to you, Sir Josse d'Acquin. The Lord awaits you.'

The guard must also have been keeping a close watch on the path up to the hilltop, Josse thought. He was impressed by the diligence with which the Lord arranged for his lands to be watched over and protected.

The Lord was indeed waiting for him, standing in the middle of his courtyard with a heavy fur cloak around his shoulders.

'You have been riding hard,' he observed. 'I am intrigued as to what pressing matter has brought you back here on a day of such bad weather. But, before we go inside and you tell me, I will call one of my men to attend to your horse.' He put up a large hand and gave Horace's damp neck a stroke and a pat; Horace nickered a soft response.

'I would be grateful,' Josse said, slipping off Horace's back.

A youth had come running from what appeared to be a stable and he took Horace from Josse with a smile.

'Your horse will be in good hands,' the Lord murmured; looking at him, Josse noticed that he was smiling as if at some private joke. 'Come in!' He slapped Josse on the back. 'Come into my hall and warm yourself. I will order some ale and—'

'No!' Josse protested. Then, remembering his manners, added, 'Thank you, but on my last visit I found your ale too good, so that I did not know when to stop.'

'Ah,' said the Lord, a definite twinkle in his eyes.

The hall was empty. Again, though, Josse had the strong impression that he was being watched.

Now, though, he was almost sure that he knew why and by whom.

The Lord waved him to a seat by the fire, taking another one himself. He fixed bright blue eyes on Josse and said, 'Well?'

As he had been riding up to Saxonbury, Josse had made up his mind that only the direct approach stood any chance at all of success with the Lord. Even then, that chance was not very good.

Still, he thought, now that I'm here I'll do my best.

Meeting the Lord's eyes he said, 'When I was last here I heard voices speaking in a foreign tongue. I assumed that it was your wife talking to her womenfolk. I also heard a woman's cry of pain and, again, assumed it was your wife, whom you had described to me as frail. I ask you now, my Lord, does she suffer pain?'

The Lord regarded him steadily. 'No more than any other old woman. Or any other old man, come to that.' He shifted in his seat, pressing a hand to the small of his back. 'The cold weather brings out the pains in the joints, you know. Me, I suffer a niggle in my backbone when an easterly blows that feels like an imp with a pitchfork. And my wife was born and bred in warmer climes, so that our northern chill affects her worst than most. She keeps inside the house in winter.'

'Ah. Aye, I see.' Was that a confirmation or not? Deciding to plough on, Josse said, 'It is quite possible, I know, that my first assumption was correct and that it was your wife whom I overheard. But I heard a man's voice reply to her in that same foreign tongue. Do any of your sons or your manservants speak your wife's language, my Lord?'

'One of my sons has a word or two. But my wife rarely speaks her native tongue nowadays. Sometimes I think that she has all but forgotten it.' Now the laughter in the Lord's eyes was very evident and the smile that he tried to control was steadily getting the better of him.

'Then, if you will allow it,' Josse said, with more confidence than he felt, 'I shall suggest another explanation for those mystifying voices that I heard, an explanation that would also, were it true, account for why it is that I feel hidden eyes closely watching my every move while I am in your hall.'

'Please, proceed. I should be most entertained to hear you.' The Lord waved a hand in an expansive gesture.

Josse took a deep breath and said, 'I know that there is a group of heretics in the area. They originally numbered seven, but one was imprisoned and is dead and one has not been heard of for some time. Of the remaining five, one, a woman, is being treated by the nuns at Hawkenlye for severe wounds to her back and her forehead. She has been branded and flogged, as had the woman who died in prison. Now, unless they have perished, the four men of the group must have found themselves a refuge. Somewhere quite close to Hawkenlye, so that they can be kept informed of Aurelia's progress and come for her when she is ready to travel.' He paused, stared briefly up at the Lord's impassive face and made himself go on. 'Somewhere where the master of the house is not afraid of the law that states that he who shelters heretics shall have his house burned to the ground. It comes to me, my Lord, that on both counts Saxonbury fits the picture that I have drawn.'

There was a long silence, during which Josse became uncomfortably hot under the Lord's intense scrutiny. He was beginning to regret his openness, and wish that he had taken the precaution of telling someone where he was going, when at last the Lord spoke.

'You have been honest with me, Sir Josse,' he said, getting to his feet. 'Wait here.'

Josse heard the Lord's heavy footsteps cross the hall and recede somewhere in the distance. He stared into the fire, watching the dancing flames, trying not to think the worst. I have my sword, he thought, and maybe I'll stand a chance if there are but the Lord and one or two of his kin at home . . .

Then the Lord came back. He was no longer alone. Beside him walked a man dressed in a long black garment tied with a rope belt. He had a wound on his forehead and he held himself stiffly, as if some other hurt pained him when he moved. He was perhaps in his mid-thirties, possibly a little older. He had a broad, chubby face, brown eyes and greying brown hair. He looked, Josse thought, very wary.

Standing up, Josse said, 'I am Josse d'Acquin. If you are whom I believe you to be, please understand that I mean you no harm and that I will help you if it is in my power.'

The man came right up to him, staring into Josse's eyes as if he were trying to see into his heart to judge whether he spoke the truth. After a moment, he said, in a heavily accented voice, 'I am Arnulf. I am inclined to believe you and to put my trust in you for, as the Lord has explained, you have come here with your suspicions and not to some fierce priest.'

'Father Micah is dead,' Josse said quietly.

'I know. The Lord told me. I did not kill him.'

'I am told that your sect does not kill.'

'That is largely true,' Arnulf said cagily. 'Although any man will kill to save his own life.'

'Such a killing is not regarded as murder under the laws of this land.' Josse was thinking of de Gifford. 'When it is a question of kill or be killed, those with authority over us are reasonable.'

Arnulf's brown eyes regarded Josse steadily. 'I do not know who killed your priest, Sir Josse. And that is the truth.'

'I believe you,' Josse assured him. 'But that is not why I am here. I have come to help you.'

Arnulf's intense scrutiny continued for a moment or so. Then, with a sigh, he said, 'I accept your help, Sir Josse. In truth, we have need of the assistance of good folk.' He turned and gave a brief smile to the Lord. 'Were it not for my Lord here, Alexius, Guiscard, Benedetto and I would probably have perished and Aurelia certainly would be in her grave. One of his sons came across us, sheltering in a ditch down below the hilltop. Aurelia was delirious and we were trying unsuccessfully to soothe her. The Lord himself came to fetch us and has protected our secret ever since.'

Josse nodded. 'Aye, and do not think, Arnulf, that he revealed your presence here to me. I—' He stopped. To claim to have worked it out for himself would sound immodest. 'Well, he didn't,' he concluded abruptly.

Arnulf gave his quick smile again. 'I was told that you are a man who keeps his eyes and ears open,' he said. 'When you were here before, you heard Aurelia crying out in her fever and her pain, and her husband trying to quiet her.'

'I thought that you did not believe in marriage?'

Arnulf looked at him with interest. 'You know about us?'

'A little. If indeed you are Cathars' – Arnulf nodded an affirmation – 'then I am told that you are here on earth under sufferance, that you long to die and be reunited with your spirits, that you do not marry and that you abstain from – er, from things of the flesh.'

Now Arnulf's smile was a positive beam. 'In essence you have it,' he said. 'Although perhaps the bare bones that you present could do with a little fleshing out. As to marriage, Aurelia and Guiscard were husband and wife before they joined us. And, although it is indeed our main ambition to reunite with spirit, yet we are sufficiently human to retain emotions such as love and dependence.' His eyes sober, he added simply, 'Guiscard was not ready to lose his beloved wife. We therefore have done what we can to prolong her life a little.'

'Are you all here, all four men?' Josse asked.

'Yes. Benedetto I believe you know of.'

'Aye, I know that he brought Aurelia to Hawkenlye and then disappeared. She is doing well, by the way.'

Arnulf smiled. 'I know. But thank you for telling me.'

Putting aside the interesting question of *how* he knew, Josse pressed on. 'You and Alexius were in prison and rescued by Benedetto, yes?'

'Yes.'

Lowering his voice, Josse asked, 'Was it he who killed the prison guard?'

'It was.' Arnulf sighed. 'It was such a case as we spoke of earlier. Alexius and I were to go to the stake. The Black Man – he who you call Father Micah – had ordained that I was too much of a threat to be allowed to live for, as he quite rightly judged, I had no intention of ceasing my evangelist mission.' He stared earnestly at Josse. 'Now I was quite happy to meet my death. But Alexius is still a youth and has not yet received the Consolamentum – you know what that is?' Josse nodded. 'I did not want him to die young and unprepared. Benedetto came for us and the guard tried to fight him. Benedetto does not know his own strength; he is a simple-minded man. He does not really understand our faith – any faith, I would say – but he is devoted to our group. We are, I believe, the closest to a family that he has ever known; his is a tragically sad story. He was a large, ungainly and slow-witted child, unloved by his harassed mother, tormented mercilessly by other children. On reaching adulthood he was employed by a man who used him like an animal. The one woman he ever encountered whom he hoped might return his feelings for her betrayed him. Then he met us.' Arnulf paused, an expression of great sorrow on his broad face. 'He would defend any of us with his life. He meant only to subdue that gaoler, but he squeezed too hard. Believe me, Sir Josse, Benedetto has suffered an agony of remorse.'

'I see.' All the remorse in the world would not bring the guard back to life, Josse thought. 'What happened to Guiscard?'

'After punishment, he and Aurelia were turned out to fend for themselves,' Arnulf said tonelessly. 'I imagine that the Black Man did not reckon they would last long for both are frail. But, again, Benedetto tracked them down and took them under his care. He had managed to herd us all together and find for us the relative shelter of a bank beneath the Lord's lands when we were discovered.'

'There were two other women with you. What about them?'

'Utta and Frieda were friends who joined our sect together in their home town of Liège. That was where I met them, and young Alexius too. I am also from the Low Countries, but I had been away on a long journey to the south. I met Benedetto in Verona; Aurelia and Guiscard joined us when we were on our way north again. They had been sent to find other Cathars and try to persuade them to make for the Midi. Their home is in the region.'

'Where they are more tolerant than in the north,' Josse said.

'Yes. I see that you are well informed. Utta and Frieda were also beaten and branded, then sent off in a cart loaded with criminals bound for a different gaol from the one where Alexius and I were confined. On the way there was a mishap – I am not sure of the details, for Benedetto was confused, but it sounds as if someone in the crowd was trying to get to a relation or friend in the cart. Anyway, there was a riot, during which Utta was thrown from the cart. While the men of the law went around bludgeoning anybody who got in their way, she had the presence of mind to pull her veil down over her forehead and crawl away. Later, when she realised that Frieda had not also been thrown clear, she tried to go after her. But by then Benedetto had found her and he would not let her go.'

'And where is she now?' Josse prompted.

Arnulf closed his eyes, lips moving as if he were silently praying. 'None of us knows,' he said heavily. 'Benedetto found a hiding place for her where he left her while he tried to find where they had taken Frieda. He was unsuccessful. When he returned for Utta, she had gone.' His brown eyes full of pain, he said, 'We all weep for her. Benedetto, who believes both her loss and Frieda's death to be his fault, has all but lost his mind with grief.'

'What will you do now?' Josse asked.

'My plan, such as it is, is to wait here under the Lord's protection' – he flashed a grateful glance at the Lord, sitting watching and listening closely – 'until we receive word that Aurelia is ready to travel. Then we shall make our way to the coast and find some way of crossing the Channel. We shall then head down to the Midi.'

'And Utta?'

'What do *you* suggest?' Arnulf's sudden anger startled Josse. 'My Lord has sent out search parties, but it is an impossible task. You must know this land far better than I, Sir Josse; can you not appreciate my difficulty?'

'Aye, I can,' Josse agreed. 'I can also see a way in which I can help you. Let me try to find Utta. As you surmise, I do indeed know this land well. I know its hiding places; well, some of them, and I am acquainted with—' He made himself stop. It was unwise to boast of knowledge of the forest people; for one thing it was arrogant, for another, he was quite sure they would not like it if they ever came to hear of it. 'I know people hereabouts,' he finished lamely.

'You are a welcome and respected guest at Hawkenlye Abbey, a personal friend of the Abbess,' Arnulf observed.

How did he know? Josse wondered. Oh, aye – Benedetto. The strong man must have been listening to gossip during his brief time within the Abbey. But no, there was something wrong with that . . .

Frowning, Josse realised that Arnulf was waiting for an answer. 'I do not deny it,' Josse said. 'The Abbess is a fine woman and also a devout nun. She is vowed to obedience.'

'Naturally,' Arnulf murmured. 'And what would she think of her friend Sir Josse d'Acquin consorting with heretics and offering to help them locate their missing lamb?'

'She – I will make sure that she does not know.'

'And how will that lie on your conscience?' Arnulf asked shrewdly. 'You who readily claim close friendship with the lady, you will not suffer from keeping such a secret from her?'

Josse met his eyes. 'Of course I'll suffer,' he said quietly. 'But I would suffer a deal more if I put that higher than helping you and your people get to safety. I'll not have your deaths on my conscience.'

'I see.' Arnulf stood silent for a moment and, again, Josse had the impression he was praying. Asking, perhaps, for guidance. 'In that case, I accept your offer of help. And I thank you.'

It was late when Josse finally left Saxonbury. Heading back for Hawkenlye, he found himself hoping that he would be able to slip down to his quarters in the Vale, get something hot to eat and settle for the night without first having to have an audience with the Abbess.

He was resolved to do what he had undertaken to do and try to find the missing woman. He was in no doubt that it was the right thing. He would then find some way of introducing de Gifford to the group and persuading them of de Gifford's sincerity. Then – maybe – he and de Gifford would manage to get the reunited six people down to the sea and away across the Channel.

Maybe.

# 18

In the morning, Helewise made it one of her first tasks to see how Aurelia was doing. She went across to the infirmary shortly before Tierce and discovered Sister Caliste crouching beside the woman's bedside, feeding her spoonfuls of broth.

She watched in silence for a moment. Then, as the woman sensed eyes upon her and, with a small cry, turned to look up at her, she stepped forward into the recess.

Sister Caliste had got up and was giving her superior a deep bow.

'Good morning,' Helewise said quietly. 'How is the patient, Sister Caliste?'

She noticed that Sister Caliste had taken hold of one of the woman's hands as if in reassurance. 'She is much stronger, my lady Abbess,' the younger nun said. 'She has slept well, her pain is less intense and she begins to recover her appetite.'

'Good, good.' Helewise was studying the woman and noting, for the first time, that apart from the red and sore-looking wound on her brow, Aurelia was very beautiful. She was dark-haired, black-eyed and her skin was a soft golden colour. But she was not as young as Helewise had thought; she guessed her age to be around the mid-thirties, perhaps more. She recalled that Gervase de Gifford had said some of the heretics were from the south; Aurelia, to judge from her dark colouring, was one of them.

Not heretics, Helewise corrected herself. I can be more definite now; she is a Cathar.

And I do not know what I am to do about her.

Aurelia was looking up at her with a doubtful expression, as if she wanted to feel that Helewise was her friend but was not sure that she was. It was an expression that tore at Helewise's heart.

With a curt nod to Sister Caliste, she turned and left them.

On her knees in the Abbey church, she waited until the rest of the community had left after Tierce. Another priest had been assigned to Hawkenlye since Father Gilbert was still not ready to resume his duties. The man would be arriving later and Helewise had to make up her mind what she was going to tell him.

She is a Cathar, she told herself firmly. That is all that I need to remember. Cathars are heretics of the worst sort, for their sect seems to appeal to good Christians and seduce them into abandoning the Church and taking up a new faith. Each time a man or woman deserts Our Lord, he suffers the agony of his passion all over again, and the man or woman's soul is lost.

I must tell the new priest the *truth* and leave the matter in his hands!

But then she saw the lovely face of Aurelia with its cruel disfigurement. It is possible that she will die if I reveal her identity, she thought miserably. Perhaps she will only be imprisoned, but then look what happened to her friend when she was in gaol. And supposing this new priest is another Father Micah? Supposing he thinks he's had quite enough trouble from these heretics and condemns the lot of them to the scaffold or the stake? He might even use duress on poor Aurelia to persuade her to give away her friends' hiding places, if she knows them.

What shall I *do*?

In an agony of indecision, Helewise dropped her face in her hot hands and prayed for guidance.

Josse had not slept well. He knew he should have notified the Abbess of what he had been doing and, moreover, what he intended to do today. But he also knew that he was going to slip out of the Vale this morning without seeing her. All of which made for poor sleep and bad dreams.

He went to fetch Horace and set out early.

\* \* \*

He rode first to Tonbridge, where he managed to locate Gervase de Gifford quite quickly; he was given directions to the sheriff's lodgings close by the castle. He told him that he had located the men from the Cathar party and that he was now going to hunt for the missing woman.

'Where do you intend to start?' de Gifford asked, having congratulated an embarrassed Josse for locating the Saxonbury hiding place.

'Oh – here and there,' Josse said evasively. He was not willing to share his knowledge of the forest with anybody, even a man with whom he had recently formed an alliance.

De Gifford was eyeing him speculatively. 'I have tried, you know,' he said. 'It is possible that I have visited the very places where you intend to search.'

'Well, then I'll just try again.' Feeling more awkward by the minute, Josse took his leave.

De Gifford called after him, 'I'll come up to Hawkenlye tomorrow morning. Meet me there, if you would, and we can discuss what progress we have made.'

With a nod of assent, Josse hurried on his way.

Going into the forest, Josse experienced mixed emotions. It was always awe-inspiring to ride those ancient tracks beneath the dark and mysterious trees, and the sheer beauty of the place gave him a sense of quiet peace. But he had experienced too many perilous moments there to feel entirely without apprehension, if not actual fear.

He rode first to the disused charcoal burners' camp close to the Hawkenlye fringes of the forest. He had known desperate people to camp there before; the old turf-roofed shacks were sound and fairly weatherproof. But now there was no sign of life. Dismounting, he checked for any areas of burned ground that would indicate a recent fire; there were none. And the crude dwellings themselves were overgrown and deserted.

He rode on beneath the trees, keeping at first quite close to the forest boundary; it was reassuring to know that he had to ride for but a short distance to be out in the open again. But, as mile after mile passed with no sign of human beings, he knew he must go deeper in.

There was one place he had to check. It was a year since he had been there and he was not sure that he could find it again. He tried to visualise the tracks and tiny paths that led to it, and thought he had succeeded when he recognised a place where he could clearly recall fording a little stream. On up the bank, follow the track to the right, then there should be a clearing with a herb garden and a hut . . .

There was the clearing. There, too, what could, with a little imagination, be a herb garden. At present, though, it was no more than bare earth with what looked to Josse, ignorant in gardening matters, like a few dead twigs sticking out of it.

He could not see the hut at all.

I must, he thought, be in the wrong place.

Muttering a curse, he turned and rode back to the stream. Perhaps he had been wrong about the turn to the right; it could have been further on. He would start again from the stream, maybe follow it for a while and see if anything looked familiar.

He dismounted, leading Horace on a loose rein; the stream was narrow and overgrown and it was likely that he would be cut and scratched by low-growing branches if he tried to ride. He was turning a long left-hand curve in the stream's course when he heard laughter.

Quickly he tied Horace's reins to a stout tree branch. Then, moving quietly, he crept on until he could peer round the bend.

And saw, kneeling on the fresh grass in sunlight that fell on a clearing by the water, a woman and a baby.

She had not heard him. She was totally preoccupied with the child, who lay on a fur rug waving its little fists in delight and cooing up at the woman, responding joyfully to her warm voice. As he watched her, she began to sing a soft, sweet song. She had her back to Josse and he could see little other than that she was dressed in a thick cloak and stout boots.

They had not said that the missing woman had a child with her. Or had they? It was impossible to be certain. If, indeed, this woman really was Utta.

There was only one way to find out.

Stepping forward on to the grass, he said, 'I believe you are Utta?'

She gave such a start of fear that he could clearly see it. Spinning round, she stared at him with eyes full of terror in a round, plump face that was white with fear.

Even as he took in the mark on her forehead – which seemed to be healing remarkably well – he was hurrying to reassure her. 'Please, do not be afraid – I am a friend. Truly – I have found Arnulf and the others and I am here to help you.'

She was shaking her head, uncomprehending, still so terrified that she was shaking. She had also, he noticed, moved so as to hide the baby from him.

'I am a friend,' he repeated, thumping his chest with his fist as if to emphasise his good intentions and trying to give her an encouraging smile.

She did not respond to his smile. But she whispered, '*Fren?*'

'Friend, aye,' he agreed. Then, speaking very slowly, 'I will take you and your baby to Arnulf and the others, Alexius, Guiscard and Benedetto. Aurelia is in Hawkenlye Abbey being looked after by the nuns, but I will fetch her when she is ready to travel. I will take you all to the coast so that you can get away out of England.'

He had no idea how much she understood. He remembered that she came from the Low Countries so, trying to recall a few words of Flemish, he made his little speech again.

This time a great beam of delight spread over her face. Responding with a long, involved sentence in her own language – of which he caught about one word in three – her nods and smiles indicated that she believed him. He was about to offer to take her off to Saxonbury there and then – he took a few steps towards her and held out his hand to help her to her feet – but she drew back.

She said slowly in her own tongue – she seemed to have picked up the fact that Josse spoke it only very uncertainly – 'I must collect my belongings. I will meet you here later. Come back later.'

'But I can wait for you here while you fetch your things!'

She shook her head. 'No,' she said firmly. 'It is as I say or not at all.'

I'm trying to help you! he wanted to shout. Then he thought, but why should she give me instant trust? Better for her to have some time to think, to test whether I am as good as my word and leave her alone to prepare. Whether I return alone.

'What is your name?' she asked him.

He told her, and she repeated it softly. Then she nodded. 'Come back later,' she repeated. 'Go away now.'

Under her determined blue-eyed stare, he decided that he had no option but to obey. With a brief bow, he retreated out of the clearing and went back to untether Horace.

He did not know how much time to give her. He rode slowly back along the stream, following it absently while he thought about the woman. After some time, he realised that the trees were beginning to thin out; another half mile or so and he would be in the open.

He rode on, drawing rein under one of the last of the great oaks. From here he could see out into the fields and hedgerows of the small community around Hawkenlye Abbey. There was nobody about, no sound but the distant barking of a dog.

He waited for a long time. Then, becoming chilled despite riding regular circles under the trees to keep both him and Horace from stiffening up, he made up his mind that he had given her long enough. He made his way back to the stream and had set out to follow it back to the clearing when she appeared, walking towards him with a small pack over her shoulder.

'I am ready now,' she said. 'Please take me to the others.'

He said, amazed, 'But where's the baby?'

'No baby.' She spoke firmly, meeting his eyes with a determined look. He thought he could see the residue of tears on her cheeks and her eyelids were red and swollen.

'But—'

'No baby,' she repeated. 'Please, take me away.'

Stunned, he stared at her. Had he imagined it? Was it not Utta's but some fairy child, which appeared to mortals then vanished back into its own world?

That, he knew, was fanciful. The child had been real enough, and for some reason Utta had left it behind.

He said, 'Was it not your child?'

'No,' she said. 'Now, we go.'

But he could not leave it. 'Will it be all right? It's cold today, and—'

'Baby will be very right,' she said, switching to his own tongue as if to make quite sure he understood.

Was it then a child of the forest people? It seemed to him in that tense moment that this must be the explanation. Utta surely would not otherwise leave a baby all alone in the forest! No woman would, certainly not one who had been playing with the child with such delight. And if indeed Utta had met up with someone of the forest folk, it would explain how she had survived out there in the wildwood.

She had come right up to him and was holding out her hand. 'I ride with you,' she announced, 'but careful, careful, hurt back.'

'Aye, I know,' he said. 'You'd best sit behind me.' Then, very gently, he took hold of her hand. Taking his foot out of the left stirrup, he indicated that she should put hers in, then, with her assistance, he lifted her up and sat her behind him on Horace's broad back.

To his great surprise, she gave a quick laugh. 'Big horse,' she observed. 'Very high up.'

'Very high,' he agreed. 'Hold on to me, I won't let you fall.'

'I trust,' she replied. 'I know, I trust.'

Giving up on trying to get her to explain her remark, he kicked Horace into a gentle trot and set off for Saxonbury.

He was moved almost to tears by the emotion of Utta's reunion with her people. Turning away from them as they demonstrated

219

their very obvious love and concern for one another and their joy at being reunited, he found himself meeting the steady gaze of the Lord of the High Weald.

'You have done well, Josse d'Acquin,' he said. 'How did you know where to look for her?'

'It was sheer chance,' he replied. 'I came across her in the forest. She—' No. Better not to mention the baby. 'She seemed willing to trust me,' he finished instead. 'I still do not understand why.'

'Perhaps she was growing desperate,' the Lord suggested. 'It must have been very hard, trying to keep herself warm, fed and sheltered out there. Possibly any friendly face would have persuaded her away.'

'I think—' He was going to tell the Lord of his conclusion that Utta must have been under the care of the forest people. But, again, he decided against it. 'I think she has done well,' he said. 'The wound on her face is almost healed and, from the way she swung herself up on to my horse, I can't think that the marks from the flogging can be paining her too much.'

'Perhaps she was treated less harshly than the others,' the Lord said. 'Either that or she is a quick healer.' Turning to look at Utta, now held in a close embrace by Benedetto, tears streaming down both their faces, he lowered his voice and said, 'How soon can you go for the other woman?'

'I return to Hawkenlye from here,' he said. 'If you will keep them safe a while longer, I will bring her as soon as she is fit to come.'

The Lord nodded. 'We will await you.'

The members of the heretic group were still wrapped up in each other. Not wishing to interrupt their happiness, Josse led Horace out of the courtyard, mounted and rode quickly away.

In the early evening, Josse watched from the shadows as the Abbess came out of the Abbey church and headed for her room. When she was inside behind a closed door, he went over to the infirmary.

'Sir Josse,' Sister Euphemia greeted him coolly. 'We were

wondering where you were. The Abbess is quite anxious about you.'

'I – er, I have been visiting Gervase de Gifford down in Tonbridge,' he replied. It was the truth, as far as it went, but still he felt the guilt rise up in him at his deceit.

'I see.' The expression in Sister Euphemia's wise eyes suggested that she did see, all too clearly. 'You've come to see Aurelia, no doubt. Go through, she's sitting up and is much better.'

He did as she suggested. Aurelia stared up at him doubtfully; struck by how lovely she was, he knelt beside her bed and said slowly, 'I am so pleased to see you looking well.'

She answered him in his own tongue, although with an accent that he did not at first recognise; it was a long time since he had talked with someone from the Midi. Listening intently, he realised that she was thanking him. That, even though he had not yet told her, she seemed to know what he was planning to do.

'How do you know?' he whispered.

She put a long finger to her lips. 'I cannot tell you. It is a secret. But I know what you have been doing and I know that you will take me to join them as soon as it is possible. I think perhaps we can go tomorrow. But very early, yes? Before anyone is awake and watching.'

Thinking that it would have to be very early indeed to be before an Abbey full of nuns rose for their first prayers, he nodded. 'Aye,' he said. 'I'll come for you before daybreak.'

She reached out and took his hand. 'I cannot move quickly,' she said. 'You need to know this, and also that you will have to help me.'

'I understand. I'll get you up on my old horse. He's steady and has a broad back. You'll think you are still lying in your bed.'

She gave him a very lovely smile. 'You are being untruthful with me, Sir Josse, but I know that you do it to reassure me and so I forgive you.' She gave his hand a squeeze then, letting him go, shifted in her bed with a small wince. 'You should go,' she urged. 'Somebody may wonder what you do here, whispering to me in such secrecy.'

'Very well.' He stood up. 'Until tomorrow.'

'Tomorrow.' He caught an echo of the smile, then he turned away.

The next morning, Helewise repeated her previous day's early visit to the infirmary. Today she went straight after Prime. She headed for the recess where, behind a curtain, Aurelia's bed was concealed, reaching it before even the infirmarer or Sister Caliste got there.

When, a little later, she was joined by Sister Euphemia, she said quietly, 'Aurelia has gone.'

'Aye,' the infirmarer replied. 'Before daybreak, I would guess.'

'Was she fit to travel?'

Sister Euphemia gave a brief tut of concern. 'I would have said not. I would prefer to have had the care of her for a few days more. Her wounds are healing quite well and her fever is down, but I fear very much that, without care, she may open up one of those cuts and the infection may come back.'

Helewise lightly touched the infirmarer's sleeve. 'It is out of our hands now, Euphemia,' she said gently. 'You and Sister Caliste have done your very best for her.'

Sister Euphemia stood looking down at the empty bed for a while. Then, with a shake as if she were pulling her attention back to more practical matters, she said, 'Aye, you're right, my lady. I'll get this bed stripped and prepare it for whoever needs it next.'

Later in the morning, Helewise received a visit from Gervase de Gifford. He began on an elaborately courteous greeting, which she interrupted by raising a hand.

'I am sure that you have not come rushing up to the Abbey this morning to exchange polite remarks with me,' she said coolly. 'Would you care to explain your mission here?'

'Er – I am still trying to discover what happened to Father Micah,' de Gifford said. 'I am ashamed to confess that I still know no more than that he was found six days ago at the top of Castle Hill with a broken neck.'

'I hope you had not been hoping for another look at the body,' Helewise said, deliberately keeping her tone neutral. 'We buried him four days back.'

'No, no, I don't think there was anything more to be learned from looking at the poor man.' De Gifford appeared to be recovering his composure.

'You have learned no more of his final movements?' she asked. 'Other than his visit to this Lord up at Saxonbury?'

'No.' De Gifford would not, she noticed, meet her eyes. Then he said, 'My lady, I was expecting to meet Sir Josse here this morning but I am informed down in the Vale, where I understand him to be putting up, that he is not here.'

'Is he not?' She widened her eyes. 'I am afraid that I cannot help you, Sir Gervase. I do not know where he is.'

She had a fair idea, but it was, she told herself, quite true to say that she did not actually *know*.

'Oh.' De Gifford seemed to be at a loss. 'I wonder, my lady, if I might pay a visit to the woman in the infirmary? The heretic woman with—?'

'I know to whom you are referring,' Helewise interrupted. 'I would gladly give my permission for such a visit, only I am afraid that she is not there either.'

She had to give de Gifford credit for quick thinking. The words were hardly out of her mouth when he made her a swift bow and turned for the door. 'If you will excuse me, my lady, I have just—'

'Just remembered an important engagement?' she asked sweetly. 'Please, then, do not let me detain you.'

For one brief moment he met her eyes. In his she saw excitement, the thrill of some dangerous task he had to do. There was something else, too; she did not think that he had been fooled for a moment by her act of innocence.

He said very quietly, 'Thank you, my lady, and may God bless you.'

Then he was gone.

# 19

Josse remembered the pre-dawn ride to Saxonbury for a long time afterwards. He remembered it primarily for Aurelia's courage.

He tiptoed into the infirmary while it was still pitch dark outside, finding his way to her bed by the soft glow of a candle on a shelf set up high in the wall.

He was not familiar with the daily and nocturnal nursing routine and, in any case, he was too preoccupied with getting Aurelia away unseen to think about why there was no nurse on duty with the patients.

Aurelia was sitting on her bed, dressed in a dark coloured robe and with a thick travelling cloak beside her. He whispered, 'Have you a pack?' and she shook her head.

He took her arm and she stood up. Then, with small steps and leaning heavily on his arm, she walked beside him along the length of the infirmary and out of the door. On the step she took one quick backward glance; he saw her lips moving but he could not hear what she was saying.

Urging her on, he helped her to where he had tethered Horace. Then, feeling her stiffen up with the pain, he helped her into the saddle. He slid back the bolts and opened the gate a little, then led the big horse outside, fastening the gate behind him. Then, trying very hard not to jog her, he got up in front of her. It was awkward and he would have felt safer supporting the ailing woman when seated behind her, but there were the wounds on her back to consider. When they were settled, he urged Horace forwards into a slow, even walk.

After quite some time, he felt her begin to relax. He encouraged Horace to move a little faster; she did not seem to protest. And, as the first rays of the early sun appeared behind them and to their left, they made their slow way up to Saxonbury.

The relatively short journey took a long time. Josse found it hard at times to restrain his impatience; as they rode on, he felt a growing sense of urgency, a feeling that he must get Aurelia to Saxonbury – and the whole group on their way to the coast – before . . . Before what? He did not know. He simply felt, with a sense of gloom that was quite unlike him, that something bad was going to happen.

Aurelia did not speak to him other than to reply to his infrequent questions about whether she was all right. Each time she said, 'Yes', and each time, he was quite sure, she probably felt like saying 'No'. Other than those brief exchanges, he was left to his own thoughts.

He went over in his mind again and again just what could go wrong. He and Aurelia would soon be at Saxonbury, she would be reunited with the others and Josse would take them down to the sea. He knew the area well enough to take them to the coast along little-used ways and he was not worried about his ability to guide them. Even if he managed to get them all lost, it was a relatively simple matter to reach the coast from Saxonbury: all you had to do was to travel due south and you could not help but hit the sea sooner or later. And there were several fishing ports along the south coast from where he ought to be able to find a craft to take the group back across the Channel.

He was not worried, either, about his ability to protect the six Cathars. He would have preferred to have Gervase de Gifford with him in case they met with trouble; he did not reckon much on the ability of Arnulf, Alexius or Guiscard to help him out if it came to a fight, although Benedetto might be useful. But it now looked as if Josse would have to do without the Sheriff's company. He could have waited for de Gifford to turn up for their morning meeting at Hawkenlye. But the opportunity to slip away with Aurelia before anybody else was about had been just too good to pass up. Aye, Josse reflected, I reckon I'll manage all right alone.

He tried to decide whether or not it was a threat from the Church that was bothering him. It was highly likely that the Hawkenlye community would be assigned a replacement for Father Micah and, if this priest shared the convictions of his immediate predecessor, then he might well set out on the Cathars' trail.

If, that was, he came to know about them.

Would he?

Would the Abbess Helewise follow her head and obey her vow of obedience? If she did, then this new priest would have to do something. It was possible that the Abbess would convince him that they had nursed Aurelia in ignorance of who and what she was, and so escape retribution for herself and her nuns. But the priest could not but make at least an attempt to track the party down and impose whatever further punishment he deemed necessary.

If the Abbess followed her heart, however, Josse was quite sure that no threat pursued the group from the Church.

What would she do?

As they began on the last long climb up to Saxonbury, Josse half-turned and told Aurelia that they were nearly there. She said nothing, but her pained smile spoke many words.

Again, the guard must have seen their approach. Drawing aside the gate, he welcomed them in with an uncharacteristically cheerful expression. 'They're all waiting,' he muttered to Josse. 'They seemed to know you'd be by afore long.'

Josse dismounted and led Horace into the courtyard. And, as the guard had said, there they all were, lined up in a row with Utta in the middle, Arnulf and Alexius to her right, Guiscard and Benedetto on her left. Behind the Cathars stood the Lord of the High Weald and his son Morcar, with two other men of similar appearance beside them. As Josse led Horace and his rider into view, they all broke out into a cheer.

It was Guiscard who first broke ranks. He came running up to Horace and, reaching up, took his wife tenderly in his arms.

Watching them as Aurelia carefully dismounted and fell into Guiscard's embrace, Josse reflected briefly that they might have taken this vow of perfect chastity but, all the same, it did not seem to have diminished their very evident love for each other. Quite the contrary.

Now the others were hurrying forward, crowding round Aurelia, patting her gently with loving hands and asking anxious questions. Coming face to face with Utta, Aurelia gave a sudden exclamation and put her fingers lightly to Utta's forehead. She asked a swift question and Utta, laughing, answered her, fishing in a pocket inside her robe and producing a small pot. She held it up to Aurelia and then, opening it, very tenderly smeared a small amount of the contents on to Aurelia's wound.

Now I would be prepared to wager, Josse thought, smiling, that Utta has there some magical remedy given to her by the forest folk. She has been treated with it, which is why her wound has healed so well. And now she is going to share it with her friend.

Aye. No matter how skilled the Abbey nuns were, the forest folk still had a few ancient secrets that nobody else knew.

After a few moments, the Lord caught Josse's eye and beckoned to him. Leaving the group to savour the joy of their reunion, Josse followed him inside the hall.

The Lord stomped over to the fire, rubbing his hands together and then opening his palms to the flames. 'The Sun is bright but he does not yet bring much warmth to those who stand still out of doors,' he observed. Then: 'Sir Josse, we have been giving thought to the Cathars' journey to the coast and we feel it is best to go immediately. Will you take them? My son Morcar has offered to accompany you, and I will lend you horses.'

'Aye, that I will, and I shall welcome Morcar's company.' Josse had assessed the Lord's big son as a useful man to have around. 'But there is a problem.'

'Yes?' The Lord's blue eyes were instantly alert.

'Aye. The woman Aurelia is still very weak and suffers much

227

pain, for all that she bears it bravely and does not complain. I fear for her if we leave straight away.'

The Lord, to Josse's surprise, was smiling. 'Now, Sir Josse, you must not misunderstand what I am about to say.' He leaned towards Josse and slapped a large hand on to his shoulder. 'I know that you have a high opinion of the skill of Hawkenlye's infirmarer and that the lady has done her best for Aurelia. But Utta has a pain-killing draught that I believe is stronger than anything within the holy confines of the Abbey. She will give some to Aurelia and thus make her more able to tolerate the journey.'

'I see.' I was right, Josse thought, about Utta having been taken under the wing of the forest folk. 'Er – did Utta say where she obtained the draught?'

The Lord did not answer for a moment. Then he said, 'Sir Josse, I have lived cheek by jowl with the Great Forest for all of my life. I have learned that, when someone comes out of the wildwood and is reluctant to speak of their experiences there, the wise do not ask questions.'

'Let us merely be thankful, then,' Josse said, 'that Utta found the right company.'

'Let us be thankful indeed,' the Lord murmured. Then, striding towards the door, he said, 'Now we must prepare our guests for the road.'

Mounts were found for the group. Guiscard and Aurelia chose to ride together; she was a small woman and the stout cob that the Lord had provided would make no great burden of bearing husband and wife together. Looking at her, Josse guessed that she had already been given some of the pain-killing draught, for the pupils of her eyes were wide and she had a vague, sleepy expression. Guiscard placed her in front of him on the cob so that she could lean against him; he had carefully wrapped her up in a thick cloak for warmth and to pad out her back. It was to be hoped, Josse thought, that she might pass much of the journey in sleep.

Arnulf and Alexius had been given sturdy ponies and a larger horse had been found for Benedetto. Josse was just wondering how Utta would ride when she approached him and asked shyly if she might ride with him. She was, it transpired, none too easy with horses.

So once again he helped her up behind him on Horace's back. Then, with Morcar in the lead on his own chestnut gelding and Josse bringing up the rear, the party prepared to ride out of Saxonbury. The Lord and his family came out to see them on their way and, for the first time, Josse caught a glimpse of the Lord's wife. She was tiny and bent with the inflammation of the bones from which so many of the elderly suffered. But her dark eyes beneath her filmy veil were bright, and there was affection in her face as she waved her visitors away.

The group fell silent as they went down the long sunken track from the hilltop. Then Arnulf said something to them, and as one they began to pray. Josse heard Utta, seated just behind him, join in and, to his surprise, he recognised the words of the Paternoster.

When the prayers were over – they seemed to take a very long time – he remarked tentatively, 'You said the Paternoster.'

'Of course!' she replied. Then, before he could ask another question, she added, 'We pray for a safe journey.'

With more fervour than he had thought he felt, Josse said, 'Amen to that.'

Considering that they were a party of whom the majority of the members were not used to riding long distances, they made good progress. Morcar appeared to know exactly where he was going and he led them along secret, hidden tracks up on the ridges with quiet confidence. He seemed to be aware of the frailty of the women and made frequent short stops. Often he would ask briefly if everybody was all right and, when they said yes, lead them off again straight away.

They stopped some time in the early afternoon to eat and drink. Josse estimated that they had covered about nine or ten miles, which he thought good going. Approaching Morcar, who was sitting by himself tearing with strong white teeth into a piece of dried meat, he said, 'How long till we reach the coast?'

Morcar squinted, shaded his eyes with his hand and stared briefly up at the sun. 'We'll be at Pevensey by nightfall, provided we meet with no mischance. We're about halfway, maybe a little less.'

'Good.' Josse was staring at the group, studying each one in turn. He saw Utta with an arm around Aurelia's shoulders, supporting her while she drank something out of Utta's flask. He wondered whether Utta's supply would last them all the way to the Midi and the relative safety of the Languedoc. 'You think we can get them a boat?' he asked Morcar.

'It should be possible.' He touched a small leather pouch that hung from his belt. 'Many a man will ferry people across the water without asking too many questions if he is sufficiently well paid.'

They sat for a while longer. Then, as Benedetto and Alexius gathered up the remains of the food and drink, Morcar asked them to remount so that they could be on their way.

It happened as they were crossing the Cuckmere valley.

The swell of the South Downs was rising up ahead of them and Morcar had taken a track that led south-east, around the end of the Downs and to the sea. The Cathars were in good heart; they knew that it was not far now to the coast and that soon they would be on their way across the Channel.

Thanks to Morcar's knowledge of the hidden tracks, they had passed not a soul on the way. But now, in the long grassy valley, they were much more exposed; somebody watching out for them would have been able to spot them from several miles away.

Josse felt his earlier unease return. Now the sensation was much stronger; he put a hand down to the hilt of his sword and then checked that his dagger was in his belt.

The Downs were huge now and right in front of them. Josse thought he could make out the ancient beacon on top of the Caburn, away to his right. Please, he found himself silently praying, please take care of them, for just a little longer . . .

The he heard the sound of a galloping horse.

It was faint as yet but, even as he stopped to listen, the sound grew rapidly louder. The others had noticed it too; Morcar had drawn rein and was twisting round in the saddle, a frown on his face.

The Cathars, every one of them, had blanched in fear. Benedetto had already slipped off his horse and was standing, arms out, in front of Arnulf, Guiscard and the drowsy Aurelia, as if preparing to defend them.

Josse had turned Horace and was staring up the road that came out of the north. From the direction of Hawkenlye Abbey.

Had she given away the secret? Had the Abbess's religious duty won out over her compassion?

Narrowing his eyes, he watched as the lone horseman came closer. A man . . . but dressed not in clerical black but in bright burgundy. And he was laughing, calling out happily, 'Sir Josse! Sir Josse! I have caught you up at last!'

It was Gervase de Gifford.

Dismounting, Josse stood waiting while de Gifford reached the group. He was so relieved to see the man that he did not think to check on how the others were reacting. Reining in his sweating horse – he had obviously been riding hard – de Gifford slipped from the animal's back and ran towards Josse.

Sensing sudden movement behind him, Josse had only just begun to turn to see what it was when a blurred shape rushed past him. Crying out in his own tongue, Benedetto was on to de Gifford before the sheriff had a chance to raise as much as a hand to defend himself.

He thinks we are apprehended! Josse realised in anguish. With his very limited command of the language, Benedetto must have heard only the word *caught* and believed that his beloved group had just met with disaster. And, simpleton that he was, he did not perceive the significance of de Gifford's smiling face nor of Josse's obvious pleasure and welcome.

Josse threw himself on to Benedetto's back. The big man had already felled de Gifford and had his hands on the sheriff's throat.

231

Josse put a hand around each huge wrist and pulled as hard as he could. He managed to dislodge Benedetto's right hand with his own right hand – his stronger hand – but could make no impression on Benedetto's left. And, in an image out of the recent past, he saw the throat of the dead prison guard and the deep impressions of Benedetto's hand. His left hand.

De Gifford, immediately feeling the slight lessening of the fatal pressure on his windpipe, twisted his head and pressed upward with his left shoulder. Catching Benedetto unprepared, he managed to knock him slightly off balance. Josse tried to grab at the big man but was thrown off as easily as a farmer tosses a hay bale. He fell heavily, banging the back of his head on the hard ground. Getting groggily to his knees, shaking his head to clear the starbursts of brilliant light from his vision, he raised his head to the struggling men . . .

. . . and saw that Benedetto was kneeling astride the prostrate de Gifford, pinning him with his huge thighs. He had pulled a long, thin blade from somewhere under his robe and was about to thrust it into de Gifford's chest.

With a great cry – *'NO!'* – Josse lunged at Benedetto. He was still dazed, still acting on his fighting instincts, and he drew his dagger without thinking. Throwing his left arm around Benedetto's neck, he dragged him backwards. With a roar, Benedetto put up his right hand and grabbed Josse's wrist in a grip that felt like an iron clamp.

In Benedetto's other hand, the thin blade was still poised over de Gifford's heart. As Josse watched, its point went into the rich brocade of the burgundy tunic. The man was about to die.

Josse drew back his dagger and thrust it into Benedetto's shoulder. With a roar of pain, the big man fell sideways, trying to reach out for the point of agony with his right hand. As he fell he twisted around, so that he landed on his own blade.

Benedetto hit the ground and lay still.

As Josse watched, eyes wide with horror, he saw a great pool of blood begin to spill from beneath the big man, its bright colour vivid against the dirt of the track.

Benedetto's blade had reached inside his chest and found his heart. Even as Josse bent down to remove his dagger from Benedetto's shoulder and feel for a pulse, he knew it was no good.

Benedetto was dead.

They wrapped him up in his cloak and laid him in the shallow ditch that ran along beside the track. All of the Cathars were in tears, men and women both; Arnulf, speaking for them all, said that the big man had loved them too well and that his love had blinded him.

Alexius, face wet with weeping, said, 'We cannot leave him here unburied.'

Josse put a hand on the youth's arm. 'We will attend to him on our return,' he said gently. 'That I promise you. But there is no time now – it will be dark soon and we need to get the women to shelter before nightfall. Aurelia certainly is not strong enough for a night in the open with no fire and no warm food.'

Alexius looked as if he would protest but then, with a curt nod, he turned away. Josse watched as he went to join the others, who had already begun on their prayers for Benedetto's spirit.

Josse felt a touch on his arm. De Gifford, still pale and with dark red bruises on his throat, said hoarsely, 'Sir Josse, I owe you my life.' He gave a deep bow. 'You have just made for yourself a lifelong friend.'

Returning the bow, Josse said, 'I would not have killed the poor man for anything less than to save another. He did not understand. He believed that you were here to arrest them and I do not think that he could have borne to see his loved ones suffer any more.'

De Gifford bowed his head. 'I believe that you judge right. Had he only given me the chance to explain, I should have told him that I had come to help, not to hinder. But as it is—' He gave a helpless shrug.

Morcar came up to them. He had, Josse had noted, seemed unfazed by the whole terrible incident; the Lord of the High Weald breeds them tough, Josse thought. Now the tall man said, 'We should be moving. Although it is unlikely, we may have been observed. The sooner we get them safely on to the sea, the better.'

Gently and with the respect due to a recent dramatic bereavement, Josse and de Gifford persuaded the group to mount up again. Then, in silence, they rode away from their fallen companion and headed on down to the sea.

They found a ship bound for Harfleur whose master was prepared to take five passengers in exchange for the Lord of the High Weald's bag of gold. Arnulf, who had recovered his air of leadership somewhat following the shock of Benedetto's death, said that Harfleur would serve them well. They would be able to journey down through Normandy and Aquitaine, cross the Loire and the Dordogne and from thence journey on to Albi.

'That is your destination?' Josse asked.

Arnulf gave a pale smile. 'It is where we are gathering,' he replied. 'Aurelia and Guiscard have friends and family there; it is their home.'

'What of your home, Arnulf?' Josse regarded him with sympathy. 'Yours, Alexius's and Utta's?'

Arnulf gave a small sigh. 'I do not believe that any of us will see our home again,' he said. 'But we shall make a new home,' he said, brightening with an obvious effort. 'Our own people are our family now and we shall all band together, all Cathars from every land. We shall gather in the Languedoc and be left in peace.'

Josse, who very much doubted it, said nothing. Instead he took Arnulf's hands in his and simply wished him good luck.

Then, as Arnulf turned to take his farewell of Morcar and de Gifford, Josse walked across to where the rest of the group stood, waiting for Arnulf to lead them on board.

Putting careful hands on to Aurelia's narrow shoulders, he wished her safe passage and a good journey. With a soft smile, she gently pulled his face down to hers and gave him a soft kiss like the touch of a butterfly. 'Thank you,' she whispered.

Utta then kissed him too, with rather more passion. Staring

up into his eyes, she appeared to be about to say something. But, shaking her head with a smile, she kept her silence. Later, boarding the ship, she turned and gave him a small last wave.

He said a prayer for her. For them all. Then he turned and, following behind de Gifford and Morcar, left the quay.

Morcar turned for home as soon as the Cathars had been des-patched; he seemed to be as fresh as when they had set out that morning and apparently had no fear of a twenty-mile journey in the gathering dark. Before he left, he solemnly took his leave of Josse, clasping Josse's right hand in his own and twisting it so that their forearms wound around each other.

'My father thinks well of you, Josse d'Acquin, and so do I,' he said. 'You are ever a welcome guest at Saxonbury.' Then, with a nod to de Gifford, he mounted up and, leading the horses that his father had supplied for the Cathars, rode away.

De Gifford watched him go. Then, slapping Josse's shoulder, he said, 'I don't know about you, Josse, but I'm cold, tired and my spirits are low. I suggest that we find the best tavern that this port has to offer and order ourselves the finest meal in the house and a large flagon of ale.'

Josse, who was struggling with emotions that ran too deep for easy comprehension, thought that was the best idea he had heard in quite some time.

The little port was quiet but a light shone out from a low-slung building outside which hung some branches from a fir tree. As Josse and de Gifford approached, they heard voices and laughter; pushing the tavern door open, they were greeted with warmth, firelight and what seemed to be a cheerful, though small, company.

De Gifford glanced at Josse. 'I think that this is the best we're going to get,' he remarked.

'It'll do for me,' Josse replied. 'Lead on.'

# 20

Josse and de Gifford returned to Hawkenlye in the morning.

When they came to the spot in the Cuckmere Valley where Benedetto had died, they stopped to locate and bury his body.

There was no sign of him.

They searched the area and, after a while, de Gifford called out. 'Over here. There is a patch of newly turned ground.'

Josse went over to where he was standing. Half under a hedge, where the soil was broken up by the roots of shrubs and grasses, there was a long area of exposed earth. It would be hidden when the hedgerow bloomed in spring but, for now, it was quite clear what it was. At one end, a strangely shaped cross made of twigs had been stuck in the soil.

De Gifford said, 'Morcar must have done it. Last night, under cover of darkness; very wise of him. He is stronger even than he looks; it can have been no easy task to dig a grave for a big man when the ground is so hard.'

But Josse was hardly listening. The cross had reminded him of something.

Reaching inside his tunic, he took out the Cathar manuscript. 'I should have given them this,' he said regretfully. 'It must be priceless and they will surely miss their treasure.'

De Gifford was frowning. 'I am not so sure, Josse. Whoever left it at Hawkenlye did so for a reason. They wanted to hide it, I would guess, in a place where it stood a chance of being safe.'

'But anyone in the Abbey who found it would take it to the Abbess Helewise and it would be destroyed! Even Benedetto must have known that!'

'I do not think that it was Benedetto who hid the manuscript,' de Gifford said thoughtfully. 'I believe it was Arnulf. As the leader of the group, he would have had the charge of their precious document and it would have been his responsibility to decide what was done with it when they realised that they could not risk keeping it with them. I think he must have slipped inside the script room while Benedetto was carrying Aurelia into the infirmary. It would have made a good diversion, wouldn't it? Every pair of eyes agog with the big man and the wounded woman?'

'Aye,' Josse acknowledged.

'And as to the manuscript being destroyed if it were to be found, you have in your hand the proof that it was not so. That Arnulf judged right when he chose his hiding place.'

Slowly Josse turned the brilliantly coloured pages. There was that strange cross again.

De Gifford said, 'What will you do with it?'

'I don't know.'

'Will you put it back in the book cupboard?'

'No. It has escaped from Hawkenlye once and I will not chance its fortune there again.'

'Very wise,' de Gifford murmured.

'I ought not to keep it,' Josse mused.

'You fear for your skin if it is found on you or on your property?'

'No, it isn't that. It's just that it is so clearly valuable and I have no right to it.'

'It has come to you, though,' de Gifford pointed out. He hesitated, then said, 'Would you like to know what I think you should do?'

Josse gave him a grin. 'Aye, I'd be delighted.'

'Put it away in a very good hiding place,' the sheriff said. 'Tell nobody where it is, not even me.'

'But why not you?'

'Try to forget about it,' de Gifford urged, as if he had not heard Josse's question. 'One day it will be even more valuable than it is today, for it will be unique. One day, who knows, maybe somebody will come asking for it. You may give it to them, you may not.' His green eyes met Josse's. 'You will know what to do.'

Before Josse could ask him to explain, he had turned away. He stood with bowed head over Benedetto's grave for a few moments, then mounted up and led the way off across the valley.

When they were approaching Hawkenlye Abbey, de Gifford drew rein. 'This is where we part company,' he said. 'I am heading home and I imagine that you are bound for the Abbey.'

'Aye.' And the Abbess too, Josse thought. He had not yet decided how he would approach her, how much of the recent happenings he was going to reveal to her. It troubled him to think of lying to her and his heart was heavy.

De Gifford was studying him. 'I think,' he said, 'that you should follow your instincts.'

'But my instinct is to tell her everything!'

De Gifford smiled. 'Exactly.'

Returning his smile, Josse said, 'I have enjoyed our encounter, Gervase. There are many things about you that puzzle me, but I do know that I trust you.'

'I am glad of it,' de Gifford replied. Then he added carefully, as if he were reluctant to ask and did so despite himself, 'What things puzzle you?'

'Your defence of the heretics, for one. Aye,' – he overrode de Gifford as the sheriff made to speak – 'I recall what you said about there being more than one way to find the truth. Nevertheless, it still surprises me that a man of the law should go so far in his defence of a bunch of heretics.'

'A bunch of heretics,' de Gifford echoed softly. 'Yes, Josse, but as I knew even before I met them, they are not just any heretics. They are Cathars.'

'Does that make any difference?'

'Yes.' The light green eyes held an emotion that Josse could not immediately read. 'I have family in the Midi, Josse. For all that she married a knight from the north and made her home here in England, my mother never forgot the land of her birth. When

my father died, she went back to the Languedoc. She became a
*parfaite* three years ago.'

'Your mother is a Cathar?'

De Gifford nodded. 'Yes. A well known and, so I believe, well
loved one. Aurelia and Guiscard know her well and brought her
greetings to me.' He lowered his head. 'Of course, she wishes that
I would join her – join her faith, too – but she respects my decision
not to.' He sighed. 'She is – all of them are – a very great deal more
tolerant than their Christian brethren, don't you think?'

Now he had raised his head again and Josse could read the
emotion that had him in its grip.

It was love.


The two men parted at the Abbey gates. De Gifford said,
'Remember what I said.'

And Josse, thinking back swiftly and isolating the one comment
to which de Gifford must be referring, nodded.

'We shall meet again, Josse,' de Gifford said. 'I do not forget
that you saved my skin. Sooner or later, I shall find a way to
repay you.'

Then, with a wave of his arm, he spurred his horse and cantered
off down the road.


Helewise had been expecting Josse for many hours. She had tried
to calculate how long his journey would take but had quickly given
up; she had no idea how fast they would be able to travel, nor even
how soon they would have set out.

She had known where he was going. She had known, too, that
he would quietly remove Aurelia from the infirmary as soon as
she could tolerate being moved. And she had finally made up her
mind what she should do.

It had cost her dear.

She had knelt at the altar for most of the night before Josse
came for Aurelia. She had gone into a sort of trance, probably
brought on by distress, fatigue and hunger; she had been fasting,
offering the discomfort and the hunger pangs to God in return

for his guidance. The two options, to denounce Aurelia or to let her go, had warred inside her head like fierce rival armies, first the one getting the upper hand and then the other. Obedience to her nun's vow, indeed, to her Christian faith, told her she must find a priest – any priest – and tell him that Hawkenlye Abbey was harbouring a Cathar. But her heart had its share of Christ's greatest gift, that of compassion, and, no matter how hard she tried, she could not make herself believe that the Saviour whom she loved wanted her to deliver another of his daughters to the pain of imprisonment and an agonising death.

In the end she had seen – thought she had seen – the tender face of Christ. And in the small hours she had risen to her feet knowing what to do.

It was on Helewise's own orders that no nun had sat quietly on duty in the pre-dawn silence of the infirmary that morning. On her orders too that the bolts on the Abbey gates were oiled to make sure that they slid back easily and soundlessly.

Later that day, when Josse and Aurelia were long gone and Gervase de Gifford had come looking for them, something deep within her had told her that he, too, was a friend to the group. That, like Helewise, he was deliberately putting aside the duty he owed to his office and following his heart. That he was helping the Cathars to escape.

She did not know why he was doing so. She was only glad, as she saw him on his way, that he was on their side.

Sister Caliste, quietly and efficiently going about her duties, had a new patient in the bed that had been Aurelia's. An elderly man had gone down with a racking cough that tore at and pained his lungs, and Caliste was dosing him with Sister Tiphaine's strongest remedy. She had also put a bowl of hot water beside his bed into which she had cast a bundle of special herbs. The steam that rose from the water was fragrant and soothing; already the old man's cough was easing.

Sitting beside him, wafting the steam towards his sleeping form, Caliste asked herself yet again whether she had done right or whether she had disobeyed and must confess and do penance. Her actions had helped someone reach safety, which must be good. But on the other hand she might well have gone against ecclesiastical rules in so doing . . .

Sister Tiphaine had explained what she must do. There was a sanctuary waiting for the Cathar woman, she said, and someone would come for her when she was ready to go. Sister Tiphaine had found the opportunity to have a quiet and unobserved moment with Aurelia, who consequently knew what was being arranged for her. Sister Caliste had but to inform Sister Tiphaine when Aurelia was ready and Sister Tiphaine would get word to the friends who awaited her. So Caliste had watched carefully, spoken to Aurelia, done all that she could to bring about the woman's recovery and to restore her to strength. And then, when the moment was right – a little before, actually, but Sister Tiphaine had urged haste and told Caliste that they must act as soon as was at all possible – Sister Caliste had sought out Sister Tiphaine and told her that Aurelia was ready.

It had been dark in the herbalist's little hut, and there had been a strong smell from something that she was brewing up in her cauldron. Caliste had delivered her message and then, with relief, turned to go. Sister Tiphaine, with a short bark of laughter as if she read Caliste's mind, had said, 'You've done well, lass. Now leave it to me. I have my own ways of getting a message out to those who dwell in the world, but you'll forgive me if I don't share them with you. But don't worry. I've been keeping Aurelia's friends aware of all that's happened here. I'll make sure they're expecting her.'

Ah well, Caliste thought now, if I tell them what I've done, I'll get Sister Tiphaine into trouble. So I'd better not.

With the serenity that was her own particular gift as a nurse, Sister Caliste put some more herbs into the bowl of hot water and recommenced waving the fragrant steam towards her patient's face.

Late in the day, Helewise heard a soft knock on her door.

She smiled. No matter how gently he knocked, she always knew it was he and not some timid novice standing quaking outside her room. Timid novices did not wear boots with spurs that rang out as they walked.

She called out, 'Come in, Sir Josse.'

He opened the door, came in and closed it again, leaning against it as if reluctant to approach her. For some moments they stared at each other. Then he said gruffly, 'They got away. I helped them. I took them to Pevensey and saw them aboard a ship bound for Harfleur. They sailed last night so they'll be somewhere in Normandy now.'

She closed her eyes in relief. She had been so afraid that he would not trust her, that, even now that it was all over, he would not reveal to her what he had done.

To think that Josse, whom she loved so dearly, could have thought her capable of betraying him, of taking an action that would probably have sent the Cathars to their deaths, had hurt more than almost anything else. And why should he not believe I would perform such an act? she had asked herself honestly. I almost believed it myself.

Behind her closed eyes she felt the warm tears begin to flow. Bowing her head, she tried surreptitiously to wipe them away.

But he must have seen.

She heard his spurs chink as he crossed the room. And, from somewhere much nearer to her, his voice, rich with sympathy, said, 'Don't cry, Helewise. This has been hard for every one of us, but most of all for you.'

'Please, Josse, don't be kind to me,' she sobbed. 'I don't deserve it and it's making me worse!'

'We all deserve kindness when we've done our best,' he said. 'Yours was no easy choice. And it's not over yet, not for you. Will you have to confess what you have done?'

Silently she nodded. She had not yet dared to think what punishment she would receive from her confessor, whoever he was.

Josse was speaking again. 'I hear from the Lord of the High Weald's lad that Father Gilbert's on the mend and about to resume his duties.'

At first she thought he was tactfully changing the subject and giving her the chance to recover her composure. Then, as his words sank in, she realised what he was telling her.

With the relief of knowing that she would be able to confess to the understanding, wide-minded Father Gilbert and not to some hatchet-faced zealot who was a total stranger, she began to cry all over again.

'He'll be by in a day or so,' Josse said comfortably. 'By then the Cathars will be halfway to the Midi.'

Through the hands with which she had covered her wet face she said, 'Thank God.'

A little later, when she had recovered and could once more sit up straight and face him, she said to Josse, 'We still do not know how Father Micah died. Do we?'

'No,' he agreed. 'I cannot make myself believe that any of the Cathars killed him. Benedetto might have done' – he had told her earlier what had happened on the journey to the coast – 'and we now know for a certainty that he is capable of such an action. He protected his group fiercely and ruthlessly and he would, I am sure, have killed Father Micah if he had perceived him to be a threat.'

'But you do not think that he did?' she prompted.

'No.' He met her eyes. 'I believe that Arnulf would have told me if he had.'

'Then who?' she persisted. 'Who killed him – or perhaps found him dead – and left him on the road above Castle Hill?'

'He had many enemies,' Josse said thoughtfully. 'Perhaps somebody took the law into their own hands when the Father's threats, to them or to one of their own, became too frightening.'

'Do you speak of the Lord up at Saxonbury?' she asked.

'No. He told me that he did not know who killed Father Micah and, again, I believe him.'

Helewise sat watching him for a while. It was possible that one of those men – Arnulf or the Lord – had been lying to Josse. But somehow his impulse to trust both of them was convincing.

Perhaps, she thought, tired suddenly, we should not dwell any more on a mystery that is never going to be solved.

As if his thoughts had run along the same lines he said after a time, 'My lady Abbess, we have to accept, I believe, that we shall never know.' Meeting her eyes, he added, 'I know I should not say this to you, but I do not think I shall grieve over long for Father Micah.'

Watching him steadily, she thought for a moment about her reply. But then she thought, he has been honest with me. I shall return the same courtesy.

With a smile, she said, 'Neither shall I, Sir Josse. Neither shall I.'

To her quiet delight, he accompanied her to Compline. It was her favourite office and today of all days she felt that the sense of completion it always gave to the day's actions and devotions was especially fitting. The matter of the Cathars *was* completed, she told herself. As far as it was ever going to be. And wasn't that a matter for secret jubilation?

Afterwards, as he strolled beside her back to her room, she said suddenly, 'Sir Josse, I understand now something that was puzzling me. When you and I spoke with Gervase de Gifford concerning the poor woman who died in gaol—'

'Frieda.'

'Yes, Frieda. Well, I told de Gifford that we would say a mass for her and he began to protest, although he swiftly recovered himself and said it was a good idea. But now I perceive his thinking. Our mass would not serve a Cathar woman.'

From the darkness Josse's voice sounded very kind. He said, 'My lady, de Gifford's second reaction was surely the true one. He knew that your suggestion came from the right motives and he applauded it.'

She smiled to herself. It was a gift, to have a friend like Josse. His was a rare compassion.

After a moment he said, 'How is Sister Phillipa's work on the Hawkenlye Herbal progressing?'

'Very well,' Helewise replied. 'She has completed some ten pages and I hope to be able to show them to Queen Eleanor soon.'

'The Queen is to visit Hawkenlye?'

'I cannot say for certain.' Helewise felt her anxieties for the Queen come rushing back. 'I am informed that she is doing her utmost to defend her son's realm and that she is demanding a renewal of the Oath of Allegiance from the King's lords and clergy. She is ably helped by Walter of Coutances and Hugh de Puiset, they say, and of course she is much loved and respected. However . . .' It would be, she decided, disloyal to refer to the particular hardships imposed by the Queen's age, and so she did not.

But Josse seemed to understand anyway. He said gently, 'It is a great burden for anybody. For a woman past her first youth it must be doubly heavy.' Then, with a note of urgency, he added, 'She will treasure her time here in Hawkenlye's peace, my lady. I pray that you will have the opportunity to succour her.'

And Helewise, moved, simply said, 'Amen.'

In the morning Josse came to seek her out and informed her that he was leaving. 'I've been away from New Winnowlands since before Christmas,' he said, 'and it's high time I went home.'

'You do not, I hope, fear for your manor?' she asked.

'No, indeed. Will and Ella are quite capable of looking after anything that arises in the normal run of events. For anything else, they knew where I was spending the Yule season.' He gave her a quick grin. 'And no doubt they would have guessed where I went afterwards.'

She returned his smile. 'As always, you are welcome here.'

She saw him off, standing by the gates and waving until he rounded the corner and was out of sight. Then, with a faint sigh and a sudden brief lowering of the spirits – gone almost before she had registered it – she went back to her work.

Josse, trotting off along the road and bound for New Winnowlands, put a hand inside his tunic to check that the linen-wrapped package was secure. He had been thinking about a hiding place for it back at his manor house and believed he had come up with a good one.

I did not tell her about the manuscript, he thought as he rode. I almost did, but somehow I stopped myself. She has been through quite a lot just recently, and every one of us has our limits.

He pictured her, the wide grey eyes troubled. Then he saw her weeping, saw himself go to stand by her side and place on her shoulder an awkward hand that wanted so much to comfort and did not know how.

Helewise.

Deliberately turning his thoughts away from her, he spurred Horace and cantered for home.

# Postscript

## March 1193

Meggie was getting used to the people who now looked after her. They were kind and tended her with loving hands. They made sure that she was fed when she was hungry and bathed when she was dirty. They found somewhere warm and safe for her to sleep. When she cried – which, for the first time in her short life, she did quite often – someone always came to pick her up, give her a cuddle and croon a soft little song until her tears ceased.

But it was not the same. It was not right, because neither the very old woman with the long silver hair, nor the slightly younger one with the brown, wrinkly face, nor the plump young girl whose breasts were swollen with milk was the person for whom Meggie hungered.

None of them was her mother.

She was too young to understand, far too young to ask questions. At four and a half months old, all she could do was frown because her sorrow hurt her, without knowing why it had come.

Lora was looking after Joanna's baby, with the help of one of the young mothers of the forest people. Sometimes Meggie would accept milk from the young mother's breast – she was still feeding her own five-month-old son – and sometimes she would screw her small face up into an expression of grief and turn away.

'I don't smell like Joanna,' the young woman remarked sadly one evening after she had finally admitted defeat.

'Milk's milk,' Lora said tersely; Meggie's quiet, heartbroken crying was affecting her badly. Glancing at the baby girl, she said, 'The child must feed. Try once more, Silva.'

But Silva shook her head. 'No, Lora. I want her to take in some nourishment as much as you do, but she's just not interested at the moment.' She picked up her own child and put him to her breast, whereupon he instantly began to suckle eagerly and efficiently, clutching at the smooth curve of his mother's warm flesh with one small hand.

'Hmm.' Lora was staring at the pair of them with an absent expression. Then, as if suddenly coming to a decision, she got quickly and gracefully to her feet and said, 'I'm going to speak with the Domina, if she will receive me. I'll try to be back afore nightfall.'

'Very well,' Silva replied, eyes on her son.

Lora picked up Meggie, wrapped her warmly – the March evening was chilly, clear skies suggesting the coming of a frost after a sunny day – and headed off along one of the faint tracks that led out of the clearing where the forest people had set up a temporary camp.

After walking for some time she reached the dell where the Domina was wont to set up her own private shelter, a little apart from her people, whenever she visited this part of the Great Wealden Forest. Smoke was rising from a fire that burned within a circular hearth of stones. From within the shelter Lora could hear faint sounds of chanting. Knowing better than to interrupt, she sat down on a fallen log, checked that Meggie was warm enough, and waited.

It was not long before the chanting ceased. From within the shelter, the tall, grey-clad figure of the Domina emerged.

Standing up, Lora said reverently, 'I am sorry if I disturbed you, Domina.'

'You did not.' The older woman sighed. 'I was aware of your presence, yours and the child's, and my own thoughts interrupted my meditation.' Approaching Lora, she held out her hands for the baby and Lora put Meggie into her arms. 'Now then, my pretty maid,' she said in a gentle voice, 'what is it that ails you? Why will you not accept milk from one other than your own mother when it is given with love?'

Meggie stared up at her, the delicate, dark eyebrows drawing together into a frown. She made a little mewing sound and the Domina lightly touched her cheek with a long finger.

Still staring intently into the baby's round eyes, the Domina said, her voice now taking on a more compelling tone, 'Return to Silva, little one. Satisfy your hunger on that which she so freely offers you and then sleep. Do not dream; do not see bad visions of what must now be put behind you. Feed, and then sleep. Sleep soundly, sleep long.'

So powerful was the Domina's magic that Lora found herself yawning hugely. With a grin, she said, 'I am grateful to you, Domina. I'd better take the child back now afore I fall asleep myself.'

'You will find that the babe will suckle now,' the Domina replied. 'And tomorrow . . .'

She did not finish her sentence and Lora knew she must contain her impatience over what the older woman intended to do. It was not done to ask questions of one so senior. With a deep bow, she took Meggie back, wrapped her in her furs and turned around to set her feet on the homeward track.

The Domina sat alone outside her shelter long into the night. The temperature fell drastically as the hours went by and a sharp frost turned the ground around her to a shade of silver that almost matched her long hair. The waxing Moon, already past the half, shone down on her, the bright light paling the stars of the Milky Way that stretched high above in an arc as if someone had hurled them from an outstretched hand.

She did not feel the cold. Her mind had left her body and the current state of her limbs and her torso was of no great importance to her. She would return to herself when she was ready, and then she would go inside her shelter to the hearth and to the drink she had set ready earlier. Once she had stirred the fire into life and added fuel, drunk her drink and wrapped herself up in her great bearskin, she would soon be as warm as she could wish.

Her deep-set eyes stared sightlessly out into the darkness. She was looking at a very different scene, one whose stage was a circle of standing stones beneath a February moon. And she was seeing herself, standing facing a young woman who wore around her neck a talisman of such power that its presence had caused the Domina's strong, indomitable heart to miss a beat.

Joanna had not realised the significance of either the gift or the giver. She had told the Domina that the claw had been given to her by a man of the tribe who had slipped away from the Yule celebrations that she had not been able to attend. When the Domina had informed her that the tribe's Yule festivities had been held too far away to make such a visit feasible, Joanna had clearly been greatly surprised. But, young and ignorant though she was in the life and the ways of the tribe, she had managed not to ask the question that burned in her eyes. She had never been told who her visitor was. Nor, indeed, what his visit implied.

And at Imbolc he had summond her. Now, turning her mind back to that night, the Domina saw them together, the young woman and the man bear, as she had watched them before. She did not need to spy on them to know what they were doing; the act that had taken place between them had been predestined from the moment that he gave Joanna the claw.

He had returned to his people after his long, long absence. He had disappeared ages ago, in a time that nobody living now recalled and that was only remembered – and given great reverence – in the songs of the tribe. Oh yes, he had come to them before, lived among them, walked and breathed as a normal man for most of those far-off and magical days. But they had all known, all of his people, just what was special about him. Some of them thought they had even seen him shift from man to bear and back again, only afterwards they could never be quite sure because of the speed with which he did it. Bears there certainly had been back then, living alongside men. Who could in truth say what had happened?

Somebody could. Somebody had known without a doubt, for he had appeared to her as he had done to Joanna. Had lain with her, many times, had impregnated her, had watched her carry and then bear the child Ursus, who grew up to wear the blazon of the

Scarlet Bear upon his shield. Who had himself given rise to a great warrior line whose deeds were still sung of by the bards and who would for ever retain a place in the hearts of their people.

Deep in her trance, the Domina turned her mind to seek out the bear man. After a long time, she felt that her consciousness brushed his. Seeing his bright eyes behind her closed lids, she asked him what she must ask. And, in time, she felt that she heard his reply.

In the morning the Domina rose early and set out on the track that led to the temporary camp. Approaching the shelter where Lora was tending Meggie, she stood outside, not speaking. Her very presence was a summons; Lora quickly got to her feet and bowed.

'It is time,' the Domina said. She held out her arms and Lora bent to pick up the child, wrapped in her furs. Without another word, the Domina turned and left the clearing. Lora, watching her go, found that she was praying. Please, Great Mother, make it all right. Please look after Meggie . . .

Then, with a faint shrug, she ducked and went back inside the shelter to empty the bowl of warm water with which she had been washing the baby when the Domina came for her. It is up to you now, Mother, she thought. I have done all that I can.

The Domina carried Meggie for many hours. When the child was hungry, the Domina drew from inside her robe a silver flask containing a mixture of honey, water and certain herbs that she had prepared herself. Dipping her finger in the flask's wide neck, she offered the liquid to the baby. Each time Meggie took it eagerly. Each time it satisfied both her hunger and her thirst.

A little after noon they came to a place where an outcrop of sandstone soared up among the trees. Viewed from a distance, it had the appearance of the top of a huge head standing out among the branches. To one side of the outcrop, some ancient, natural force had carved out a cave. It extended some ten or fifteen paces back inside the Earth and its sandy floor was dry.

The Domina found her way to the cave entrance with ease. It was she who had discovered it, many years ago. She knew it was a place of strong Earth power and she had tucked away a memory of it in her mind, knowing that, one day, it would be useful.

She stood in the shelter of a large boulder that stood beside the cave entrance. Then, absolutely silent in her movements, she peered around the boulder. A hearth had been set out a couple of paces inside the cave mouth. The fire was low now, although there was a neat stack of small logs nearby. Beside the fire was the skinned body of a hare, wrapped in a variety of leaves, all of which the Domina knew to be edible and reasonably nutritious.

Good. The occupant of the cave certainly seemed to have remembered how to live out in the wildwood.

The Domina went on into the cave. Bedding was rolled up and tucked away on a rock shelf where it would stay dry in case of a sudden shower that blew rain inside the cave. Another lesson well learned.

Meggie stirred in her arms. The Domina debated whether to give the child some more of the mixture in the silver flask but decided against it.

She found a boulder close to the hearth and sat down to wait.

It was the baby who noticed first. The Domina, gazing down at Meggie's wide eyes, felt the child's sudden unnatural stillness and she knew. Old as she was, she who had seen human beings interact with the Earth and with each other for more decades than she could now recall, still there was room in her heart for wonder. *Great Mother*, she prayed silently, *what a gift you have bestowed upon us in the bond that ties mother to child, child to mother.*

Because someone else also now knew who awaited her by the hearth. Breaking into a run, dropping her carefully gathered herbs from hands that suddenly didn't care, Joanna came racing into the clearing, around the great outcrop and into the cave. Ignoring the Domina, eyes only for her baby, she cried, 'Meggie! Oh, my sweetest child!' and the ache and longing in her voice brought tears to the Domina's old eyes.

She gave mother and baby a few moments simply to rejoice in each other. Then, observing the wet stains that were spreading over the front of Joanna's robe, she said, 'You have kept yourself in milk?'

'Yes,' Joanna replied.

Good, the Domina thought again. For all that she had no idea what was to come, she kept hope alive. She kept her milk flowing, in case her child should be returned to her.

'Then I think,' said the Domina, 'that you had better feed her.'

Looking up at her briefly, with a quick smile Joanna opened her robe and did so.

Joanna had been living in the cave for a month. The Domina had sought her out in the forest and taken her there.

She had not known why this terrible thing was happening to her. She had been ordered to pack a small amount of essential kit – warm sleeping furs, her knife, her flint, a light drinking vessel – and told that she must leave Meggie behind. Her heart almost breaking, Joanna had obeyed. The Domina's dark eyes had compelled her, and there was no question of rebellion.

As they had walked the long miles to the cave, Joanna had a dreadful thought. When she had found Utta, when, later, she had done what she had to do to save not only Utta but herself and Meggie too, she had believed that act to be what the Domina had prophesied: *What you have done before you can do again.* Now she quaked with fear that it was not what the Domina had meant at all.

That what she had referred to was the giving up of a child.

Joanna had asked Josse to find a household for her son Ninian and, having let the boy go, she had known she would never see him again other than in the black depths of her scrying stone.

Was this, then, the second test that she must pass? The abandoning of her second child, her daughter, her Meggie, her beloved?

Not daring to ask, she had followed the Domina along the forest paths with silent tears coursing down her face.

When they reached the cave that was to be Joanna's dwelling place, the Domina said, 'You have taken life. Two souls have you sent into the abyss. Concerning the first, I know all that I need to know, for you have already told me and I have seen it. I know that you told me no lies. Concerning the second, I wish you now to explain.'

So, sitting on the sandy floor of a cave, lost so far within the forest that she knew she would never find her way out, Joanna told her tale. She told of how she had found the woman, Utta, and taken her back to the hut in the forest to look after her. How she had discovered the sickening brand on the woman's forehead and known that H meant heretic. How she had taken fright and removed Utta, Meggie and herself to the safety of the refuge in the yew tree.

How the Black Man had come looking for his prey. Looking for Utta. How Meggie's soft little sound of love had alerted him and how he had advanced towards the foot of the tree. Then Joanna forgot the Domina beside her, forgot that she was telling a tale, for she saw him begin to climb, saw every detail unfold before her eyes as if it were happening all over again . . .

*Down in the lower branches of the yew tree, the Black Man, suspended from the rope that he had slung and tied, raised his head and saw her. Instantly he looked surprised; he said, panting with the exertion of the climb, 'What in the devil's name are you?'*

*I have no brand, Joanna thought, and he is expecting to find a heretic woman. She was just wondering whether she might after all be able to convince him that she was no concern of his, no threat to him, and persuade him to go away and leave her alone when he laughed his ghastly laugh again.*

*'You're one of those filthy, pagan forest dwellers, I'll be bound,' he said, speaking as if he had no idea that she understood, that she spoke his language or, indeed, any language at all. 'One of that vermin crowd who need to be hunted down like treacherous plague rats and*

*burned on the heretics' pyre.' His pale face spread into a grin that was more like a rictus. 'It's good work for the Lord that I'll do this night, a forest bitch and her pup both thrown to the flames.'*

*Then, reaching out with his right arm and getting a good grasp on the next handhold, he gave an upwards thrust from his legs, clasped around the rope, and got his torso across the branch.*

*He turned up his face and stared triumphantly at Joanna.*

*'Thought you could get away, didn't you?' he murmured softly. 'Thought you were too clever for a man of God? Well, let me tell you, my lass, I—'*

*But whatever he was about to say would never be known. Joanna drew back her left foot and, with all the strength in her leg muscles of more than a year living the tough life of the wildwood, she swung it forwards again and kicked the Black Man on the point of his chin.*

*His head rocketed backwards, the momentum of Joanna's kick sweeping him off the branch and on, on, over in a back flip. He was more than halfway through the revolution when, face first, he hit the ground.*

*Even from upon the branch, Joanna heard the crack as his neck broke.*

'Then,' she said, recalling the Domina beside her, 'I slipped down from the tree and went to see. He was dead. So I called up to Utta that it was safe to come down and she climbed out of the tree as well. We knew we must get rid of the body and I wanted to carry it a good distance away and bury it. But Utta said that was not right, because it would mean he died without any prayers being said for his soul. She was a good woman for, although he was her sworn enemy and would have slain her without mercy, she still had a thought for his immortal soul. So I put Meggie in her sling and Utta and I carried the Black Man between us up to the road that runs up from Castle Hill towards Hawkenlye Abbey. We left him there on the track. We knew someone would pass by before too long and that they would report the body, probably to the nuns of the Abbey. Then he would be almost certain to be buried according to the rites of his own religion.'

'You knew, then, who this man was?' the Domina asked.

'No. Merely that he was a man of the Church, for he had implied as much in his own words.'

The Domina nodded. There was silence for a long time and then eventually she spoke.

'It is no crime among our people to take the life of one who would take our own, or that of one we love,' she said. 'That first time, you slew a man who was on the point of taking the life of your daughter's father. The second time, the man that you killed was intent on taking three lives, those of you and your daughter and, had he known she was there, that of the heretic woman too.' Turning her deep eyes on Joanna, she said, 'You are not here in the cave as a punishment.'

'Oh.' Every fibre of Joanna strained to ask, *Why*, then?

Eventually the Domina answered the question Joanna had not dared to ask. 'You have taken life,' she said distantly, as if her thoughts were too profound for words. 'These acts must be assimilated, both into your own soul and into the great web that is the life of the tribe. You will stay here alone and think on what you have done.'

Questions rose up in Joanna, demanding answers. How long must I stay? What about Meggie? Will I be allowed to return? How do I *assimilate*, as you order me to do?

But already the Domina was rising to her feet and walking in her stately manner towards the cave mouth. She did not even turn to say goodbye.

Joanna was going away.

She was packing up and leaving her beloved little hut. Not for ever – or so she fervently prayed – but for a long time.

So much had happened there, or nearby. She had taken in a stranger and it had almost cost her her life. And Meggie's life. The safety of her home now felt less secure than it had done. He might not have found it but he had come very close. And he had discovered the refuge in the yew tree, although quite how, she still had no idea. Perhaps it was as she had always thought, and it had all happened by mere mischance.

Also she knew she had to make reparations for what she had done; the month of contemplation and meditation in the cave had merely been the start. There were rules in her new world just as there had been in the one she had left over a year ago. She had had her reasons for her actions and she knew she could defend them. But defend them she would have to do. The prospect frightened her, for all that Lora and the others tried to reassure her. In the end, seeing that she was about to be overwhelmed by her dread, Lora had said, 'Live in the now, my girl. Let tomorrow look after itself. If you spend all your time in fear of what may be to come, you won't appreciate the beauty of today.'

It was sound advice, Joanna knew it. Also, Lora's words echoed what dear Mag Hobson used to say. Still did say sometimes, her faint voice sounding as an echo of Lora's. It was a great comfort.

As she finished her packing and fastened her leather satchel, Joanna sat down beside the hearth and looked around her little home. Mag's home. Everything was spotlessly clean and tidy; she wanted to leave it so in case someone should happen upon it and investigate within. Perhaps, recognising it as a dwelling that was loved and cherished, they would leave it alone. Just to be on the safe side, however, Joanna intended to put another hiding charm on the place.

Later today – in only a little while from now – she would put Meggie in her sling, pick up her bundle and set out on the long, secret road that led north-westwards. It was one of the old straight tracks, made – or so her people said – by the Great Ones of an earlier time who could feel the Earth's pulse beneath their feet and who let Her power lines ordain where their paths led. It went as straight as any of the old roads that the Romans built, heading always for that distant destination.

Mona's Isle. The very name made something within Joanna quake and turn over, like a fish caught in a sudden eddy.

There she would begin receiving instruction. Some of the great ones of her people – the Domina included – would teach her. She could hardly believe it, but it seemed to be because of the bear claw. And, more significantly, who had given it to her. The Domina had told her about the bear man. A little, anyway. Just enough to make Joanna both dread and long to see him again.

Thinking of that made her fears return. So instead she turned her mind to her little house. What would she miss? The song of the birds at dawn. The cry of the vixen and the occasional distant howl of the wolf. The flowers and the herbs in her garden, the rows of simples, ointments and remedies that she had made, bottled and labelled with her own hands.

Josse.

His image was suddenly there before her eyes, unbidden. She had seen him that day when he had come for Utta, and it was only because she had been so quick in slipping into hiding that he had not seen her too. She had gone foraging, leaving Utta happily playing with Meggie beside the stream. Returning, she had heard his voice. Her reaction – the reaction of her body that had loved him and lain with him – had all but taken her breath away.

Utta had asked him to return for her later. Then, as soon as he had gone – was it not just typical of big, kind Josse, Joanna now thought, to understand Utta's fear and do exactly as she asked? – Utta had sought out Joanna to return Meggie to her and to say goodbye. It had been heartbreaking; Joanna could still remember Utta's halting words of gratitude and love, still feel the tight hug and the warm tears on her cheek that might have been Utta's or her own. Then Utta had gone, and Joanna and Meggie were once more alone.

Josse.

He had asked her to marry him once but she had declined, knowing that his heart was not really in it and that he loved another. Also, she knew she was not destined to live the life of a knight's wife in his cosy manor house; her way was very different.

Josse.

He had planted his seed in her; she had conceived and borne him a daughter. And he did not know. She wished there were some way that he *could* know without its changing anything. But she did not believe that was possible.

Josse.

'I am going away,' she said softly to him, wherever he was. 'Not for ever, they say. But it may be for a long time.' She sighed. 'I loved you, in my way. Perhaps I still do. But it is not destined that our paths run together, not for the moment, anyway.'

No. Her path, or so she understood, was very different.

She got to her feet, gently arranged Meggie in her sling, then picked up her pack. She checked that the fire was quite dead, that everything was as she wished, then went out through the low door and carefully fastened it behind her, concentrating hard and quietly chanting her strongest spell. Then, stepping back a little, she imagined the hut disappearing into its surroundings.

'Wait for me,' she said aloud. 'I'll be back.'

Then, squinting up at the Sun, she turned on to the track that led off into the north-west and strode away.